THE TRAVELER

MEASURED TIME

BOOK ONE

To Bob,
You never travel alone when you bring a book.

Lynn Perez-Hewitt

L Y N N   P E R E Z - H E W I T T

PAGE PUBLISHING, INC.
Conneaut Lake, PA

First originally published by Page Publishing 2020

ISBN 978-1-6624-2568-4 (pbk)
ISBN 978-1-6624-2569-1 (digital)

Printed in the United States of America

For Diamond Jim
Who will always fly First-Class on my flights of fancy.

ACKNOWLEDGMENTS

I wanted to tell a good story, and I didn't do it alone. I am profoundly grateful to my husband, friends, colleagues, and even strangers who, when I said I was writing a novel, asked about it and then wanted to read it. A handful of early readers endured drafts and stumbles. Thank you, Peggy and Jim Halderman, for your practical, thoughtful feedback, as well as critical insights into physics. Thank you, Dr. Marilyn Newsom, not only for being an enthusiastic reader, but for sharing your medical knowledge to keep me from missteps and mistakes in that realm. Thank you doesn't begin to say it to Linda Peterson, my skilled and tireless editor. Three, count 'em three, drafts benefitted immeasurably from her keen eyes and pointed questions, leading me to a better story.

To gifted musician and friend, Terry Pollock, who gave me permission to mention the name of his band and that crazy song called, 'Trading.' It was perfect and added that special southern Arizona magic to my tale. To early readers Elizabeth, Mary, Teresa, and many more, you all gave me an opportunity to face my fears and share the manuscript.

Thank you to NaNoWriMo, for helping me get back in the writing saddle. Eternal gratitude and sore muscles to Anytime Fitness, without whose stationary bike and rowing machine too many key plot twists and character conversations would not have been devised. Not to mention my gym rat buddies who encouraged me, and in the case of Heather, provided me critical industry knowledge on road surfaces. Much appreciation to Page Publishing and the eternally patient Nora Custead for steady guidance through the publishing process.

And the spark of a story would never have become the flame of a novel without Diamond Jim, husband, friend, supporter, and best sounding board ever for my untethered imagination.

CONTENTS

Cast of Characters 11
Prologue 13
Chapter 1: Day One, Vento Junction, Arizona,
September 8, 2008 15
Chapter 2: Day One, Vento Junction, Home of Don Grant.......20
Chapter 3: Los Alamos, New Mexico, September 1944.............32
Chapter 4: Day One, Vento Junction, Arizona,
September 8, 2008 36
Chapter 5: Los Alamos, Late August 1944 42
Chapter 6: Nicholas Nishimura, Los Alamos, August 1943........44
Grace Nishimura, Vento Internment Camp 1943.....47
Chapter 7: Day One, Vento Junction, Arizona,
September 8, 2008 49
Chapter 8: Los Alamos, New Mexico, September 1944.............52
Chapter 9: Day One, Indio, California, After the Phone
Call, Late...54
Day One, Nick's Notes..57
Chapter 10: Day Two, Vento Junction, Arizona,
September 9, 2008 58
Trip to Indio, California..59
Chapter 11: Oak Ridge, Tennessee, Early-December 1944 65
Early Evening, Same Day 67
Chapter 12: Day Two, Indio, California, Grace's House..............72
Day Two, Nick's Notes 73
Chapter 13: Day Three, Indio, California, September 10,
2008 Grace Nishimura Acevedo's Home 74
Vento Internment Camp, Late Spring 1943 79

Chapter 14: Day Three, Los Angeles, California, Home
of Rick Stanton, September 10, 2008......................82
Chapter 15: Mac MacLane, Fall 1946............................95
Chapter 16: Day Three, Los Angeles, Stanton Home,
September 10, 2008 100
Day Three, Nick's Notes................................105
Chapter 17: Day Four, Los Angeles, the Next Morning at
the Stanton Home, September 11, 2008 107
Stanton Home, Los Angeles, California 109
At The Institute..112
Chapter 18: Stanton Home, 2008................................119
Chapter 19: The Institute, Los Angeles, California, June
3, 2000...122
Chapter 20: Day Four (Still), Interstate 10, Heading East
from Los Angeles, September 11, 2008 131
Chapter 21: Still Day Four, Indio, California, Grace
Acevedo's home, September 11, 2008....................138
Day Four, Nick's Notes................................149
Chapter 22: Day Five, Interstate 10, Driving East to
Vento Junction, Arizona, September 12, 2008........150
Meanwhile, Back in Indio at Grace's Home...........152
Day Five, Nick's Notes 152
Day Six, Nick's Notes 153
Chapter 23: Grace's Home......................................155
Day Seven, Nick's Notes................................157
Chapter 24: Day Eight, Vento Junction, Arizona,
Apartment of Ben Grant, September 15, 2008 158
Day Ten, Nick's Notes................................159
Chapter 25: Day Thirteen, Vic and Don Exchange
E-mail September 20, 2008–October 2, 2008........161
Nick's Notes, September 24, 2008.......................169
Nick's Notes, October 1, 2008 169
Chapter 26: Near Eloy, Arizona, Day 26, Friday, October
3, 2008...171
Later That Day..175
Nick's Notes, October 8, 2008 177

Chapter 27: Vento Junction, Arizona,
             Friday, October 10, 2008 178
             Nick's Notes, October 10, 2008 185
Chapter 28: In the SUV with Michelle and Ben Heading
             to LA from Indio..187
             In the SUV, Heading to LA with Vic at the
             Wheel and Don in the Passenger Seat................188
Chapter 29: The Institute, Los Angeles, California,
             October 10, 2008..191
Chapter 30: Still at The Institute, October 10, 2008.................200
             October 10, 2008, Nick's Notes 203
             October 15, 2008, Nick's Notes 205
Chapter 31: Near The Institute, Los Angeles,
             October 17, 2008 206
             Nick's Notes, Wednesday, October 29, 2008 211
Chapter 32: Somewhere on the Oregon Coast, October
             30, 2008..212
             Nick's Notes, October 31, 2008 219
Chapter 33: The Institute, November 1, 2008 220
Chapter 34: The Institute, November 3, a Few Weeks
             Before Thanksgiving 2008...................................228
             Nick's Notes, Wednesday, November 5, 2008.........229
Chapter 35: Thursday, November 6, 2008 231
Chapter 36: Saturday, November 8, 2008 234
Chapter 37: Saturday, November 8, 2008 At The Institute 236
             Nick's Notes, Sunday, November 9, 2008 238
             Nick's Notes, Wednesday, November 12, 2008.......238
Chapter 38: Thursday, November 13, 2008, The
             Commons at The Institute 240
             Nick's Notes, Wednesday, November 19, 2008.......243
Chapter 39: November 20, 2008, Vento Junction 244
             Vento Junction Juvenile Facility...........................245
Chapter 40: Around the Kitchen Table at Don Grant's
             Home, Later November 20, 2008 248
             Nick's Notes, Wednesday, November 26, 2008.......251
Chapter 41: The Institute, Thursday, November 27, 2008.........253
Epilogue 263

CAST OF CHARACTERS

Donald "Don" Sullivan Grant, b. 1946, retired high school science teacher, Vento Junction, AZ

Benjamin "Ben" Sullivan Grant, b. 1974, history teacher, Vento Junction Community College

Charles "Charlie" Sullivan Grant PhD, b. 1978, physicist

Nicholas "Nick" (a.k.a. Brown) Nishimura PhD, b. 1920, Pasadena, CA, physicist

Grace Nishimura Acevedo, b. 1928, Pasadena, CA, sister of Nick

Hector Acevedo, b. 1925, New Mexico, husband of Grace. Married 1946. Deceased 2006

Daniel Acevedo, b. 1947, attorney, son of Grace and Hector, father of Nicola

Victory "Vic" Acevedo, b. 1948, actress, daughter of Grace and Hector

Nicola Acevedo, b. 1977, graduate student in physics at UCLA, daughter of Daniel Acevedo

Richard "Dick" Stanton, PhD, b. 1918, physicist, best friend of Nick Nishimura

Elizabeth "Betsy" Baldwin Stanton, b. 1920, teacher, wife of Dick, mother of Rick and Rosemary

Richard "Rick" Stanton, PhD, b. 1947, professor of physics at UCLA, advisor to Nicola Acevedo, husband of Jane MacLane

Patrick "Mac" MacLane, b. 1918, colonel, stationed at Los Alamos 1943-1944, founder of The Institute

Martha O'Hara MacLane, PhD, b. 1922, professor of math and physics at Stanford, wife of Mac MacLane, mother of Jane and Robert

Jane MacLane Stanton, b.1947, daughter of Mac and Martha, married to Rick and head of The Institute

Mitchell "Mitch" Stans, b. 1978, head of security at The Institute, adopted son of Rick and Jane Stanton

Suzanne Brown, PhD, b. 1978, biomedical engineering researcher at The Institute

Nicholas G. Fabian III, b. 1982, Sligo, County Sligo, Rep of Ireland, cybersecurity specialist at The Institute, former geologist

Clary McGonigal, b. 1990, Sligo, County Sligo, Rep of Ireland, geology prodigy at The Institute

Theresa Cisneros-Johnson, b. 1928, Los Alamos, NM, teacher, grandmother of Elizabeta and Mercedes

Elizabeta "Beta" Gonzales-Thompson, b. 1984, twin sister of Mercedes

Mercedes "Mercy" Gonzales-Thompson, b. 1984, twin sister of Elizabeta

Michelle Matthews, b. 1978, Chicago, IL, journalist

Father Joseph (Father Joe) Benedict Perez, b. 1932, Parish priest of Our Lady of Victory, Indio, CA

PROLOGUE

The sun was setting, and the New Mexico sky was fiery orange and neon pink as Mac MacLane lit a cigarette and thought about what was ahead. September in the high desert was still hot during the day, but the nights were darn nice. He looked out at the horizon and hoped the Tricksters were ready, because tomorrow was the day. The war in the Pacific wasn't going as well as the newspapers said. The OSS needed to catch a break. The Tricksters might provide it. He sure as hell hoped they would. Nerves were frayed and tempers were running as hot as the days were.

All the scientists were on edge. The cocktail party tonight should help. They all needed to blow off some steam. Everyone felt the pressure, but especially young Nishimura. With his family in one of those Camps, this effort to help end the war was very personal. For his sake Mac hoped it all worked. Tomorrow they would succeed or fail. There was no in-between for any of them.

He ground his cigarette out with his boot. Time to go let off some steam.

CHAPTER 1

DAY ONE, VENTO JUNCTION, ARIZONA, SEPTEMBER 8, 2008

He walked across the street with the light. There was a cluster of people, and he followed their lead. It was midafternoon and a man in a suit stood out—a man in a suit wearing a fedora like he meant it was odd. But the people kept on walking, kept on thinking their own thoughts, while he began to collect his. And those thoughts were jumbled. Where was he? Why didn't his Japanese features cause alarm? But he kept on walking. Practical questions cropped up. Would his money work here? He thought he heard English. Where was he? Could he be understood? He was hungry, and he didn't see any diners, but he smelled food. All the things Mac told him about blending in and being casual in his actions so he wouldn't attract attention raced through his mind.

And then he saw a car. But not like any car he was familiar with. Now he knew he needed to find out the when of where he was. Trees looked like trees. Streets looked like streets. Women wore tighter clothes. But that wasn't a bad thing. Men wore denim pants, and it looked like their underwear was showing—strange times. He continued walking.

The street was a mix of small store fronts and brick buildings that might have apartments, but how did these people live? After another block, he found the source of the smell. It was a burger joint. He went in. It was bright, and he sat down. No waitress came to his table. He watched people, and they were standing at a counter where a kid in a funny outfit punched his fingers on some kind of flat machine. Then he noticed that the bright wall above the kid was actually a menu. He saw a ninety-nine-cent burger and figured he had that much, and it sounded like American money.

He went up to the line and listened as people ordered food. When it was his turn, he asked for the ninety-nine-cent burger. The kid mumbled some questions to him, and he asked him to repeat himself. The kid mumbled again. He still couldn't understand the kid, but it seemed the kid understood him. The guy behind him grumbled out loud about, "The kids these days."

He thought, *I guess some things don't change.*

The kid slid a wrapped burger on a plastic platter of some sort across the counter. He took it and sat down to eat, carefully placing his fedora on the seat beside him. The older guy who had complained about "kids these days" had his platter and caught his eye. He motioned to see if he could join him. The two men sat eating their burgers. The older man spoke first. "Haven't seen a fedora like yours in quite a while. Nice to see a guy in a suit and a sharp hat."

He thought about his response and then said, "I like the feel of a good suit and a sharp hat."

The older man nodded. "My dad used to dress like that every day when he went off to work, even after the Depression. Then the war came, and he went to work in a factory. Then I only saw the suit and hat for Sunday."

Drips of information collected for him. The Depression he recognized. The War he recognized maybe—could be a different war. He still didn't know when today was.

The two men finished their burgers. He followed the older man's lead and tossed the paper wrapper in a bin marked trash and stacked the platter above it. They walked out the door together. The older man hesitated and said, "If you don't mind my asking, you don't look like you're from around here. My name's Don, Don Grant."

Nick smiled and offered his hand. "Thanks, Don. I'm Nick Brown, and no, I'm not from around here. Can you point me to a hotel or a place where a guy can get a room?"

"Glad to meet you, Nick. Can't say that this hick town has much in the way of rooms. You can drive to Tucson and find lots of places but not much here in Vento Junction."

Nick responded, "Well, I'm on foot. Is there a bus I can catch?"

Don chuckled, "You sure aren't from around here. There's no bus. Hey, I live alone now, and we've got a spare room. Why don't you come home with me? You're welcome to spend the night."

Nick thought he would accept. His prospects were bleak for the night, and he needed to learn more before he could make his next move. But he needed to check out his host, at least a little.

"Pardon me for asking, but why are you doing this? Inviting me to your home?"

Don paused. "I was a high school science teacher for more than thirty years. I've seen my share of lost kids. Lots of them spent time in my home when they were sorting themselves out. You have a bit of that look about you." Don walked over to a large pickup. He motioned for Nick to get in on the passenger side. Once seated Don put a strap across his chest and clicked it in place somewhere. He looked over at Nick and said, "Better buckle up. The sheriff will give me a ticket if he sees you without your seatbelt."

Nick fumbled before finding a strap like Don's near his right shoulder. He pulled on it, and it readily reached across his chest. Then he groped for how to make it click. Don pointed to a red tab. Nick slid the metal tab in beside it and heard a click.

Don started the truck. It sounded powerful, and when it pulled away from the curb, it seemed to glide. It was smooth and quiet. Not at all what Nick was used to when riding in a truck. They sped along through town and into a neighborhood of pretty fancy houses. Small yards. No fences. No sidewalks. As they continued, the houses became more modest. Soon they pulled into a short driveway. Don pushed a button near his visor, and the garage door lifted. They drove into a large garage with a smaller vehicle to one side. Don said it was a golf cart and that everyone had one.

Nick found that if you pressed on the red button, the seatbelt released. They got out of the truck and entered the house through a

17

door in the garage. Nick was struck by the bright colors and modern gadgets in what must be the kitchen.

"Take a load off," Don offered, "while I turn on the news. How 'bout a beer?"

"Sure." Nick nodded. "You don't have to ask me twice." Nick smiled. This was indeed familiar territory.

Don reached into the large two-door appliance and retrieved two bottles of amber liquid. "My sons introduced me to this Mexican beer called Corona. I really like it."

Carefully taking off his fedora and setting it on the kitchen table, he looked toward the doorway to the next room. Then he heard a man speak. He looked around. Maybe it was a radio in the next room. *Good,* he thought. *News should be helpful.*

He walked into the next room and was startled to see a box with what looked like a movie playing—a color movie. But it was a man and woman sitting at a desk talking about an accident, then an arrest, and then a guy talking about the weather. This was very strange. Now he was pretty certain he had landed at some point in the future. He certainly had no such movie boxes in his lab before he had left.

The talking wrapped up with a brief sports segment. He heard familiar names like: Cubs, Yankees, Sox, and that the Cubs were losing, the Yankees were winning again—some things didn't seem to change. Then the movie shifted to some angry guy talking about "the war in Iraq." *Iraq?* Nick thought. Not Japan and not Germany. He had to find out when this was. He scanned the room for a newspaper. He saw one across the room.

First, Nick decided to find out more about his host and his attitudes. "So, Don, this place is near that camp, right? Where the Japs are?"

Don turned to look at Nick with his eyebrows raised. "That camp went to ruin not long after the war. Never should have even been a camp. We never should have imprisoned our own people. It's a stain on our history and our character."

Nick looked at his host with a serious tone. He replied, "I'm relieved to hear you say that. They were my family in that camp."

Don continued his thoughts. "Americans have made a lot of mistakes. Slavery, the way we treated the Chinese workers who helped build the railroads, the European immigrants, but the way we put our friends and neighbors into prison camps just sticks in my craw."

"Mind if I read your paper?" he asked Don.

"Sure. Not much good news in it." While Nick began to scan the paper, Don moved into the kitchen to give this strange young man some space.

The paper was dated Sunday, September 7, 2008. Nick thought it was a good thing he was sitting down. He had jumped forward sixty-four years. He would be eighty-eight years old if he was still alive. The crazy machine he, Dick and the Tricksters had been working on in the lab had worked. But since Dick had not been able to predict how far he would go, Nick wondered if his best friend also factored in time with distance. And would they be able to get him back? How could they even find him if they didn't know he had gone forward in time? Was he somehow still connected to 1944?

Don stood at the sink washing his hands and thinking about the young man he had brought into his home. He definitely looked Asian. A shock of close-cropped straight black hair, wide set eyes over a fine nose. His lips mostly in a straight line like he was thinking hard as he absorbed his surroundings. When the engine of the truck had roared to life, a wide grin had transformed his face into an image of youth.

Don wondered what his son Ben would think about his most recent stray.

CHAPTER 2

DAY ONE, VENTO JUNCTION, HOME OF DON GRANT

Nick decided to find out some more about his host. Don readily shared that he was a widower, had been living in Vento Junction since before he retired, and his son worked nearby at the Community College. Don had been a high school science teacher. Retired a few years. His wife had died two years ago of cancer. She had been a smoker. Just couldn't quit even though she knew it would kill her.

Cigarettes kill you? thought Nick. This was news to him. Maybe they're different in this time. He'd better hope. He liked a smoke and had been wondering where he could get a pack. He'd wait on that thought.

He decided to be bold. "Say, Don, I left in a hurry today and didn't bring a change of clothes. Any chance you have some old work clothes I can borrow?"

"Sure, loads of 'em. Let me just rummage around a bit. You look like my younger son's size. Got a couple of his things still here."

Leaving his bottle on the kitchen table Don left the room to get the clothes. Nick continued to look for scraps of information. He saw a book on the shelf in the living room titled *The Greatest Generation* about World War II. He walked into the next room to get a closer look at the book. He took it down and began to flip through it. He was startled by some of what he saw, but it seemed like the war had been won by the United States. What had happened? How did they do it? Maybe he would ask Don.

Right then Don returned with a pair of denim pants and one of the underwear shirts Nick had seen guys wearing on the street. Don pointed down the hall to a bathroom and a bedroom Nick could use. He headed off to change and sort out his thoughts. So much to take in…

When he had changed into the fresh clothes and hung up his suit Nick looked in the mirror. He looked like he would blend in now. That might be handy. He went back to join Don, who was putting down a small silver box on the coffee table.

"I just talked with my son. He's going to stop by for a minute on his way home. He checks on me pretty regularly to make sure I'm doing okay. He's not too sure about me living alone, but I'm used to it now."

The two men drank their beers and watched the small movie box until there was a noise outside. "That must be my boy," Don said.

A minute later, the front door opened, and a younger version of Don entered. He hugged his Dad and looked over at Nick. Don introduced them. "Ben, this is Nick Brown. Nick, this is my son, Ben. How 'bout a beer?"

"Sure, Dad. I'll get it." Ben walked into the kitchen and returned with a bottle for himself, two more, and an opener. "So, Nick, what brings you to this corner of the earth?" Ben drew on his beer.

Perhaps it was the beer. Perhaps it was Don's comments about the internment camps. His gut that told him to trust this father and son. The fact that Don had taught science didn't hurt either. Later, he wouldn't be able to decide exactly what it was that caused him to trust them, maybe thinking about his own father, but trust them, he did.

"What would you say if I told you that this morning I was in New Mexico and a machine brought me here this afternoon."

"I'd say a plane could easily do that, but why here?" said Ben.

Nick clarified, "Well, actually it wasn't a plane. I stepped into a box, and the next thing I knew, I was on the sidewalk. Here. And it was 1944 when I left."

Both Don and Ben spent a minute taking in that little detail of Nick's travel.

Don nodded and spoke first. "That explains the suit and the fedora. But, son, in 1944, wouldn't you have been in one of those internment camps? Is that why you were asking about the Vento Camp? Were you here?"

Nick relaxed. Don seemed to accept his tale of time travel. Ben was silent.

Nick went on, "Yes, I was here, in this internment camp at first. They took my family in 1942. But my work in physics at Stanford caught Oppie's interest. They pulled me from the camp and moved me to Los Alamos in 1943. I've been working there ever since. My folks are still in the camp."

Don shook his head. "Sorry again about those camps. Glad the government finally apologized about those."

Ben wanted to find out more about this visitor and his outrageous story, so he spoke up. "What work were you doing at Los Alamos?"

Nick decided to try to connect some fact and conjecture. "Since it's now 2008, you probably know we were working on a weapon."

They nodded.

He continued, "Maybe you don't know that a team of physicists were also working on molecular transference. It didn't seem too out of reach to move atoms from place to another if we were also going to smash them."

Ben shook his head. "We all know about Oppenheimer and the atomic bomb. Two of them got dropped on Japan at the end of the war. That was also the last time they were used. But transferring molecules—that's out there. We never heard anything about that."

Don seemed to be lost in thought. "I did hear that they did more experiments there. That Los Alamos was about more than just the bomb."

"But, Dad, if that was the case why didn't we ever hear anything?"

"Son, you know the government can keep a secret when it wants to, and this would have been one helluva secret."

Nick continued, "The experimental mechanism had been primitive to start. Sending an object somewhere close and bringing it back. We didn't know where the item traveled to, but we had gotten better at bringing them back. The war effort was tense. We were competing with the Germans and didn't know how much progress they had made. The army was putting pressure on all of us to get something they could use. I volunteered to be the first human to be sent."

Ben and Don nodded and waited for him to continue.

"So this morning, the team gave me a little money, wished me well, closed the door and here I am. I just don't know if or when they can get me back. It took a lot of juice to run the machine. It may be a while before they have the power to try to get me back. And they may not know that I traveled in time. It's a new twist in the works."

Ben was the first one to speak. "So they *will* try to bring you back."

"That was the plan." Nick paused. "I think the notion was that this kind of transfer could be used to gather military intelligence to help with the war. I'm pretty sure sixty-four years in the future wasn't what they had in mind at all."

Don spoke now. "Well, we can tell you how and when your war will end. You've seen the one book,"—he pointed at the book near Nick—"but a lot more boys and innocent people will die before the war ends in Germany in 1945 and in the Pacific later that year."

Nick shuddered slightly. Another year of death. He wondered if there was anything he could learn here that could end the war sooner. So he asked them.

"Did anybody try to end the war sooner? They couldn't possibly have just gone on bombing and shooting each other."

Ben shook his head sadly. "It was the atomic bomb that ended the war in the Pacific. Hitler committed suicide in Germany when he saw that he couldn't win. The world can never forget the genocide of the holocaust. That's an international stain never to be forgotten." Don and Ben shook their heads. Neither of them knew what to say now, but Ben had a thought. "Come with me to the den. We'll hit the Internet. Maybe we'll find something."

"Genocide? The Internet?" Nick was baffled. What the heck.

"Come on. I'll explain it as we boot up Dad's laptop. "Dad, is it in your office?"

Don was already heading to the room down the hall that was his retirement office. He headed for a flat black rectangle sitting on a desk. "Here you go. You know the password since you set it up for me."

Ben smiled at Nick. "You have a lot to catch up on. The European recovery was possible because of the Marshall Plan that the United States funded. Germany is still stained by the mass killing of Jews, homosexuals, gypsies, so many people. And then when we won the war in the Pacific, the deal was that Japan disbanded their army. Over the next decades, they built their economy with the money they saved not having to pay for an army, and now they are known for technology. The United States invents it, but the Japanese perfect it, among the new gadgets are laptop computers."

Nick said, "Boy, what sixty-four years will do. They'll never, ever believe this when I get back… if I get back."

Before the screen lit up, Ben asked Nick, "So any idea of the kind of info you need? Physics, history? We'll have access to just about anything you can ask for."

"Here?" Nick asked.

"It's not what's in books anymore. It's on the Net. You'll see." Ben wondered how Nick would react to Google.

They sat side by side at the desk. Ben sat in front of what he called a laptop. Don pulled up a chair on the other side of him.

Ben said, "Okay, let's just go for it and see what we get if we search for time travel and Los Alamos."

Nick watched as letters appeared on the screen. Ben pushed a key and what appeared to be typed listings popped up on the small movie screen.

"Where's the projector?" he whispered. Ben smiled. "No projector. Its wireless. Used to be over the phone lines, but now we don't even need those."

Nick muttered, "And we thought time travel was outrageous."

"It still is, I'm afraid. We have lots of great tools, but we can't cure cancer and people still go to war."

Ben was making the screen change. He had found a scientific paper that had recently been declassified. It was by a Nicholas Nishimura from Stanford in 1939.

Nick blushed, "That's me. We decided that Nick Brown might be safer just in case a Japanese name wouldn't bring a friendly reception." Ben nodded, understanding.

Ben decided to search for "Nicholas Nishimura" to see if there was anything that might be helpful. There was a Wikipedia entry. They all moved in closer and read the few paragraphs.

> Nicholas R. Nishimura, 1920–1944. Killed serving his country. Noted physicist was working on experiments to aid military intelligence effort. Nishimura's work in teleportation had offered great hope for cutting time in delivery of supplies to troops overseas. When human transport was attempted Nishimura volunteered. The experiment ended unsuccessfully, and the scientist was declared officially dead in October 1944. Work was terminated on teleportation experiments. Notes on these and other Los Alamos findings were made public through the Freedom of Information Act.

Ben straightened up. "The writer was listed as Charles S. Grant, PhD. That's Charlie who wrote this."

Nick asked, "You know him?"

Grinning, "I think I do. My brother Charlie has always been into more science fiction than science. But this has got to be him."

Nick sounded more urgent now. "Can I talk to him?"

"Last we knew Charlie was living with our aunt in Flagstaff. Dad, will you give her a call?"

"Sure. Just remember Betty is hard of hearing."

Ben sent the Wikipedia entry to a printer down the hall. Nick was pensive and then said, "I guess I didn't go back."

Ben said, "At least not to 1944. Let's see if Charlie found anything that even Wikipedia wouldn't accept."

As they waited for the document to finish printing Ben explained about Wikipedia, the online encyclopedia written by many people.

"What a concept. Regular people get to write encyclopedias now?" Nick wondered.

"Kind of," Ben replied. "There are people on staff who review the entries before they're posted—before they're put up for the public to read. It could be that Charlie had more information, but maybe it seemed too far-fetched to be included."

As they drank their beers, they talked more about what they had found. Don found his address book and called his sister. She wasn't in, so he left a message.

Nick looked baffled. "It sounded like you spoke to someone."

Don grinned. "This is technology even I can explain. We can now have our telephones connect to a tape recorder. When someone calls and you're not home, they can leave a message. No more missed calls."

"But how many people have telephones?"

The two Grants laughed and sputtered out together, "Everyone." Nick shook his head.

Don continued, "And now with cell phones, it's crazy."

"Cell phones?" Nick was really curious.

Don reached into his pocket and produced the little silver box Nick had seen in the truck.

Don announced, "This is a cellular phone. You can call anywhere in the world with this, from almost anywhere."

"And you don't have teleportation." Nick was shaking his head, trying to make sense of the science and technology he had just learned of. Computers the size of a placemat or smaller. Everyone had a telephone. Phones so small they could be lost in your hand. A source of information at your fingertips. Just ask a question and there was the answer. My God. What would he find out about next?

His astonishment spilled out of him. "You can pull information from thin air. You can talk to someone on the other side of the world using something smaller than my hand. Someone must be doing teleportation, even time travel. They must."

Ben said, "It does seem logical. We can do amazing things. Fly planes remotely. Use lasers for guidance. Nanotechnology. Yeah, it does seem like it should be possible."

Just then Don's cell phone vibrated. Nick asked, "No ring?"

Don said, "This way it doesn't bother other people when I'm out." He answered the call. It was his sister.

"Hi, Betty. Yeah, I just wondered if Charlie was around. Just saw something he wrote, and I might have some information for him. Yeah, that would be great. We'll look forward to his call." Don closed the phone. "Charlie's on campus but should be home in about an hour," Don reported. "He's been working on something at the lab."

Ben explained, "Charlie's a physicist. He's teaching a few classes." Ben paused before going on. "He's been fired from his last few jobs. He keeps writing research grants to study time travel. Oh, he uses other descriptions, but the physics community is on to him. So he only works a little here and there."

Nick was thinking out loud, "That explains his interest in an obscure scientist from 1944."

Not too much later, the phone buzzed again. This time Ben answered. Since the brothers hadn't spoken in a while there was some catching up before Ben could broach the topic on all their minds. Finally, he plunged in, "So, Charlie, have you ever heard or read of a scientist named Nicholas Nishimura?" There was a pregnant pause.

"Why do you ask?"

Ben replied, "His work is pretty interesting, don't you think? Even promising?"

Charlie was getting suspicious. "OK, you guys have found something I wrote, and you want to give me a hard time. Not funny, big bro."

"Not this time, Charlie. This is different. I ask you about Nick Nishimura because I just met him."

Charlie's uncharacteristic reply came back over the line, "OK, that shouldn't be possible."

Ben shrugged. "Well, Charlie, you of all people should know that it is."

"It is?"

"Yes, it is."

"You're putting me on, and I think it's pretty rude and childish."

"Charlie, I'm not. He's here. He's right here with me at Dad's house. When he got up this morning it was 1944. And he's taking all this future stuff pretty well, considering. From cars, trucks, the Internet, winning the war. The sixty-four years he just skipped represents a lot of change. But the fact is, he's surprised we don't have time travel, given all the other amazing technology we take for granted."

Charlie grumbled, "Well, when you put it that way, I suppose it is pretty amazing."

Ben smiled, "So, Charlie, is your car gassed up?"

By now, Charlie was grinning because it showed in his voice. "I can be behind the wheel in half an hour, maybe less."

Ben was pleased. "We'll be waiting for you. Oh, and bring your research notes with you."

Ben hung up the phone and turned to Nick and his dad. "He'll be here in about four and a half hours. What do you want to do until then?"

Nick thought for a minute and said slowly, "Do you think you could find out what happened to my family?"

Ben and Don looked stricken. "Nick, I'm so sorry we didn't think of that. Of course, we can do a search. What was your dad's name? Do you have other family members we can look for?'

Nick said, "My dad was Henry. Henry R, for Richard. My mother was Sunny or Suzume. My younger sister's name is, or was, Grace."

Ben cleared the screen and began typing. "If Google doesn't find anything, we can try Ancestry.com. Where would they have gone after the camps closed?"

"We lived in San Tierra, California. I have to imagine they would have tried to go back."

"What did your dad do, before the camp?"

"He taught science at South Pasadena High School." Nick became pensive. "What happened after the war? Did people get their jobs back? Their lives back?"

Ben grimaced. "It really depended on the community." He stared at the computer screen. "I found something."

Don was looking over his son's shoulder. "Sorry, son, it looks like we found something, an old newspaper reference. Sounds like San Tierra wasn't too welcoming after the war."

Ben had a thought. He started searching for post WWII repatriation of Japanese-Americans. He typed faster. "I found a site. I've got them. They ended up in Indio. I even see a mention of your sister."

Nick wasn't sure he wanted to know more, yet he did. It was all so much, so fast. "Can you find out if anyone is still in Indio?"

Ben kept typing and sucked in his breath. "I found a notice of your sister's marriage. She married a man named Hector Acevedo in 1946. Both of your parents were mentioned in the notice. Did you have an uncle named Gregory?"

Nick shook his head. "I haven't thought of Uncle Greg in ages. He was kind of a black sheep. We didn't see much of him when we were growing up. I guess the camps brought them back together."

Ben continued to type. "I've got a listing for Grace Acevedo in Indio."

Don reached for the phone. Nick reached out his hand and said, "I'm not sure."

Don said, "Son, when you get to my age you don't wait to call family."

Nick nodded. "But I shouldn't be the one to talk to her."

Don and Ben nodded. Don picked up his cell phone and Nick heard high-pitched tones. The phone rang. Fortunately, it was the same time in California as Arizona, and it was just late afternoon.

Ben looked at Nick. "Did you have daylight savings time in 1944?"

Nick nodded. "Yes, they still have it? I thought it was just during the war."

A message machine picked up. Don said, "This is a message for Grace Nishimura Acevedo. My name is Don Grant and I have some new information about your brother Nick. Please give me a call." Don left his number and hung up.

Nick dropped into a nearby chair, suddenly overwhelmed. "Thanks, thanks so much. This morning they were all alive. Now I have to think about what sixty-four years has done to the family I knew."

Ben looked at his dad. "We need some food. Shouldn't be doing all this stuff on an empty stomach and beer."

Don looked over. "Horseshoe for takeout?" Ben nodded.

Don dialed and said into the phone, "Hi, Dee. Three burger platters and three pieces of that fine apple pie you all make."

Nick was still trying to absorb all of this when Don's phone rang. Don looked at Nick, who nodded, then grabbed the phone. "This is Don Grant."

The voice on the other end of the phone was not what he expected. A young woman spoke. "This is Nicola Acevedo. You left a message for my grandmother. She's unable to manage phone calls right now. You said you knew something about my great-uncle Nicholas. You called him Nick."

"Yes, Miss Acevedo. What was the family told about his time in the military?'

"We were told he died a hero. That was all."

Don said the next bit very gently, "Did they return his remains to you?"

An equally soft tone responded, "No, no, they didn't."

"Do you know anything about what your uncle was working on before he..."

"He was a scientist, a physicist," she broke in. "I've looked into his published papers. My best guess is that it had to do with translocation of atoms. I always figured he was blown up in an experiment gone wrong...and the government didn't want to admit to it."

"You're not too far off," muttered Don, "but he didn't blow up. He wasn't just translocated. He was sent to the future."

She gasped, "That's not possible. How do you know any of this? Can it be possible?"

"Because I met him today. He's twenty-four years old and sitting in my living room."

There was silence from Nicola's end of the conversation. "Miss Acevedo? Are you still there?"

"Well, I haven't time traveled if that's what you're asking."

"No, I'm concerned that what I've just told you gave you an emotional and physical shock and that you shouldn't be alone."

"I'm not alone. Abuelita's right here."

CHAPTER 3

LOS ALAMOS, NEW MEXICO,
SEPTEMBER 1944

Richard "Dick" Stanton looked at the metal box that had just sent his best friend into the unknown. The air in the room smelled of ozone and burnt insulation. He both regretted his departure and envied his adventure. This damn war was full of such contradictions. Other scientists in the room shifted around uneasily where they sat and stood. What does one do after the launch of an experiment? Champagne? Cigars? "We don't know if it's a success yet. We don't know exactly where Nick went. And God alone knows if we'll be able to get him back." He muttered softly under his breath, he hoped.

The power drain to run the transport experiment was profound. The other labs were not happy with them. It would be days before they could attempt to reach Nick, and he knew that.

The handful of men in the room began to recover from the drama of the launch. One by one they shuffled papers at their gray government issue metal desks and put them in their briefcases. The New Mexico monsoon was running into September and the skies were about to start to release torrents of much needed rain. They wanted to get to the lodge and cocktails before the gravel road became impassable. Finally, it was just Dick and one of the military types still in the room. For an army guy Colonel Patrick "Mac" MacLane wasn't bad. He appreciated rules and knew when to enforce them and when not to be in the room. As Dick made ready to leave, the colonel stopped him.

"Dr. Stanton, I need to have a private talk with you. Do you have some time?"

"You know you can call me Dick, Colonel. And sure, you want to talk now? Here?"

"Dick, thanks. Not here if that's okay. Let's take a walk. And call me Mac, please."

Dick packed his briefcase, putting a few of Nick's items in his pile. Just in case, he wanted to keep his friend's papers safe. As the two men left the gray metal Quonset hut, they squinted against the thundering sky. The intense rains of monsoon season were not something he experienced growing up in Southern California. They stayed next to the buildings, heading in a direction away from the main compound of labs, offices, and living quarters. As they reached an empty lot with a staff car, Mac motioned Dick inside. "Let's get under a roof before this gets started." Mac looked over at Dick. "On a scale of 1 to 10, what chance do you give today's experiment of success?"

Dick paused. "I hope for Nick's sake, it's a 10. As a scientist, I give it a 6. It went just like the other successes. And we just don't know."

Mac thought about that answer. "Do the other scientists share your feelings?"

"Pretty much. Although a few are more skeptical. Though Simon seemed to think everything was perfect. That's an odd attitude for a physicist, but better than doom and gloom I suppose."

Mac said slowly, "Maybe not. We have some concerns about Simon."

Dick almost stopped breathing but reminded himself to keep pulling air in and pushing it out. "What kind of concerns?"

Mac's shoulders straightened. "We have reason to be concerned about Simon's credentials."

Dick was dumbfounded. "You guys didn't check him out? My God, I went through weeks of interviews and background checks."

"So did Dr. Constantine, but recently we have begun to question the truthfulness of some of the third party work we relied on."

"You don't think he's a physicist?"

"No, we don't. We think he's a spy."

Dick was dumbfounded. "A spy." He kept his voice low and his temper steady. "I haven't been impressed with his work, but a spy?"

"It's not our best day when we have to admit that we think we screwed up. But we think Dr. Simon Constantine is not what he purports to be."

"But why? And why our experiment? Why not the weapon in Building G. Yeah, we all know. Don't get your feathers ruffled."

Mac's jaw was tight. "Because transference of supplies and people is more powerful than any weapon of destruction."

"So now what do we do? And what the heck does this mean for Nick?" Dick was shaking his head, thinking about what this might mean for the safety of his friend.

Mac was grim. "Well, it means that we're going to slow our efforts to get him back. It's got to appear like the experiment isn't worth stealing. We may even make it look like they're pulling the funding on the project for now. We want to see if that will flush him out."

"Will you let us work on getting Nick back anytime soon?"

"That depends on Dr. Simon Constantine, or whatever his real name is."

Dick Stanton began to take in the implications of what he had just heard. "How long are you willing to wait to find out?"

"I'd like to say as long as it takes, but that's not really feasible. Probably the end of October will seem natural. We'll be watching Simon closely to find out if he can be trusted."

"So how will this go down? You or someone from your side arrives in the lab and just says 'Halt?'"

"Almost. With the power drain, they have a good cover to slow the experiment. It will sound more official than that, but there will be an excuse given to slow the trials for a while. If we can't get this sorted out by the end of October, all of you will be reassigned to other projects. At least for a while."

"What happens to Nick? What the hell happens to my friend? I thought you never left a man behind?"

Mac frowned. "I'm not happy with this either. But when this transport thing works—and I believe it will—it's critical that it not fall into the wrong hands."

Dick was relieved he had grabbed Nick's loose notes from his desk. He thought about the small black notebooks Nick kept in their quarters. That would be his next stop.

Mac continued his train of thought, saying, "We'll set up secure communications with all members of the team. I hope it won't come to this, but if it does, you will all be dispersed to different projects beginning November 1. We want and need to sort out the Simon Constantine situation as soon as possible."

The two men realized that while they had been talking, the rainstorm had begun in earnest. A real gully washer, as the locals would say. Too bad for all that new gravel the NM highways folks had spread out. Mac fired up the engine and drove them slowly toward the lodge and dormitory where Stanton stayed. He and Nick had shared a room, and he wanted to get there and secure Nick's personal things. Not knowing how soon things would change or where he might be moved, he was concerned about making sure he took care of his friend's things.

The two men said little on the short drive to the lodge. When he got to their quarters, he felt hollow. He had expected quiet during his friend's experiment, but things felt different now with the knowledge that Nick would be away longer and that he himself could be leaving.

It was unsettling and very unsatisfactory to be facing even more uncertainty than before, before this morning. Just this morning, he and Nick had joked about what they would do when he returned. Now the plan to crack open the bottle of pre-war Scotch seemed sad rather than celebratory.

As he walked toward their door, he saw Theresa, their young Indian maid. Nick had become fond of her, like the younger sister he was missing. Theresa drew closer. She spoke softly to him, "Do not worry about your friend. The spirits watch him."

CHAPTER 4

DAY ONE, VENTO JUNCTION, ARIZONA, SEPTEMBER 8, 2008

Don recovered from hearing that Nick's sister was alive and near the phone. He wanted to know if she was well and thought how best to ask, when Nicola answered his unspoken question.

"She's sharp as a tack and in great shape. Let me see if she wants to talk to him."

Don relayed the information as Nick began to focus on the moment. He had looked like he was far away just a minute ago. He rose and moved toward the phone.

"Grace? Is that you?"

"Nicky, it's me," a thready but familiar voice responded. "But how can it be you? You died in 1944."

"I'm not back from the dead if that's what you mean. It's a long story, but there was an experiment in New Mexico. Remember the government work? Well, the experiment was just this morning to me. In 1944. And then I ended up here in Arizona in 2008."

"This sounds like some story, Nicky." Grace was understandably skeptical. "How do I know it's you?"

"I don't know."

Ben piped up, "We can e-mail a photo of you with today's front page. Ask if Nicola has an e-mail address."

"Grace, I feel like I'm speaking a foreign language, so bear with me." He spoke haltingly over the phrases that were new. "Does Nicola have an…e-e-e-mail…address? Apparently, we can take a picture and send it that way."

Then Nicola was on the phone as Ben intervened. "Sure, I have e-mail. Why don't you give me yours first?"

Ben smiled at her safety precaution. "Of course. I understand. I work at the local community college. I'd do the same thing in your place." And he spelled out his e-mail for her.

They had left the food on the table when the phone rang, and all of a sudden, the food smell was overpowering. Nick realized how hungry he was. The burger he had earlier was more of a snack. Maybe moving your molecules through time and space made you hungry. Who knew? The three men ate in silence with the TV for company filling them in on more news of the day.

Breaking the silence, Ben began to fill Nick in on some of the household gadgets that people of 2008 took for granted. Dishwasher, garbage compacter, microwave oven, icemaker in the door of the refrigerator. The motion-sensitive lights in the carport were a big hit. They all knew they were filling time before Charlie arrived. After their brief meal, Ben took out his cell phone and took a photo of Nick with the paper he had picked up when he got the food.

Nick tilted his head and said, "Wait, I thought that was a phone. Now it's a camera?"

Ben grinned, "They're actually called smart phones now because they can do much more than call. I can e-mail this photo from the phone to Nicola. In fact, I just did."

Nick just shook his head. He wished his friend Dick was here to see all this technology and knowledge. Dick! What had happened to Dick?

"Hey, Ben," Nick said. "While we're waiting for Charlie to arrive maybe we could look up some of my scientist buddies and see if the In-ter-net has anything to tell us about them." Nick stumbled a little over some of the new vocabulary he was hearing.

Ben shook his head and headed to the den to collect the laptop and bring it to the living room. "I can't believe I didn't think of that. Usually I'm the one asking what else or why and here I am just numb." As he talked, he opened the laptop and refreshed the screen. "What name shall I try first?"

"Dr. Richard Stanton. He was my best friend. He and I both went to Stanford and were inseparable until the Camps. When I got pulled out and sent to Los Alamos, I was relieved to see that Dick was there too. He hadn't completed his PhD when I left him, but I'm sure he would have gotten it as soon as he was able."

They all waited for Google to search for Dr. Richard Stanton. Unspoken was the question, "Did he survive the war?" Nick had to believe he had.

Ben smiled," You're right. He did get his PhD. In fact, more than one. He taught at UCLA for more than forty years. He retired in 1986. Then he went to work for a Think Tank."

Nick shrugged. "Think Tank?"

"A place where they pay you to think, but then they own whatever your thoughts might produce." Ben sounded cynical.

"And how is that different from the government?" Nick was serious.

Ben spoke knowingly. "Because the Think Tank pays better than Uncle Sam—much better. And not everything you work on gets turned into a weapon. Even better, they can offer state-of-the-art labs. Universities don't have the budgets they used to. Or the corner on the market," he muttered.

Ben kept on reading. "The Think Tank is headed up by a guy named Patrick MacLane. There's a link to him. I'll check it out."

Don whispered to Nick, "A link takes you to another page of information."

"Oh," Nick added, trying to log all the new words and info. "That makes sense."

"Hey, this is pretty interesting. Nick, do you remember a Mac MacLane from Los Alamos?"

Nick's eyes cleared from the fog of overload. "Yeah. He was there. We didn't see a lot of him. But what we did see was usually okay—he wasn't as buttoned up as the rest of the uniforms. We'd have cocktails sometimes."

"Well, this Think Tank is his baby—the one where your friend Dick went after UCLA."

"Where is this Think Tank?"

Ben grinned. "Pasadena. Right down the road from UCLA."

Nick smiled at this bit of connection and then thought to ask, "Do you know if either of them are still"—he hesitated—"alive?"

Ben nodded. "Looks like your friend is. A bit grizzled judging by the photo here, but it's recent."

Nick leaned in and had to suppress a gasp. His friend Dick at ninety—not an image he had ever contemplated. "He looks in good health. What about Mac?"

He retired from the think tank a few years ago, but The Institute he started seems to be thriving."

"Maybe a field trip is in order." This time, it was Don who spoke. "I know something about the passage of time, and I don't think we should wait too long."

They all turned when they heard the sound of a car pulling in and a door slamming.

Dan and Ben nodded. "Charlie."

The cyclone known as Dr. Charlie Grant plowed into the room and stalled. Shaggy dark hair and a day's growth of beard darkened his sharp features. The wind and momentum knocked out of him by what he saw in front of him. In his dad's living room, gathered around a laptop, were his dad, his brother, and an Asian looking stranger. A 24-year-old stranger who matched the 1939 photo of Nick Nishimura in the Stanford yearbook.

Not often at a loss for words, Charlie chose to sit down and try to close his mouth.

Don smiled and said, "Nick, this is my other son, Charlie. The one who knows your work." In saying this, Charlie learned several facts. His dad followed his work. His dad and brother had shared it with the stranger. And he might just be able to speak again but not right away.

The magnitude of the moment was not lost on the two scientists in the room. The one whose work had made his presence possible and the one whose belief in the work had caused so much career frustration.

Charlie swallowed, looked at Nick, and asked, "Does anyone else know you're here?"

Nick replied, "Just my sister and her niece. If they have received the e-e-e-mail with my photo and today's paper."

Charlie sounded worried. "Did you tell them not to tell anyone?"

Nick shook his head. "It didn't occur to me. Why are you concerned?"

"The government is different now than when you were working for them."

Nick pointed out, "They were secretive in 1944."

Charlie was grim. "They have moved beyond secretive."

Nick was puzzled. "What comes beyond secretive?"

Charlie dropped his voice to almost a whisper. "Protective custody."

"You know this from personal experience?" Nick was starting to share Charlie's concern.

"I was interrogated about my research a few years ago. I lost my job but not my freedom. And I gained a new respect for the long arm of the law." He used air quotes when he said "law."

Nick caught on. "I doubt Grace or Nicola will say anything. They were understandably suspicious at our call. That said, though, we might proceed more carefully from this point forward."

Ben nodded, "Good point. We were thinking about calling the Think Tank where Nick's former colleagues are hanging out."

"Holy shit, no!" Charlie was agitated. "Not till we've checked it out. Trust should not be freely given in our current environment." Charlie was somber.

Nick looked alarmed. Don smiled. "Son, we've had many years of peace. And we still have enemies. I think what Ben and Charlie are trying to say is that your knowledge would be greatly desired by the new enemy."

Nick was taking this all in. Sixty-four years in the future and there were still enemies and his work put him at risk. "OK, then how do we proceed? Who can we trust?"

Don's phone rang. He reached for it and grumbled, "I can't believe I forgot Sam! I took her to the groomer earlier and plain forgot. I'll be right back."

Ben looked at Nick. "The dog."

Nick was nonplussed.

Charlie added, "I wondered where Sam was. Well, maybe not the first thing I wondered, but she's always with Dad."

Don called over his shoulder, "Anybody need anything while I'm out?"

Nick thought to himself that he wouldn't even know where to begin listing what he needed.

As the door closed behind Don, Charlie turned to Ben and Nick. "Okay, we have to have a plan. First, tell me all the websites you've visited. Where have you left your tracks?"

CHAPTER 5

LOS ALAMOS, LATE AUGUST 1944

Nick lifted his glass to his colleagues, Dick and Mac, at cocktail time, the colonel was just Mac. "Well, we've had some success, but I'll be damned if I know why."

Dick returned, "Do we care? We've been at this for the last year and we've just had a breakthrough."

Mac joined, "I think I share Nick's concern. If you don't know why, then you can't repeat your work with any confidence. Yes?"

Dick nodded. "OK, yes. We do need to look at what's changed. Review all our notes, because something has changed, and we need to know what. They may call what we're doing 'the Trick' and us 'the Tricksters,' but we know it isn't."

Nick was thinking and slowly talking, "How wide will we cast our net for change? My soap? The food?"

Mac thought about it. "Something more universal but benign, or thought to be so common as to elude our awareness."

Dick nodded. "OK, not your soap, which by the way hasn't changed even though our maid is sweet on you."

Nick was sharp. "Her name is Theresa."

Mac tried to focus the train of thought. "OK, we're agreed it's not the soap. Think, you guys. If you haven't had too much Old Crow for your brains to work. What's changed around you? People, tools, supplies, anything?"

"Well yeah, the damn dust is worse. I cough a lot more. Ever since they brought in that gravel to make the road better." Dick made a good point. The place was even dustier than usual.

Mac lasered his eyes to the young scientists. "OK, scientists, what do you think? Something like gravel? The dust? Could that be the variable you can't or haven't accounted for?"

Nick had perked up. "We need to know where it came from. If it's from nearby, then it's less likely to be our factor. Mac, can you find out?"

Mac had a sly grin, not all from the booze. "I'll look into it tomorrow. May take some time. What do I say if someone asks why I want to know?"

Dick smiled, "Tell them it's for the Trick. That ought to sway them."

Mac nodded, "Well, the gadget has a lot of sway. We'll see how far I get with the Trick."

They refreshed their drinks, satisfied that they were onto something, maybe.

CHAPTER 6

NICHOLAS NISHIMURA, LOS ALAMOS, AUGUST 1943

Between the train from Southern Arizona to Northern New Mexico and then the road to this remote place, Nick was exhausted. He had lots of questions and, so far, few answers. There were a lot of military uniforms so far and no scientists that he could see. And now some young Indian girl was his guide to a dormitory.

"What is your name?" she spoke very softly.

Nick was taken by surprise. His guide had left him with his thoughts up until now. "Nick. What's yours?"

She lowered her head and her voice. "My English name is Theresa."

"You have another name?" He was curious.

"Yes, I have a name among my people." Her voice was stronger.

"What is that name?" He was more curious.

"It is only for my people. Not for you." She looked away.

"OK. I think I understand. My grandparents were private about family stuff from Japan. It could be like that for you too." Nick was sympathetic.

"So, Theresa, do you go to school around here?" Nick thought this might be a safe topic.

"The Catholic Mission has a school for girls. I no longer attend. I must work to help my family."

"That's hard. I hope this job helps a lot." Having a conversation wasn't easy.

"What subject was your favorite?"

"I like chemistry and history." She smiled at him at the mention of her favorite subjects.

"It's an interesting combination. Is it organic chemistry?"

"Yes, I was able to bring in many items from my village for experiments." Theresa had warmed to the topic.

"What kind of items?" Nick wondered what organic items were around the area.

"Plants, crystals, things like that. My people, my family, are healers. I'm curious about why some things work sometimes and not others." She was opening up.

"Now I'm curious too. I'm new here and don't know what my schedule is, but I'd like to continue our talk. I'm a scientist, and we're curious about a lot of things." Nick was intrigued.

Dick Stanton knocked on the door frame. "Not to interrupt, bud, but we have some research to do."

"Dick!" Nick was surprised and happy to see his best friend. "I had no idea you were here!"

"No one does. That's the idea. This place is remote for a reason. All my family knows is that I'm working on something for the government. That's all I was allowed to say. They can send letters to a mail drop and maybe they get to me." Dick was a little frustrated.

"Enough of that." He pulled his thoughts back to his friend. "Are you settled? Wanna meet the guys?"

Nick looked at Theresa. She smiled then looked serious and said, "I am here four days each week. Usually after lunch. I try to spend time with the children in the mornings."

Dick raised an eyebrow. "Are you flirting with the nicest maid in town?"

Theresa blushed.

"N-no," Nick stammered. "We were talking about chemistry."

"Of that I have no doubt." Dick was teasing his friend.

Nick glared at his friend and turned to Theresa. "Never mind him. I do want to learn more about this area. When are you here again?"

"The day after tomorrow." She gathered her things to go to the next messy room.

The two young scientists took off at a quick pace to catch lunch and get to the Tech Area.

Nick began to meet regularly with Theresa to learn about the rocks and plants nearby. It was Theresa who told him he should meet Edith Warner and have a meal at her house by Otowi Creek.

Dick chuckled. "Lots of scientists go there to eat. It's plain but decent food and a chance to get a break, not to mention her chocolate cake."

Nick feigned offense. "When were you going to let me in on this?"

"All in good time, Bucko. The muckety-muck gadget guys go there once a week. We probably want to avoid that night. Even here, we keep secrets from the gadget guys."

"Well, what are we?" Nick wanted to know.

"They've started calling us 'the Tricksters.' And if we can pull this off, it will indeed be quite a trick."

Nick stared at his friend. "Well, do you think we can do it?"

"I know we can. I know you and how smart you are. If you're working on it, it's real."

"Now you have an idea why I spend time with Theresa to learn all about her native teachings. There's a rich history of power and healing here."

"So that's why? That's the only reason?" Dick was having fun with his shy friend.

"Come on. She's my little sister's age. I do like her, though. And she's smart and different from the girls in California."

"No, I get it. I think. Do you really think our surroundings can play a part in the experiment?" Dick got serious.

"I really don't know, but this science is sensitive. We don't know yet how to make it do what we want. And we need every edge we can find." Nick was just as sober as his friend.

"Well, OK. Let's find a time to go off campus and meet Edith." Dick was lighter at the thought.

Grace Nishimura, Vento Internment Camp 1943

Grace missed her brother Nick. When he was plucked from the isolation of the camp, her loneliness was so much worse. She worried about her mother and father all the time. The first place had been awful. Vento was a little better, but it was so different from home in San Tierra. At barely sixteen, she was enjoying an active social life. At least until December 7, 1941. Then it seemed that even her friends shied away from her. Her boyfriend had stopped calling. When she saw him at the Roller Rink, he admitted that his folks didn't want him to see her. She was stunned to think that anyone who knew her or her folks could think that their loyalties were anywhere other than with the country of her birth. But apparently, they did.

The camps were lonely, but at least everyone was sharing the isolation and the betrayal. At first, she couldn't even send letters to her girlfriends and former teachers. All but the letters to her teachers had been "returned to sender." Now the only one she wrote to was her former high school science teacher. Her time in the camp had allowed her to think about what she wanted to do when she got out. She had decided to become a nurse.

In the camp she had been helping at the camp's medical clinic. The nurse, Doris, appreciated her help. The clinic helped more than the internees. They also helped many of the migrant workers who couldn't afford a regular doctor. That's how she had met Hector. He was the boss of the crew of workers from nearby. They had followed the harvests, but since the war started, it was harder to follow the crops. Gas was so dear, and when you were the lowest rung on the social ladder, you didn't get many ration coupons. Hector and his crew had been "hired" to build and maintain the camp. Something was always breaking, and someone was always getting hurt. Because Hector spoke English, he was the one to bring the injured worker to the clinic. As time went by, he began to bring younger kids and then pregnant mothers. The variety kept Grace and her new friend, Doris, plenty busy.

It was not entirely a surprise when Hector started a conversation one afternoon when she was cleaning a cut so that Doris could stitch it up.

"Where are you from?" A typical opener, she thought.

"San Tierra."

"Really? Where's that? In America?" He seemed surprised.

She frowned. "Yes, it is. It's not too far south of Pasadena. I was born there. My dad taught high school in Pasadena, California."

"Then why are you here? I thought you were all Japanese?"

"No. We're Japanese-American. My grandparents came from Japan, but my parents and my brother and I were all born in California."

She turned the tables on him. "What about you? Where are you from? Mexico?"

"New Mexico," he smiled. "I'm Mexican-American. My parents are from Juarez, across the border, but moved here as kids themselves. I was born in Las Cruces."

They laughed at each other, but as the laughter subsided, they looked around, and they were still at an internment camp. There were towers with men holding guns and lots of barbed wire. And there was still a war going on. And her brother was gone with no word about why or where.

DAY ONE, VENTO JUNCTION, ARIZONA, SEPTEMBER 8, 2008

Charlie was giving Nick the Cliff Notes version of the past sixty-four years in government, science and spying. Nick was shaking his head. "Are there no good guys anymore?"

Ben offered, "It's not as clear as it was in WWII. Shades of gray make it harder for all of us. There's a little right in every wrong and vice versa. Face it. What was done to your family in the name of national security was wrong."

Nick nodded. "No argument on that front."

Charlie added, "The government did finally apologize for the internment camps—not until Ronald Reagan was President, but it finally happened. And there was some financial compensation too." Charlie moved closer and lowered his voice. "That brings us back to the plan. Who and what sequence *is* the problem of the day?"

Nick thought out loud, "We've contacted Grace and Nicola. I think they're next. They might be able to help us reach out to the others. Especially if we're not ready to show our hand yet."

Ben nodded, but Charlie was hesitating. "What do we know about them or their lives? I know they're family, but family can turn on you."

At that moment, the room was filled with a flying, yipping fur ball, followed by Don. Charlie scooped up the deliriously happy dog for some serious reconnecting. Ben looked at Nick who said, "Sam, I presume?"

Ben supplied, "Full name Samantha Jane. She's a miniature Australian Shepherd. We grew up on a small ranch and got used to having herding dogs around. Now she's just a pet who herds us."

Nick was shaking his head slowly. "This too is new. We didn't have a pet—few people did. Too costly. It was the Depression, remember?"

"Dad," Charlie directed himself, "we're deciding on next steps. What do you think?"

Don rubbed his chin with his hand. "Well, it all started in California, the family, Stanford, Nick's work. I think we go back to the start."

Nick added, "What about Grace and Nicola? When do we and how do we meet with them? How do we investigate them as Charlie recommends?"

Ben smiled. "I think between Dad's charm and a few simple searches we can do that. We probably want to be in California, though, when we search so that Vento Junction, Arizona, stops being a hub." Charlie's healthy paranoia was rubbing off on him.

They decided to rent an SUV in Tucson for the trip and be comfortable. Ben explained the concept to Nick—both car rental and SUV. It was another head shaker.

Don put the news on, and they all focused on something other than what they were about to do. After the news ended, the TV stayed on as background while the talk shifted back to "the plan." Ben found the Rand McNally road atlas since they had opted to stop using any search engines. With Charlie, they plotted the route to Indio. They agreed that it should be a four- to six-hour drive, depending on traffic and how often they stopped.

Nick, meanwhile, had been watching TV. Transfixed by the drama on the screen with some skin showing—not really racy, but… He spoke softly. "Things really have changed."

Don spoke up. "Yeah, the sexual revolution pretty much changed things forever."

"Sexual revolution," Nick repeated.

"The mid-1960s. Women got the pill and it all changed," Don offered.

"What pill?" Nick was focused.

"The birth control pill," Don replied.

"You can control birth?" Nick was baffled.

Ben clarified, shifting his gaze. "Actually, it's pregnancy control. It allows women to control their menstrual cycles and avoid pregnancy."

"So how does that tie into a sexual revolution?" Nick wanted to know.

Charlie chimed in. "With the risk of pregnancy removed, men and women could have sex without the danger of it resulting in a child and costing them their freedom. People began living together without marrying. They still do. I tried it."

"So how does that work?" Nick wanted to know.

"The sex part or the living together?" Charlie smiled.

Nick was honest when he said, "Both."

"Well, sex got easier because women started asking for what they wanted in bed. Living together is never easy, and sex doesn't always help—in fact, sometimes it muddies things," Charlie shared.

"How fast does a woman…" Nick began.

"Jump in the sack?" Charlie finished for him. "Depends on the woman. Sometimes it's a one-nighter. Sometimes longer."

Ben looked at his dad's bookshelves and saw the dated volume he thought might help Nick. "Here. It's an oldie, but it should shed some light on the time period."

Nick accepted the yellowed copy of *Our Bodies, Ourselves* and sat down. Ben and Charlie smiled at each other, sharing the thought that Nick might not fall asleep right away that night.

Don made a list of tasks and supplies for the morning, and they each drifted off to their beds to get some rest for who knew what lay ahead.

CHAPTER 8

LOS ALAMOS, NEW MEXICO, SEPTEMBER 1944

As Mac left Stanton, he was flushed with the shame of failure. Not only had he probably just sent the guy's friend to, at best, an uncertain future and worst case his death, he had let a rat into the mix. Well, not him personally, but the team who was to have done the vetting answered to him. They probably grilled the young California scientist with the Japanese looks and last name and then let the spy from Greece waltz right in. He had been an exchange student at Cal Tech when the war broke out and it was too dangerous for him to go home. Or that was his story. Since Oppie knew him, he sailed through. And if there was one, there could be more. Mac would make this right if he had to stay with it even when this damn war was finally over. When the war is over—what a thought. He'd been to London and saw what the bombing had done, to the buildings, but not to the spirit of the people.

He collected his thoughts and entered the Officers' Quarters. A couple of guys looked over at him. He shook his head. No news is no news, but it felt like bad news.

Almost Three Months Later, December 2, 1944

On a troop train, heading east to Oak Ridge, Tennessee

Dick Stanton was tired of being shipped around and hoped this place in Tennessee could be "home" for more than a couple of months. Since leaving New Mexico, he had heard from a few of his fellow Tricksters. They were scattered from coast to coast. They still couldn't say much. Telegraph was the best way and still they had to find you to give you the telegram. And now the train was dropping him at a place made of mud. He'd heard it called Atomic City. That would be full circle for him. Still no word on Nick. He got a wire occasionally from Mac. Nothing of substance, but he was a man of his word.

CHAPTER 9

DAY ONE, INDIO, CALIFORNIA, AFTER THE PHONE CALL, LATE

Nicola watched her grandmother's face soften as memories flooded in. Her *abuelita* did not speak of the war and the camp unless she was remembering her romance with Hector.

"*Abuelita, que tal?* Are you here with me?"

"No m'*hija*. I'm in a first-aid clinic in Arizona with a kind young man who didn't see an enemy when he looked at me."

"*Abuelita*, you know what a contradiction it always is for me when Spanish comes from your not-Mexican face," Nicola said it with love. The comment wasn't new, and they both smiled.

"Your *abuelo* Hector was the best thing to ever happen to me. I have to thank that wretched camp for that. I would never have left California back then, and I would have missed him. And I probably would have followed my dad into teaching, not nursing. So many paths changed by the war.'

Nicola loved her *abuela* and understood that the memories were in preparation for whatever was in that car from Arizona heading their way.

"Abuelita, I googled the man who called me. He does teach at that community college. He's kind of good-looking, in a cowboy kind of way."

Grace knew she was being teased. "Now, *m'hija*, don't get my hopes up. You keep telling me you only have time for science and research."

They both laughed at the familiar back and forth. "Now really, *abuelita*, what do you remember about your brother? You don't speak of him."

"That's because he died so young. Or at least that's what we were told. Nicky was so smart. We were so proud of him. When we were shipped off to the camp, I wasn't surprised that he didn't stay long. That brain was needed to fight the war."

Nicola turned to face her. "Was he part of building the bomb?"

"They wouldn't tell us. Just that he died as part of the war effort. Back then you just put a gold star in your window. We couldn't even do that. We didn't have our own window at the camp. We mourned privately. So many families lost sons and brothers. And some never even knew the little that we did. At least we knew Nicky was a hero."

"So what happened to Great-Uncle Nick's stuff?"

"A sweet young man came to the house after the war and brought us his personal things."

"Who was that?" Nicola was intrigued.

"It was so long ago. I have his name with the box. It's in the closet in the guest room."

Nicola went to find the box. Grace continued to let her mind wander.

"*Abuelita*, this says Captain Richard Stanton. Can that be right?"

"Yes, honey, that sounds right."

"*Abuelita*, why didn't I know this?"

"Why would you need or want to know?"

"Because Dr. Richard Stanton is kind of a famous scientist. And his son is my advisor."

Nicola pulled out her phone and started tapping. "What are you doing?" Grace was curious.

"I'm looking for Dr. Richard Stanton's bio to see if there's any mention of New Mexico."

"But why would there be?"

"If he had Great Uncle Nick's things, then he knew him. And if he knew him, he may know what happened to him."

Grace shook her head. All this fuss, and for what? Maybe nothing. Just stirring up memories long put to rest.

"You do what you need to, *hija*, I'm going to go to bed. Don't stay up too late."

Nicola continued her search.

> Richard H. "Dick" Stanton, PhD. Born Pasadena, CA. March 15, 1918. Richard Stanton joined the War effort in 1943 as part of an elite team of scientists working on special projects in New Mexico. He completed his military service in Oak Ridge, Tennessee. Following his marriage to Elizabeth "Betsy" Baldwin in 1946, Memphis, TN, he returned to California to complete his dissertation, earning the first of two advanced degrees. He was a professor of physics at UCLA for four decades, retiring in 1986. Following his retirement, he joined the research staff at a think tank in Los Angeles. He and his wife had two children, Richard "Rick" Stanton, Jr. (Jane) and Rosemary (Edward) DeWarren. His son also teaches at UCLA, and his daughter is a popular author of science fiction.

As Nicola searched the university website for faculty profiles and other media sources for mention of Dr. Richard Stanton a bright-colored flyer on the kitchen table caught her eye.

Abuelita Grace used the kitchen table like an inbox. This flyer announced a Classic Car Show this weekend. Starting today. Several vintage cars were featured from 1940, Oldsmobiles, and Plymouths.

Nicola got an idea for a way to arrange the meeting with the strangers the next day.

Day One, Nick's Notes

I have never believed in luck. But today has made me rethink that belief. Perhaps science had some help. I survived the teleportation experiment, though our focus on moving from here to there interfered with our considering the possibility of moving from between days and years.

The luck is very real. Being found by Don Grant then meeting his sons, who have many of the skills needed to survive this next stage of the experiment. First, learning that I traveled to the future, then learning that Grace is still alive, sixty-four years later!

While I trust Don, Ben, and Charlie, they are making me aware that trust should not be readily given. That it was easier to tell friend from foe in 1944 than in 2008. I will respect their guidance and not trust easily, I hope.

The technology and science of 2008 is the stuff of magicians and wizards. And still they tell me they do not have time travel or teleportation.

DAY TWO, VENTO JUNCTION, ARIZONA, SEPTEMBER 9, 2008

The trio plus one and Sam headed out early. The days were still hot near the border. Charlie navigated, Ben drove, and Nick and Don sat with Sam and watched the countryside speed by.

Nick asked, "When do you think we'll get to Indio?"

Charlie thought, *It's at least five hours, maybe a little longer. But certainly before dinner, even with stops for Sam, and Dad.*

"Are there trains anymore?"

Don frowned. "Not like in your day. Lots of freight, but very little passenger traffic. Ever since the Interstate Highways were built, people can drive and not be controlled by schedules."

"Interstate Highways?" Nick asked. "Uh-huh." This was Ben. "In the 1960s. The highway system is an Eisenhower left over."

"General Eisenhower?"

"Yes, but he was President Eisenhower then, when the highways were built. After the war, he was still really popular and was elected president."

"What year?"

Don paused. "Well, I think it was, well, the election was in '52, so he would have been from '53 to '61. He followed Truman."

Nick was confused. "Truman? Harry Truman, the vice-president?"

"Sorry, son." Don shook his head. "FDR died in office, and Truman stepped in. It was 1945. Truman was actually the one to decide to use the atomic bomb to end the war."

Ben weighed in, "I've got a few history textbooks back at the house. They might be a way you can catch up at your own pace. It's got to be a lot to take in."

Same Day, Indio, California, September 2008

Nicola woke her grandmother as the sun began to warm the air and remind them of the heat that was coming. After giving her a cup of coffee, she asked, "Abuelita, what kind of car did your father have before the camp?"

Her grandmother took a minute to clear her head of sleep. "It was blue, navy blue, really big. Not a Ford. Starts with an *O*, I think."

"Oldsmobile?"

"That's it."

"Do you think your brother Nick would recognize it?"

Now Grace was following her thinking. "If it's him, he would definitely know that car."

Nicola switched screens on her phone to dial Ben.

"Ben here." He spoke loudly to be heard over the car noise.

"Hey, Ben, it's Nicola. I have an idea. There's a classic car show in Indio starting today. Let's meet there. The flyer says they have some 1940s vintage stuff."

Ben caught on. Not only could they avoid being in Grace's home for the first encounter, they could have something familiar… for Nick. "Great idea. Will you text me the address? We should be there in about two and a half hours."

"I'll do it right now." Nicola was smiling.

Grace got ready for the day then puttered around the house thinking about what might be about to happen in a few hours. The Super Walmart was about ten minutes from the house. The parking lot was enormous, and these kinds of events drew people from quite a distance.

Grace and Nicola arrived at the store and chose a place near the front in the shade. They had a good view of people arriving for the car show, and Grace didn't need to stand in the heat. Nicola had brought cold water from home, and they both sipped as they scanned the groups arriving.

Nicola saw them first. An athletic-looking older man with a dog and three younger guys, one with Asian features. She watched them as they cruised the vehicles. When they reached the 1940 Olds aisle, she poked Grace.

"It's showtime, Abuelita." She walked around to help Grace get out of the car. They casually walked toward the group. Sam saw them, maybe smelled them, first. The guys followed Sam's gaze.

Nick's focus was on Grace's face, as was hers to his. "Nicky, do you remember Daddy's car?"

"How could I forget? I wanted so badly to drive it when I got my license, but his answer was always 'not yet.'"

They stared at each other without moving. Ben moved toward Nicola to introduce himself. "What gave us away? Four guys and a dog?" he chuckled.

"Not even close. I was watching Abuelita, and she caught her breath when she saw him." Don and Charlie came over to say hi, along with a very happy Sam. The brother and sister had begun to speak softly to each other. Grace began to cry softly, and then they were in each other's arms.

"How can this be?" Grace was in a daze. "You're so young."

"If I tell you I woke up two days ago in 1944, would that explain it?"

"Not even close." Nicola was moving toward Nick while Ben was moving toward both of them. "I think it's time to go somewhere more private for the next part of our conversation, don't you?" He was looking at Nicola. Nick didn't know about video cameras and a 24/7 news cycle.

"Of course, you're right. Let's go to the house. We've got food and beer."

Charlie perked up. "Did I hear beer?"

Don laughed, called Sam, and they headed for the SUV.

Nick look wistfully at the Oldsmobile but sensed the concern of both Ben and Nicola and trusted them. "If you don't mind, I think I'll ride with them." Nick pointed to his family.

"Of course." Ben nodded. The groups split off. Nicola explained which car to follow.

Grace began to share memories. "I've missed you. The camp was hard on Mommy and Daddy. It changed them. I'm a nurse, and I can tell you they weren't the same after the camp. This isn't scientific or medical, but their spirits weren't the same after."

She continued responding to his raised eyebrows. "What happened after the camp? Oh, we tried to come back. We weren't welcome. That's why we came to Indio—a new start. Hector's family had cousins here. We were welcome. Daddy was able to teach high school. Hector was a fireman and then the fire chief. I was on staff at the hospital. Mommy and Daddy came to live with us when they couldn't live on their own. Our kids were little, and they had a chance to know them.

Grace was far away as she told the story. It was important that her brother hear what happened after he was gone.

"Nicky, we were so proud of you. Mommy and especially Daddy. He knew what you worked on was important to our country."

At this, Nicola weighed in. "What *were* you working on? And you should know that Dr. Richard Stanton's son is my PhD advisor."

"Whoa." Nick almost physically leaned back. "That's a lot to take in. Dick Stanton got his PhD. And he has a son? In what discipline?"

She smiled. "He's emeritus now. His son is in his late fifties, and it's Quantum Physics."

Nick got quiet. "We were working on molecular transference."

It was only a matter of minutes, and they pulled up to a neatly kept ranch house with a grassy yard. In the second car, Sam was excited.

Nick helped Grace get out of the car. They couldn't stop looking at each other for such different yet similar reasons. Nicola went ahead and unlocked the door. Sam sniffed the yard and marked her first visit.

Once inside, they all filled the kitchen as Grace and Nicola began to pull food and beer from the fridge. Once the guys had their drinks, Nicola showed them the patio and encouraged them to give the womenfolk some space. Ben raised an eyebrow at her, and she chuckled, "I know, I know. I'm a feminist, trust me, but Abuelita needs my help and a little room to absorb this."

Once settled on the lawn chairs, the guys looked at Nick and then at Charlie. "It's a lot to take in, isn't it?" Charlie observed.

Nick grinned. "I guess you're the master of understatement."

"Not likely. A few of my previous deans would have said the opposite."

Ben started, "So she *is* your sister? We found the right person?"

"Oh yes, she's Grace. A lot older, but of course she would be. It's been sixty-four years since I had a letter from her and longer since I've seen her. She was 16 the last time I saw her. It was 1943 at the camp. I was only there for a year or so, and then the army came for me."

Don weighed in, "She looks great for eighty-two years old. And I'm glad she didn't have a stroke when she saw you."

Nick was taken aback. "I hadn't even thought about the shock for her. I was just so happy to know that someone in my family was alive. And I didn't even do the math. I think I need to start thinking things through."

"And now we have another clue," offered Charlie. "The Stanton family of scientists. If Nicola's advisor is Dr. Richard Stanton's son, then we have a lead on your work all those years ago."

"My God, you're right. So I'm twenty-four in 1944, and Dick was a couple of years older. So he'd be ninety. I hope he's still alive, much less up to seeing me. I know you found his photo, but anything can happen." Nick began to stare out to the horizon.

"We'll get Nicola out here and plan our next steps." Charlie was all over this; after all, she knew his work.

Ben stepped into the flow. "Hang on. Let's drink our beers, have some food, and be deliberate and careful with who we reach out to and what we say. This could get away from us, and there'll be no getting it back."

Nick was puzzled. "What are your concerns? These people know me, or at least knew me."

Ben took a stab at explaining it to the time traveler. "They knew you sixty-four years ago, and here you are still twenty-four years old. You know the Internet we used to look people up with. It's also used to spread news, scandals, outrageous stories. And once something is on the Internet, it's everywhere and you're not in control."

Don offered, "It's not like when we got our news on the radio and in the newspapers. Today, we get news every minute of every day if we turn on the TV or the computer. Ben's right. Slow and steady needs to be our approach."

Charlie was gazing into the distance. "So maybe we need a backstory for Nick. Shirttail relative came to visit. Named after his war hero, great-uncle?"

"And he's going to need ID and a social security number. I wonder how we manage that?"

Grace was in the doorway. "I may have an idea on that. I've done some work over the years helping immigrants, and I have some resources." Nicola came up behind her and hugged her. "She's done a lot more. You still have some tricks to share, huh?"

Ben rose. "Are we eating out here? Is there something I can do to help?"

Nicola smiled. "Yes, we're eating out here. There's a table propped up over there. I'll bring you a cloth and silverware."

There was movement for a few minutes as a place was cleared for the table, the cloth was spread, and places set. Nicola began bringing out platters of tamales, a bowl of beans, another with salad. "Anyone for another beer?"

Don started thinking ahead as the group relaxed. "So is there a motel that takes dogs around here?"

"You are welcome to leave her here while you go to the Holiday Inn near the Walmart. It's clean and reasonable. Nicola is in the guestroom here, so Nicky, I think you need to stay with the boys." Grace was grinning.

The sounds of glasses and beer bottles clinking, silverware, and passing plates filled the backyard. Sam sat near Don, waiting her turn.

"I have some rice in the frig. Would that be okay for her tonight? Tomorrow, we can pick up some food for her," Nicola said.

"What am I thinking? We've got a bag of her food in the SUV." Ben jumped up.

Don held up his hand. "Sit down. Sam's not starving. She can wait until the end of our dinner but thanks."

The talk turned to Nick and his extraordinary story.

Charlie jumped in. "I knew it. I've studied your work."

"You have?" Nicola was intrigued. It hadn't occurred to her to check up on Ben's brother.

Charlie bowed to her. "Dr. Charles Grant at your service."

"Oh my god, you're Charles Grant? I've studied your work. I know you're onto something. I keep tracking your moves. Where are you now?"

"Northern Arizona University. They seem to tolerate what they refer to as my 'hobby' reasonably well."

"Hobby? This work is a lot more than a hobby," challenged Nick.

"Molecular transference is fringe science, and what we're really talking about is teleportation." grimaced Charlie. "This is a helluva lot more than the double slit experiment."

"Well, I'm walking, talking proof."

"And that's why we need to keep a lid on this." Ben was very, very serious.

OAK RIDGE, TENNESSEE, EARLY-DECEMBER 1944

It took Dick Stanton a while to adjust to Tennessee. It was cold, wet, and muddy this time of the year, pretty much like New Mexico. But the work here was not research, so he wasn't sure what role he'd find to fill. He didn't have to wait long. Right after he was shown to his barracks, such as they were, he was directed to a blocky building surrounded by a wooden walkway. Turned out to be important since the mud was more like wet cement. He'd have to get some mud boots if he was going to be here for any length of time.

The CO directed him to an office with a desk and a chair. As he walked toward it, the CO said, "Glad to have you here, Dr. Stanton. I hear you're a whiz with statistics. That's what we've been looking for. I'll have Betsy start bringing you the reports we need you to interpret."

Dick was stunned. This wasn't anything he was prepared for, trained for, anything at all for. Damned Army. He needed to get out of here, but a pretty young woman had just walked in with a sheaf of papers.

"Please come in and close the door," he said seriously.

"I don't close doors to rooms with strange men. So who are you and what have you got in mind?"

Dick blushed. "It's not what you think. I'm Richard Stanton, Dick. I just got here from New Mexico. I'm a research scientist in physics. I am not a specialist in statistics, and somehow that guy out there thinks I am."

"I heard him call you doctor." She was still suspicious.

"I'm working on my PhD. I've done all the work, but the war interrupted the presentation of my doctoral thesis. So I'm almost a doctor."

"Well, all of us are almost something. I'm Elizabeth Baldwin, Betsy to my friends. I graduated with a math degree from Smith. I saw an ad in the *New York Times* for a job for the war effort. And here I am. Welcome to Mud City."

Dick felt his shoulders start to drop below his ears as he began to see a solution. "A math major. So statistics are something you're pretty good with?"

"I've been producing the reports for the past year, but I lack certain qualifications to satisfy the brass."

Dick was confused. "What qualifications? You were a math major at Smith. It doesn't get better than that."

Betsy leaned against his desk. "*That* was a good answer. You're right. My brain is damn fine. But I'm not a man, and that's the truth of it in this *man's* army."

Dick almost dropped his jaw. "You're kidding. You're doing the work and they think a guy could do it better?"

"Listen,"—Betsy leaned in—"all the real work around here is done by women. Men are all away fighting. This is important, or so we're told, but not important enough for men to do."

"The last time I checked, I was a guy," muttered Dick.

"I can't tell you why you're here and not 'over there,' but I'm glad you're here. I need someone to take my work and present it so we can make some progress here."

"Show me what you've got. I'm sure you can bring me up to speed. What *is* happening here?"

"Mining uranium. It will be shipped out west for something."

"I think I know the reason. The place where I was stationed was working on a project that's going to need a fuel source. Uranium pretty much fits that bill."

"Holy…we've heard rumors of something big. How big *almost Dr. Stanton*?"

"Big enough that I think I'm glad I'm in Tennessee." Dick was thoughtful now. "Betsy Baldwin, I have a proposition for you."

She raised her eyebrows. "I'm listening."

"With your expert help, I'll prepare interpretations of the statistics. We can keep our heads down and hope that we can stay far away from the New Mexico project for as long as it takes." He hesitated. "And I'd like to take you to dinner to seal the deal."

Betsy paced the small office. When she stopped in front of him Dick looked up as she began to speak. "I can do the first. The part about interpreting the statistics. Keeping our heads down sounds sensible, so I think I can do that. Dinner, just you and me…I have two roommates who would never forgive me if I had a dinner date and kept them in the dark. So you can take three lovely ladies to dinner or go alone."

At this, Dick grinned. "I have three younger sisters at home. I think dinner with three smart cookies will be a gas. Where do I take you ladies around here?"

"Leave that to me, *almost Dr. Stanton*. A car will be in front of your barracks at eighteen hundred hours. Be ready."

As Betsy left the office, Dick leaned back in his chair with a wide grin on his face. This post wasn't so bad after all.

Early Evening, Same Day

Dick Stanton's new friends picked him up right on time. The gathering gloom hid most of the ugliness of the place as they rolled out of the confines of Atomic City and into the countryside.

"Hey, where are you all taking me? Should I be concerned about kidnapping?"

Mavis Black, Blackie to all, giggled and said, "What a great idea. Why didn't we think of that girls?"

Gertrude "Trudy" Brown poked her friend in the side. "Don't even joke about that stuff around our driver here you ninny."

Their driver, a young man looking barely old enough to drive, grinned. "I hear nothin', ladies. I'm just here to make sure you make it to the holler and back A-OK."

Betsy patted him on the shoulder. "Thanks, Eddie. How's that math homework coming along?"

"A lot better since you helped me with the thinkin' part, Miss Betsy."

Dick kept his thoughts to himself and smiled broadly. This was turning out to be a lot more interesting than it first seemed.

After a lot of twists and turns on rutted roads the battered army truck pulled up to a house on the edge of what might have been a village in a foreign country. A swarm of raggedy children raced from the house and jumped up and down shouting, "Miss Blackie, Miss Trudy, Miss Betsy."

"OK, you hooligans, who finished their homework?" Blackie demanded.

"Me, me, me, I did, me too." They were all answering at once as the women, the driver, and the newcomer made their way up the muddy path to the small wooden structure.

The screenless front windows were slightly open to let in the clean evening air and the smell of food, great food, was a magnet.

"Susanna, come meet our new friend," Betsy called out to the kitchen.

They were now standing in a small front room with several roughhewn tables set for four. It was a restaurant. The newcomer was dumbfounded. Way back here, American ingenuity was on display.

Susanna walked toward them, wiping both hands on a worn dish towel. "Now you gals didn't say nothin' about bringin' no menfolk along." She smiled while chiding them.

"Well, this one just kinda fell in our lap and you know they don't let us out at night alone, so we had to bring Eddie to drive us." Trudy was explaining while walking toward the kitchen.

Susanna was on to her tricky ways. "Now you just set yourself down there while I gets to finishin' your suppers. You knows I don't like you in my kitchen."

"Oh, we know all right." Trudy was not chastened. "But one of these days, I'm gonna get to watch you make all this heavenly food."

The girls chose a table near the open kitchen door and began to fill Dick in. Betsy started. "It was pretty early on after we three arrived when we realized that Susanna, who was working cleaning offices in our building, was cooking food for the guys on the side."

Blackie jumped in. "She was a caterer and didn't know it. So we decided to help her out with some business know-how. My dad had a restaurant back in New Jersey, and I knew I could help."

Trudy continued, "So we offered to come home with Susanna one day and help her grow her business. We knew we could share our ration coupons and so could all those guys she cooked for. When we looked at this room it begged to have a few tables, so Susanna could begin to cook and serve right here."

"Susanna's husband, George, couldn't join up because of a mining injury so we asked him to make the tables and benches. Watch for splinters. They're not all completely smooth." Betsy laughed.

Dick was fascinated as one of the youngsters began to bring out plates filled with steaming food. A smaller young'un' brought out forks and spoons. Betsy reached into her pocket and handed-out cloth napkins all around.

Jars with a clear liquid appeared. "Don't worry. It's water," laughed Blackie. The hard stuff takes a special order.

As they all fell to eating the amazing food, Dick assessed the situation. A Negro cook and cleaning woman being helped by three smart civilian women being underappreciated at a military facility. Seemed familiar except in New Mexico it was the local Indian girls, and his friend Nick who had been helping them out.

"Is this restaurant open for breakfast and lunch too?" Dick wanted to know, planning for tomorrow's meals.

"Oh, no. From seven to eleven, it's a school for the local kids," Blackie said proudly.

"Yessir. We got permission to come here three mornings a week and teach the three *R*s to these lucky kiddos." Betsy was grinning widely.

Eddie piped up, "Me too. I never got to finish school, so this is great for me. I drive the gals here and get to stay and learn."

Dick started thinking about his friend Nick. "Do any of the men help with the teaching?"

"You have to be kidding." Betsy was not kidding. "The men around here care about one thing. Getting production up at the factory. Respecting or paying attention to the people who are hosting us, much less giving anything back to the locals, did not and does not occur to them."

Dick nodded. "It was the same where I came from. Nose to the grindstone for the war effort, but a few of us took time to get to know our neighbors and lend a hand when we could."

Betsy listened carefully to this and thought again that perhaps this new scientist was a good thing in her life.

All too soon, the dishes were cleared, pie was served, and then Eddie gathered them up for the trip back to what his new friends called Atomic City. Dick stepped toward the kitchen to call to Susanna. She came shyly to the doorway. "Thank you, ma'am, for the best meal I've had since my own mother cooked for me in California." And he shook her hand. She put her face in her dishtowel with shyness. "Oh suh, you don't gotta thank me. These gals is all the thanks I needs for my young'uns and my man George."

"Be that as it may, this was a wonderful evening and I look forward to many more."

The girls began to tug him away toward the doorway so they could all get back before curfew. Betsy whispered to Dick. "That was nice of you. It means a lot to her."

"I meant every word. She deserves our respect for her hard work, and her food is fantastic."

Betsy whispered again, "You're not like the other men they sent here."

"How so?" Dick was curious.

"They're all puffed up wanting to seem really important, when they're not. You're smart but don't seem to need to push our faces in it."

"Well, I would hope not. This war is big enough for all of us to play a part. If we're lucky we get to know what part. Otherwise, we just take it on faith."

"Almost Dr. Stanton, we're gonna all get along just fine." Betsy reached for his hand, shook it, but didn't let go.

CHAPTER 12

DAY TWO, INDIO, CALIFORNIA, GRACE'S HOUSE

The sun had set when the group grew quiet. Nick broke the silence, "I need to know what happened with the experiment." Looking at Grace, he continued, "You may have been told I died in 1944, but we now know that to be less than the full truth." Charlie started to sputter, and both Don and Ben put hands on his shoulders.

"Here's my concern. Did our work continue secretly? Could I be pulled back across time at any point? How do I make the best use of the time I have here in the face of not knowing?"

Both Nicola and Charlie looked at each and then spoke, not to Nick, but to each other. "I haven't come across any hints in my research to indicate that you did anything other than cease to be a scientist in 1944," Charlie said softly.

"Neither have I, but I haven't looked for anything coded or hidden. I took at face value that Dr. Nicholas Nishimura and his work were dead." Nicola was thoughtful.

Ben spoke up. "That does shift gears a little. Nicola, perhaps you could e-mail your advisor and see how his dad is doing and if he's up for a visit from a 'family friend.'"

"Whose family shall I say is asking?" she wondered. "Well, if Nick is a shirt-tail relative of the Nishimura clan, he could be a long-lost cousin. We had a Great-Uncle Greg, who was a black sheep of sorts."

Grace added, "We lost track of Greg even before the camp. After the war, he was nowhere to be found, and then life went on. I went to school, got married. You know the rest."

Nick smiled slowly. "I don't. I'd like to hear it."

"I'm guessing Dr. Stanton, Junior's dad, is still in the Los Angeles area." Nicola's brain was spinning. "I'll send that e-mail right now. Time waits for no man…or woman."

Don decided someone needed to be practical, "OK, folks. It's getting late and it sounds like we could have a long day tomorrow. Grace, if you and Nicola still are willing, we'll leave Sam with you. She likes your yard and it will be easier to find a motel without having a dog along. Boys, let's give our hostesses some time to rest and prepare for tomorrow."

"Yikes. You're right, it's after ten p.m. Time flies when you're talking about time travel," Ben joked.

They said their goodbyes. Nick hung back with Grace until the SUV fired up and the lights went on.

Day Two, Nick's Notes

The urgency to know, not guess, about my circumstances is growing. So far, we have no evidence that I went back, but that doesn't mean there wasn't an unsuccessful attempt to recover me.

The drive from Arizona to California in what is called a sport utility vehicle was fast, smooth, and almost quiet. Talking with Charlie was refreshing, another like-minded scientist.

Meeting Grace and her granddaughter made this time jump very real. Hearing about the years I missed was difficult. I wish I had met her husband.

Tomorrow we continue our trip to Los Angeles and see my old friend Dick. I hope he has answers.

CHAPTER 13

DAY THREE, INDIO, CALIFORNIA, SEPTEMBER 10, 2008 GRACE NISHIMURA ACEVEDO'S HOME

Nicola had a reply in her inbox first thing in the morning. Dr. Stanton, Jr. was intrigued by her request. He reported that his Dad was 90, but still sharp and in good shape. He revealed that he did indeed still live in Los Angeles. Nick was right. Nicola replied and asked how soon a visit could be arranged. Then she put on her robe to join her grandmother for breakfast.

Grace was alert and making coffee. Nicola reported, "Looks like a trip really is on the agenda. I got a reply from my advisor. His dad is in great shape, at ninety, no less. Now I'm waiting to see how quickly we can get a visit arranged."

Grace shook her head. "I had not even considered that Nicky could be pulled away from us, again. We need to know if he stays. How can we find out? How can we help him?"

Nicola added, "We need to know if he *wants* to stay. Did he have a girlfriend? Someone whose heart broke when he didn't come back?"

"We didn't hear that much from Nicky about his personal life, other than spending time with the other scientists. They were all about the same age. And it was wartime. No one was counting on anything permanent."

Sam was standing near Nicola, her tail wagging. "Want some breakfast, girl?" And then came the sound of tires in the driveway.

"Our visitors have returned. Hope you made a big pot of coffee, *Abuelita*."

When a knock sounded on the door, Sam was right there with a happy *woof!*

The door opened, and Nick was first in the door, followed by Charlie, Ben, and lastly, Don. "I smell coffee, and we brought Mexican pastries from Safeway," announced Charlie. They filled the small kitchen, especially with Sam wiggling from man to man. She had adopted Nick as her own now too.

Nicola reported the news from Dr. Stanton Jr. and jumped when she heard the tone her laptop made when an e-mail arrived. She went down the hall to check. While she was gone the coffee was poured and the pastries began to disappear. She came back quickly, smiling broadly until she noticed the diminishing treats. "Hey, you guys, leave some for the ladies! Especially when I have great news. Dr. Stanton Sr. is visiting his son, and we can drive in and see him this afternoon."

Backs straightened and they all started to shift around. Ben asked, "How long do you need to be ready to travel? Will you come with us or drive your own car?"

Nicola looked at Grace. "I think I can come with you. Perhaps she and Sam can stay here while we make our trip. The hours on the road could be hard on both of them, and we don't know how long we could be there."

"That's sound thinking, young lady." Don smiled. "This has been a lot for your grandmother to take in."

Nicola was on her feet. "I'll be ready in ten minutes."

Charlie reached for the next to the last pastry. "Sounds perfect to me. I'll just do some carb loading before the drive."

"Carb loading?" Nick was puzzled.

Ben explained, "He's joking, but the concept is that before exerting lots of energy, your body can be better prepared by eating carbohydrates, like bread, pasta, pastries. But Charlie is joking. There will be very little energy exerted riding in the SUV."

"Ohhhh. We didn't do that in my day. We just ate what was around and available. Things were a lot better at Los Alamos than the camp, or even for most families during the war." He looked over at Grace. "I know I just got here, but I think I have to do this. If I can learn what happened after I left, well, I don't know, but I know I have to find out more than I know now. And if my friend Dick is still with it maybe he can tell me, us, about that day and what happened after. Maybe it's crazy, but all of this feels crazy to me."

"Oh, Nicky, I know you do. We all want to know if you get to stay. Do you want to stay?"

That stopped Nick in his steps. "I hadn't thought of it as a choice until just now. Unless I hear something from Dick Stanton today about the state of the research, I think I have few reasons, if any, to return, and it could be dangerous for me knowing what I know now."

Charlie offered, "If you changed history by returning, it's possible that none of us would even be here. There's been a lot written about this topic. A lot of it thought-provoking and not very positive."

Nick shook his head slowly. "I hadn't even considered the impact of my returning to my original time. Do you think just even having been gone and returning could create harm?"

Charlie continued, "That could depend. In our timeline, you were declared dead. We don't know how many hours or days they waited to make that declaration. If they could snag you and bring you back, that could change."

Ben stepped over to Charlie. "I don't think you're helping here, little brother."

"But he's not wrong." Nicola interjected as she came back into the kitchen. "This could be a big mess of timelines and lives that we need to sort out, and the sooner the better."

Grace stood with her hands on her hips. "Then you need to get on the road so Nicky can make up his mind, *if* he has a choice."

The others had left to check out of the Holiday Inn Express. Grace pulled out a chair for Nick to join her at the kitchen table. Nicola drifted in quietly and stood listening in the doorway.

Nick took Grace's hand, sat down, and said softly, "Tell me everything, please. Everything I missed."

"Oh, Nicky." She pulled back a little but left her hand in his. "There was a lot more good than bad, but there has been sadness. Let me tell you about the happy times."

Nicola moved to put the kettle on for tea, an old habit from her grandmother Sunny.

"I was just sixteen, and we had gotten to the camp. It was so awful. You remember, yes?"

"It was a lot more recent for me. Only two years ago, in fact." Nick smiled ruefully.

"It's so hard to think that you were just there, the war years, so hard. Anyway, you remember then that Doris, the nurse, was nice to me. She needed my help, and I needed something to do. And the first-aid clinic was how I met Hector."

"He was your husband?"

"And the love of my life. Who knew the camp would bring me love? But it did. He was a few years older, just nineteen. He had wanted to join the army, but he was the breadwinner for his family, so he had to stay. That was hard on him. But the army tracked him down as a civilian in California and gave him work building the camp. He was a good worker and managed all of the men. He was lucky that he liked the work and the camp commanders liked him. He worked hard, and so did his crew. And they were honest. But they got hurt often. They were always being told to work faster, faster. They built roads, shelters. Hector was the boss and would bring the guys in. Doris was my boss and my friend. She figured out that while she fixed up the guy that was hurt, I could talk with Hector. That's how we fell in love. Two Americans with a heritage that kept us out of the War. By the time the war ended and we were finally able to leave, Hector had asked me to marry him. Daddy had given his permission. We all moved to Indio, where Hector's people are. San Tierra didn't want Mommy and Daddy back. Maybe the town had always been against us, but after the war, it was bad. Even our house had been taken. And Daddy couldn't get his old teaching job either."

"What do you mean he couldn't get his old job back?" Nick was astonished.

"Just that. A lot of people held onto their prejudice. San Tierra is still unfriendly." Grace shook her head.

"Anyway, Daddy got a job teaching science at the Catholic High School. You haven't met Father Joe yet. He's like a brother to me and was such a help to Hector. It was his predecessor that was brave and hired him. It was an all-boys school back then. It's co-ed now. Actually since 1964. But Daddy didn't live to see that. He always felt badly that the girls weren't getting the same chance to learn. He only lived another ten years after the camp. After Mommy died, the rest of his spirit left him."

"When did Mother die?" Nick was trying to take this all in. Of course, they had been alive a few days ago to him.

"Two years before Daddy, 1954." Grace's gaze was very far away. "But you need to know that Hector's family loved them. The Mexican families here love and revere their elders like the Japanese. We were so lucky to be loved here." Her eyes glistened with the memories.

"Victory and Daniel were still so small when their Nishimura grandparents died. But at least they have some memories and lots of photos."

"Could I see them?" Nick too had been far away but returned at the thought of something he could touch.

"I'll get the albums." Nicola rose to find them.

"Well then, how did you become a nurse?" Nick was returning to the story of Grace.

"Oh, I started at the local hospital's school of nursing. They gave me a scholarship because they knew Hector's family. Pretty soon, we were part of the community. It made it easier to keep moving forward. When I went to nurses' training, Hector became a fireman. Every little boy's dream. He was a good one. And it was what finally killed him, but that's not part of this story."

Nicola returned with a couple of thick photo albums with black construction paper pages. Grace and Nick sat side by said as she pointed out family gatherings over the years. "Mother and Father look so old, but they were only in their fifties." Nick was puzzled.

"When I say the camp was hard, it was hard. Food wasn't good, what there was of it. We had to work. We were prisoners, Nicky. Remember?" Grace was trying to be gentle, but the reality called for truth.

Nick hung his head a little. "I was able to leave so soon after we got there. Probably only a year or so. My memories of the camp are almost two years old. It doesn't seem like much when we have sixty-four years between then and now, but so much happened."

Vento Internment Camp, Late Spring 1943

Hector Acevedo was smitten. The shy girl at the first-aid clinic had touched his heart. Apparently, she was as American as he was. The unfairness struck him suddenly. Until then, he hadn't questioned Order 9066 from President Roosevelt. The people in the camp looked like foreigners. They could be planning to attack. Now he looked at them and thought, *What if Mexico had attacked? It could be my family in a camp.* He had to tell her he understood, but how?

The answer came quickly. One of his crew had slipped while using a scroll saw and cut his forearm. Hector put him in the old pickup truck and sped off to the first aid clinic at the nearby Internment Camp called Vento. It wasn't near any town, but it was close to where he and his crew were working. The guards were understanding and didn't stop him on his frequent trips to the clinic.

When they got there, Doris, the nurse on duty, came out to the truck.

"Whatcha got there, Hector?"

"Bad cut on his arm. He was working with a saw and slipped." Hector filled her in while scanning for "her." What did she say her name was? It wasn't Japanese.

"Where's your helper?" He decided he needed to find out.

Doris was cleaning the cut and preparing to stitch it closed. "Oh, Grace is with the little kids today. She's teaching them their ABCs."

"What's the situation with her?" He decided to ask more.

Doris glanced away from her work and arched an eyebrow. "Grace had just graduated from high school when her family was sent here. She was planning to be a science teacher. When I learned that, after she got here, I grabbed her. She's very sharp, calm, and great with the kids, who are always needing some kind of patching up."

Doris was carefully stitching the cut closed. If these guys weren't so busy with building out the local military projects the stitches might not have been necessary, but she'd learned after several of the guys had re-opened wounds that stitching was safest.

"When will she be back?" Hector really wanted to talk to Grace. Her name was perfect for her.

Doris smiled. "She'll be here tomorrow. But don't hurt yourself just to come back. Sadly, she won't be going anywhere until this war is over."

A few days later, it was his mother who needed first aid. Doris had said she had something called diabetes. Her blood sugar was off. He had just found her lying on the couch at home. In a panic, he drove her to the Clinic.

Grace was there. "It's my Mom," Hector blurted out. "Doris says she has something wrong with her blood."

"I remember your mom. It's diabetes. Let's get her inside. If she's not alert, that means she needs her insulin. Do you know if she had her shot yesterday?"

Doris arrived just as Grace and Hector were settling his mother on a cot.

Grace looked at Doris. "It's her diabetes. I'm thinking her sugar is high, and she must have missed her insulin shot."

"Smart girl. I think we have notes on her dosage from the last time she was here."

Hector waited while Grace flipped through the clinic notes to find his mother's name and last visit. "I guess I should help her keep track of her shots."

Doris spoke to Hector. "I expected your mother for her shot yesterday. What happened?"

Hector was confused. "She didn't tell me. I would have brought her. She probably didn't want to bother me."

Doris continued, "She needs the shot especially if her diet is going to be unpredictable."

"She's visiting me and my brother. She lives in Indio, California. I think she has a clinic she goes to there."

Doris nodded to Hector. "That's good for home, but when she visits you, she needs to come here every day."

Grace was looking down and smiled. She had been following the exchange with Doris. Hector saw this and was glad his mom had to come here every day. He could definitely bring her.

CHAPTER 14

DAY THREE, LOS ANGELES, CALIFORNIA, HOME OF RICK STANTON, SEPTEMBER 10, 2008

Richard Stanton Jr., called Rick by family and friends, was more than curious about the request from Nicola Acevedo. He knew her to be an extraordinary young woman, a fine student, loyal to her colorful family and known in some circles for her interest in what some called fringe science. He wondered if this fell into that fringe area. When he had called his dad this morning, speaking with him had rekindled questions that his dad had never answered to anyone's satisfaction.

Nicola said she would text him when she knew an approximate arrival time. He knew it was three or four hours from Indio. Plenty of time to corner his dad about what he did during the war. Rick had a strong sense that this shirttail relative had something to do with Nicola's interests in teleportation, and because she wanted his dad present, maybe that mysterious period in 1944 that his dad wouldn't speak of might be explained. Or not, but this promised to be an interesting day.

Three hours later, he was pouring a cup of coffee for himself when the senior Stanton walked into the kitchen and sat down. "Got any more of that? I'm going to need some to have to face this after all these years."

"Why do you say that, Dad?"

"What do you think the chances are that this has to do with your student's thesis?"

"I don't think it has anything to do with her current work and everything to do with her obsession with teleportation."

"Smart boy. Neither do I."

"You know, I was involved in a couple of projects near the end of the war. But you don't know about the first project. I was stationed at Los Alamos with all the guys working on the bomb."

"Holy crap, Dad. Why didn't you ever mention that?"

"Why do you think? It was hush-hush then and no point to rehash that now. Unless this shirt-tail relative knows something. We left some loose ends."

"What kind of loose ends? That doesn't sound like you, and I don't like the sound of that." Rick leaned in.

"As well you shouldn't. Loose ends were, and maybe still are, people." Dick stirred his coffee. "We had a CO named Patrick MacLane. We all called him Mac. He's your Jane's dad. But you know that. He was a few years older, ancient to us. He tried to protect us, but the war machine was bigger than all of us. When our experiment didn't *work out,* we all got shipped off to other posts. I heard from him occasionally. After the war he was the man behind The Institute that I've worked with. And he has never stopped looking."

"Looking? Looking for what? What do you mean *didn't work out?*" Rick was puzzled. "What does this have to do with the bomb?"

"Nothing. We weren't working on the bomb. We were working on molecular transference."

Rick nearly rose out of his chair. "What?"

"And it wasn't a 'what' we were looking for. It was a 'who' that we were missing."

"Okay, this is going to take a lot more coffee and maybe something stronger." Rick was shaking his head.

Dick paused. "Let's just see what kind of a visitor shows up at our door. In the meantime, do me a favor and use your university ties to look up Patrick MacLane. I'd like to know what the internet has to say about my old CO and the founder of The Institute. It might be important to see what the wide-world thinks it knows about Mac."

Dick Stanton looked out the window of his son's living room and blanched. "He's the spitting image of him."

"Of who?"

"Of the guy that's haunted me since that day in 1944. That's who."

I repeat, "Who are you talking about, Dad?"

"Nick Nishimura. My best friend from school and—" He was stopped by the doorbell.

The door opened on a motley crew of five. Three younger men, one young woman, and a fatherly guy. Rick opened the door and welcomed them, greeting Nicola warmly. "Hi, Nicola, how've you been and who's the gang of four with you?"

"Hi, Doctor. Thank you so much for making this visit happen. Let me introduce my new friends. Dr. Charlie Grant, his brother Ben and their dad, Don. And the newest member of the troop, Nick Brown."

While they had been in the SUV, Nick had shared the alias he planned to use, and they all agreed to use it until they could tell which way things were going during the visit.

As they filled the living room, Rick asked if anyone would like coffee or tea or to use the restroom. As he collected their requests and pointed the way to the restroom, he assessed the group and his father's reaction. Dick Stanton had taken his favorite chair at the far end of the long rectangular room and was gazing at just one of the visitors, Nick Brown.

After they all had their beverages and had reassembled, Dick blurted out, "You're the spitting image of him."

"Who?" Rick asked.

"My best friend." His eyes began to fill. "I haven't seen him since September 8, 1944."

"You didn't forget," Nick almost whispered.

"How could I forget? How could I forget my best friend?" Dick was speaking to his memories in anguish. "I killed him."

Nick rose to go closer to the older man. He got down on one knee. "You got old."

"Nick, we talked about this." Charlie cautioned.

"But he's my best friend. And he didn't kill me."

Dick Stanton made a sharp observation. "You just used the present tense, young man."

"It's still the present for me." Nick couldn't stop himself as the others alternately shook their heads or were stunned. "It was 1944 a few days ago. And now my sister is old, you're old. I don't recognize anything, and I'm not dead."

Dick spoke softly, "No…you're definitely not dead."

Rick spoke up. "Dad, I think it's time you filled us all in on what happened that day and may be the years since."

"It started in 1943. Oppie gathered scientists from all over to come to Los Alamos to work on his 'gadget' and there were others working on our project to aid military intelligence. We had been experimenting, successfully, with sending bundles of bandages across the compound. Maybe five hundred yards. But the pressure was on. It was July and then September 1944, and the brass were pushing for results. No one wanted the war dragging out another year. If our work could speed the end, we were pushing hard."

Nick added, "I wanted my family out of the camp, so I volunteered to be the first live subject to be *transported*."

Charlie wondered, "You couldn't have tried a rabbit or a rat?"

Dick smiled. "Didn't have those in the compound. And food was scarce. The predators in the desert took care of all the small wildlife."

Nick looked at Dick. "I know what it was like for me. I stepped in front of that light, felt a tingle, and walked out into Arizona 2008. Scared as hell. Not knowing where I was. It wasn't until I was getting something to eat and met Don that I began to think that not only had I been transported but that it wasn't 1944 anymore."

"What was your first clue?" Charlie grinned.

"Well, the cars, the menu at the diner, the way people dress, especially the women. It got strange really quickly."

"What did you think when you realized what happened?" Dick wanted to know.

Nick looked kind of dazed, but Dick continued. "I'm *still* trying to figure out what happened. Aren't you? Theresa wasn't worried. She said the spirits were watching."

A car pulled into the driveway. Rick said, "She needs to hear this too. She has as much invested as the rest of us." The door opened, and a stunning redhead walked in. When she saw the group gathered in her living room, she froze. "Rick, honey, what's going on?"

"Everyone, this is my wife, Jane MacLane Stanton. Honey, we have Nicola Acevedo, my advisee, Don Grant, and his sons Ben and Charlie, and Nicola's Great-Uncle Nick Nishimura."

Jane reached for the back of a chair and sank into it. "Nick Nishimura? The same Nick Nishimura that your dad and my dad have looked for all these years?"

Nick spoke up, "Your dad? Colonel Mac MacLane?"

"One and the same on both counts." This time, it was Dick who spoke. "So you didn't die in the experiment?"

"That has yet to be seen," hesitated Nick. "Will I be grabbed from this time and sent back?"

"That's really why we came right away when Nicola found out you were here." Charlie spoke to Dick. "When Nick told us what happened and we couldn't find any accounts of the experiment, we couldn't assure him of his status. I've studied Nick's work and never found anything about New Mexico."

Jane spoke. "There's a good reason for that." She looked around the room, gauged their ages, then looked at her husband. "This is going to take something stiffer than what it looks like you're all drinking."

Rick went to the liquor cabinet, reaching for a bottle of amber liquid. "Bourbon okay?" Everyone nodded. He started passing glasses and then the bottle. Glasses were filled, some asked for ice, and then Jane began again. "Right after the experiment, my dad found out there had been spies in your midst." She looked at Nick and her father-in-law. "So after a *reasonable amount of time* and efforts to find the spies, Washington scrapped the mission. My dad had to tell you everybody would be reassigned. That no one could look for Nick."

"That didn't sit very well with us," muttered Dick.

"With my dad either." Jane's voice was strong. "He's an honorable man, and he knew it wasn't right to stop the work."

"Well, what happened?" Nicola prompted.

Dick spoke. "I got sent to Oak Ridge, Tennessee. Atomic City they called it. Where the uranium for the bombs was coming from. Awful place, but I met your mother there. I'm grateful something good came from it."

Jane added, "Dad stayed in touch. He wanted Dick to know if anything shifted in the brass's thinking about molecular transference. But it was as if it never happened. Except they all knew it did. After the war Dad came out here. He was at loose ends and thought he'd try to track down the guys from Los Alamos. He visited Stanford and ran into my mother, Martha O'Hara."

Nick perked up, "Martha O'Hara, Dr. Martha O'Hara?"

"One and the same, star pupil." Jane smiled at him.

"Is she—"

"She and Dad were a bit older than you, so no, they're both retired. In fact, that's how I know what I know about the whole 1944 experiment. When dad realized he was developing dementia he confessed some things that he neither wanted to forget, nor to blurt out without context."

Rick started. "After the war there were a lot of smart guys at loose ends, Jane's dad among them. My dad finished his PhD and began teaching, but there was an opportunity to do some good, but not at the university and not through the military."

Nick was puzzled. "Then what else is there?"

Jane smiled. "A think tank. They called it The Institute. It sounded smart and serious and it worked to attract a lot of talent. Once my mom and dad teamed up it started to come together quickly. Of course, Mom had some resources from Stanford. There were people with money who wanted to do research outside standard academic boundaries."

"As long as Martha and I were on the Advisory Board, people knew it wasn't going to get crazy. Little did they know." Dick smiled slyly.

Nick brought them back to the experiment. "Did you try to run the same tests we did? Did you ever try it with anything living?"

Dick shook his head. "Oh, we tried. That's when I began to think I had killed you. The mice didn't do too well. They vaporized. I didn't tell Theresa."

"Shit. How many?" Charlie was morbidly curious.

"We stopped after a while. Probably a couple dozen. We could never recreate what we had done in New Mexico." Dick was puzzled.

Nick leaned in. "Theresa? She's alive. Are you in touch with her? What happened to her?"

Charlie asked, "Did you ever go back? Try to recreate it on site?"

"After the war, everything changed. Our buildings were left to fall apart or be moved. The entire Los Alamos project shifted into different buildings. It would continue for the long haul. So the answer is yes and no. We all went back. Mac tried to swing whatever clout he still had. No dice. And Theresa is fine. We stay in touch."

Rick gauged the room. "Pizza anyone? I think we're going to be a while."

Heads nodded. Rick left the room to make a call to order food. Jane continued, "The Institute began doing really good serious work in all areas of physics. There was interest in weapons, but a lot more interest in helping countries in peacetime. Helping recovery efforts. Things were pretty well wrecked when the war ended. Pacific islands were decimated, Europe was in shambles. And because of the Marshall Plan, there was money to be had for research to help rebuild."

Nick looked at her. "Now I'm totally lost. How would our experiment have helped rebuild?"

"It was still about moving stuff. Transportation takes roads that we didn't have, landing strips we didn't have, equipment we didn't have." Dick was recalling.

"But it didn't work."

"That does not mean we didn't keep trying. We did that for several years. We did other science, but a few of us knew the real reason for The Institute." Dick smiled.

"By the time I was in high school, I knew I wanted to follow dad, so I applied to Stanford. Wasn't accepted. Went to Cal Tech.

And I met Jane there. We had met a few times growing up when the families would get together, but nothing ever clicked until then. A little slow on the uptake."

"You made up for it once you figured a few things out." Jane grinned. "I knew I wanted to work at The Institute. Dad wanted one of us to carry on the work. Dad realized he was missing a step a few years ago. He called us all together. It was heart-wrenching. Mom would have stayed on, but she knew she had to be by his side. It sounds so old school, but they have a love that defies time and illness. Even though they still are 'here,' it hasn't been the same for us without them."

A dog barked. Everyone looked out the window to the back-yard. Nick thought it looked more like a mountain goat, but the tail wagged like a dog. Rick and Jane both rose to address the creature wanting attention.

"Anyone afraid of an Irish Wolfhound?" Rick laughed. Everyone migrated to the backyard to meet the furry family member while they absorbed all the information that had been shared.

In the backyard, the dog trotted from person to person to be greeted, petted, oohed, and ahhhed over. Nick hung back. More than everyone else, he was turning things over in his mind. Did all this mean he would be here for good? It wasn't the dog that gave him pause. So much information. When he felt a cold nose push his hand, he smiled and decided the present was a good place to be for now.

The pizza arrived, and as the patio was prepped for food, Nick wandered over to his old friend. "So where does the work stand now? Do I need to worry about being snatched back to 1944 or some other year?"

The two old friends grabbed two chairs and stared at the melee with pizza, dog, young and younger people. Dick spoke. "There was talk that some of our work was stolen by a spy. We tried to follow it to see where it could have gone. When the war ended, Russia ceased to be an ally. We entered something called the Cold War. They had the bomb, we had the bomb, and no one wanted to die. It was a standoff."

Jane wandered over. "One of the things The Institute kept an eye on was that talk of a spy. We actively tracked Simon Constantine until he died in Istanbul in 1979. We tried to find out who his contacts were. None of the scientists who came over here from Eastern Europe ever seemed to be clear on what he worked on, but they all knew the name."

"So you think somewhere in a foreign country someone may be able to send me somewhere else?" This could be a concern for Nick.

Rick weighed in. "No, we don't. No one since you two has ever been able to even move bandages. But that doesn't mean we're complacent. The Institute has files on every pertinent experiment in every part of the world. And anyone worth their salt wants to work there. We have the best of everything." Rick was proud of what they all had done.

Jane chimed in, "Though there seems to be some chatter about the topic of late."

"Chatter? What does that mean?" Nick was clearly lost in the current jargon.

Charlie weighed in, "It's slang for talk that's been picked up through wiretaps, e-mail, or other ways of listening in on conversations."

Ben spoke up. "Technology has improved since your time, Nick. We can now listen in on telephone conversations and electronic messaging without the people having the conversation being aware."

"And that's legal?"

"Well, mostly." Charlie and Jane spoke in unison and started to laugh. Jane continued, "We like to think it's legal when the good guys do it."

"And we're the good guys, right?"

"Yes, Nick. We're still the good guys. And there are lot more bad guys now." Don smiled ruefully.

"So getting back to the chatter. Am I at risk? Are my molecules going to get scrambled without my permission?"

"We don't think so. You still need to be in proximity to the source of the light in the double slit experiment although some of the results have led us to believe that not everything shifts as one mass or unit," Rick explained.

"So that's what you're calling it?"

"Actually, it's been called that for two hundred years," Charlie smiled. "You guys just took their idea and made it real on a large scale."

"So does anyone know where this chatter is coming from?" Nicola was serious. "They might not be able to send Uncle Nick back, but they might find out he's here."

"You think the light waves could leave a signature?" Charlie was intrigued.

"Maybe. Has anyone looked into it?" Nicola was getting lost in her thoughts.

"Are you saying you want to change your thesis topic again? This would be the third time, young lady." Rick looked almost hopeful.

Now it was Jane's turn. "Or do you want to finish what you're working on and join The Institute to follow this line of inquiry?"

"The institute? Work there? Oh my God! That would be a dream come true for any scientist, much less one with a personal interest in the topic."

"I'm officially jealous." Charlie was glum.

"Not so fast, Dr. Grant. We've had our eye on you for a while." Jane was grinning. "You're just kind of hard to keep track of. It's a good thing we have some digital media specialists who are able to find you in key chatrooms." Jane shared.

"Not to be repetitious, but it *is* my molecules we've been discussing. You're confident that I'm here and can stay here?" Nick was seeking certainty.

"Buddy, you're a scientist. How certain do you want? Our side isn't doing any scrambling of molecules, and our spies don't think anyone is close enough to you to interfere." Dick was smiling. "So I think you can start adjusting to 2008."

Ben spoke up. "Grace mentioned arranging for ID for Nick. It will be suspicious if he doesn't have a Social Security Number and driver's license."

Jane's ears perked up. "And how does she think she can make those items appear?"

"Abuelita has worked for a long time as an immigrant advocate, and my father is an immigration attorney," Nicola said proudly.

Ben looked at her. "You never mentioned your dad. What's his name?"

"Daniel...Acevedo." And the room went quiet.

"*The* Daniel Acevedo? The guy who is usually in front of the Supreme Court? That Daniel Acevedo?" Jane was staring at Nicola.

"That's the one. My dad. He was deeply affected by what Abuelita and Abuelo went through during the war. He made it his life's work to defend people wrongfully treated because of their place of birth or heritage." Nicola was clearly proud.

"Maybe we should ask if you have any other famous relatives. Got anyone else you think we should be aware of?" Ben was very curious.

"Well, my Aunt Victory has gotten some attention."

"No way. Victory the actress?" Don was clearly impressed.

Nicola was serious. "Indeed. One and the same. She was named for everything that happened after the war—many victories. When she decided to be an actress, her Spanish last name was a problem. So she's just 'Victory,' and it's worked for her." Nicola was petting the dog and not looking at anyone.

"Nick, you've got quite a family to get to know." Dick was enjoying this way too much.

"And how do you think we should introduce him? Got any ideas?" Jane was thinking about secrets versus publicity.

"We really hadn't gotten beyond ID for Nick and trying to find out if he was going to disappear," Ben admitted. "But if we think he's here to stay we need a plan."

"I think The Institute can help." Jane spoke. "We're used to working with foreign citizens, people who need to keep a low profile, people with high profiles. All of the above. Let us start working on a plan."

"How many people are going to be let in on the truth?" Don wondered.

Charlie chuckled. "This is kind of like witness protection in reverse."

Nick was puzzled. "Witness protection?"

Nicola said, "It's offered to people in criminal cases when the risk that their testimony is so damning that the criminals will kill them rather than allow them to testify."

"That happens?" Nick was alarmed.

"It's a very different world from the one you knew." Dick shook his head. "It did seem that things were simpler then. We knew, or thought we knew, who the bad guys and the good guys were."

Nicola spoke again. "Except of course for the internment camps and the treatment of women."

"Yes, that was a stain on our character that will never be cleansed. And it seems the prejudice against people who are different never does go away. People may say all the right things, but attitudes run deep, especially attitudes based on irrational fears." Rick was serious.

Ben jumped in. "Are you perhaps speaking about the Democratic candidate for the presidency?"

"I could be. Personally, I think he's the most qualified guy we've had in years. That makes me worried for his safety." Rick stared at his knees.

"Why would you worry about a candidate's security?" Nick had a lot to learn.

Charlie was glum. "Because too many angry, ignorant people have guns and are willing to use them."

"This doesn't sound like the country I knew a few days ago."

Jane leaned over. "A lot has changed in sixty-four years. And we will bring you through it, but probably not tonight. Everybody agreed on that?"

Don was the first to speak. "Hell, it's a lot for me to take in and I lived it. We definitely need to be more measured with his reintro-duction to the good old US of A."

Charlie had his mouth full but said, "Pizza anybody. This is great stuff."

Everyone lightened at that and ate more. Rick and Jane's dog Feynman moved from person to person hoping for a careless slip of the fingers. The sun had set, and the temperature was dropping, as it can happen near the coast. The group moved their food, drinks, and furry helper inside.

"What happens now?" Nick was wondering aloud.

"You mean what happens to you?" Jane, the manager of the group, scanned the room. "That's a fair question. I think we've agreed that you need to stay under wraps. You need a place to be safe. It would be helpful to have a group to host you to continue your work."

Now it was Rick's turn. "Well, we're empty nesters and it sounds like The Institute is about to play a big role in Nick's immediate future. Why not let him stay here for a while?"

The room murmured. Charlie and Nicola looked at each other. "You also talked about us working at The Institute. When might that happen?" Nicola was being practical.

Jane replied, "I can't speak for HR, but I'd imagine soon. Especially in light of bringing our new research scientist on board and up to speed quickly."

Dick and his son looked at Nick. "This is all happening really fast. Do you need some time to walk along the beach, ride a bike, listen to music, just let this sift through your head?" Dick was a little worried about his friend.

Rick was thoughtful when he added, "It might also be a good idea for you to have a physical and get some vaccinations."

Charlie perked up. "Yeah, we have no idea what may have happened to his heart or any other key functions. A baseline would be a good thing to have. And I hadn't even considered all the vaccines that he hasn't had, polio, diphtheria, tetanus, yellow fever."

"I don't think we're sending him to a tropical island quite yet," Jane was laughing. "But all the childhood stuff that he would not have had the benefit of, sure. He needs it."

"Does Grace have any contacts with doctors who don't ask questions about adults with no vaccines?" Ben looked at Nicola.

"She has every back channel known at the border. We can make this happen. Besides, I should call her and see how she and Sam are doing."

CHAPTER 15

MAC MACLANE, FALL 1946

When the peace finally came in 1945 and soldiers began to shut down operations, Mac wanted to make sure that he had what he needed to continue his search. It haunted him that young Nick Nishimura had vanished. That his buddies couldn't track him. He hoped that with time science would find a way. Until then he wanted to get as far away from this man's army as he could.

He was from Chicago, but Southern California sounded good now. The sun, the shore. Bleak Chicago winters held no interest. He knew his parents would want him home, and there was always a job in his dad's firm. But if he'd learned anything about himself after six years in the army, he was his own man. So he sent a telegram to his dad letting him know that he was heading west.

After he got to San Francisco, he realized a lot of guys had the same idea. There were former soldiers everywhere you turned. He ended up visiting Stanford University one September morning. As he headed for the student union to find a cup of coffee, he nearly ran into a woman walking too quickly. After he steadied her and apologized for being in her way, she paused, "You're not a student that I recognize, and I know the faculty. Who are you?"

"I used to be a soldier, now I'm a civilian looking for someone I know or something to do." Mac found himself being more honest with this woman than he had been with himself. "My name's Patrick MacLane, used to be Colonel MacLane. Now just Mac."

"Well, Colonel Patrick 'Mac' MacLane, I'm Dr. Martha O'Hara. I teach here at the Farm."

"The 'farm'?"

"That's what it used to be, so that's what we call it. And it's so rural and great out here."

"What do you teach, Dr. O'Hara?"

"Martha, please. I'm in the sciences. Physics mostly."

"I worked with some young physicists during the war." Mac smiled at the memories.

"Would I know any of them?" she asked innocently.

"I don't know if I ever asked where they went to school. One was a Japanese-American kid. I really liked him."

"Not Nick Nishimura?" Martha was staring at Mac.

"In fact, yes, he was one of the guys. Did you know him?"

"He was my star student. I was sad and angry that the war took him from his studies. Especially the way it happened. Goddamn internment camps. God forgive me."

Mac was excited in a way he hadn't been since before the war ended. "Hey, would you like to grab a cup of coffee or lunch?"

"I'm supposed to teach a class in a few minutes. Let me meet you in the Union in about forty-five minutes. Please be there. I have to know what happened."

"Oh, I'll be there, Martha. You can count on that." As she hustled off to teach her class, he thought, *Maybe you can help me find out what happened.*

In less than forty-five minutes, Mac had a table at the student coffee shop and was thinking about how crazy the world was. This morning, he was at loose ends. Now he was having coffee with a beautiful scientist and everything was looking up. The coffee shop was paneled in light wood. The tables were not too close together, and they were big enough for textbooks if students wanted to study. A friendly middle-aged woman was at the counter to take his order.

"What can I do for you, soldier?" she asked him with an unmistakable Irish brogue.

"How did you know?" He was curious.

"Your eyes. You gauged the room when you walked in. You're a little older, although we're getting more older students now. Yes, mostly the eyes. You've seen life that these youngsters haven't."

"Got me." Mac smiled. "Is it so obvious?"

"Not to them. They are all sunshine and hope. And it makes me happy to see that. We've been too long without it."

"Wise beyond your years, ma'am. I *have* seen too much, but my life is starting over. Right here, I think. See that lovely lady walking in the door? That's who I'm meeting."

The woman grinned. "Then you'll have your hands full if you're telling me you're meeting Martha O'Hara."

"That's exactly who I'm talking about." Mac wondered what was up.

Martha walked directly over to Mac at the counter and demanded, "Now, Mother, what have you done to make my new friend look at me like that!"

"Mother?" Mac was dazed.

"I graduated from Smith and then dad died. Mother and I decided that if Stanford would take me, they might take her too. This coffee shop is her domain."

Mac grinned widely. "Then it's my lucky day. Two smart women have just entered my life right when I need them."

"Good answer, boyo. I'm Annie O'Hara at your service. And I've a wee flask behind the counter for the late afternoon. If you catch my drift."

"I'm in love. Take me now." Mac was glowing with happiness at just what a lighthearted pair he had chanced to meet.

"Annie, may I buy your daughter a cup of coffee and maybe lunch?"

"You certainly may, but you'll want to be taking her to a finer place than this."

"Soon, but we need to make a plan. I've always found coffee to be useful when making a plan."

Annie was smiling at Martha. "Smart and handsome. Good work, lass. I told you none of them smarty-pants scientists were what the good Lord had in your future."

"Oh God, here she goes. Grab a cuppa and go to that far table. The BLTs are great here. Ma, we'll take two." Martha took control.

Happy to get away from a mother with wedding plans in her eyes, Mac went where he was directed. After they sat, all he could do was look across the table and smile at Martha. "You have no idea how good it is to be here and be here with you," he stated.

"You're right. The war was very different for us here. We saw lots of sailors, some soldiers and flyboys. But all the action was far away. I told myself that teaching these boys was my way to help the war. I don't know if that was true or just something I clung to because I didn't know what else to do. Oh, I went to parties, danced with guys being shipped off, was at the Red Cross table every chance I could. But it never seemed like enough."

"Well, let's be in action now. There is a lot of work to do, and I need to find smart people to do it." Mac was excited.

"OK, you've got my attention. And I'd like to know what happened to my students too."

The sandwiches arrived, and they dove in. Hunger had sneaked in while they had been planning their futures. As they finished the food, Mac began. "Dick Stanton was yours too? I thought as much." When Martha nodded vigorously. "Both Nishimura and Stanton were working on moving supplies from one place to another. Molecular transference was what they called it. The boys working on the bomb were in one lab, and they were in another."

"Moving supplies? Pencils?"

"We started with bandages. Figured we could get to ammo as we got better, but the war was heating up in the Pacific, and the brass in Washington wanted to see results. Moving a roll of bandages five hundred yards wasn't enough for them. Especially because they were really after intelligence."

"What do you mean? That's huge. That's so much more than we thought was even possible."

"I agree, but these aren't scientists. They're politicians and soldiers. They don't see how far we've come; they see how far we have to go. We were told to speed up the experiments. The bomb boys were already blowing up prototypes. We needed to show something."

"I don't have a good feeling about this."

"Smart lady. You're right to have a 'not good feeling,' but maybe not quite what you're afraid of."

"September 8, 1944. Nick put on his best suit and hat, stepped in a chamber in front of a beam of light, and disappeared. He did not show up across the compound. We don't know what happened." Mac was pained to repeat this.

Martha was confused. "No trace of him? Nothing?"

"No trace. So we think he made it—we just don't know what that means."

"But the report I got was that he was killed in action." Martha was puzzled.

"That was the best the War Department could come up with. Disappeared in the process of an advanced physics experiment was not one of their choices for the telegram." Mac was being ironic, he hoped.

"We have to find him."

"That's what I hoped you'd say." Mac began to smile. "This is where the plan comes in. I have a little money and access to more. You know scientists. We need to set up a way to continue the work that Nishimura and Stanton started."

"Well, I'm still in touch with Dick. I'm sure he'll be on board. I can start a list of talented people looking for interesting work." She looked at Mac. "So what's your job going to be?"

"I'll find the money and protect you from the bad guys because they are still out there. We shut down the project because of just that fact."

"Spies?"

"You might want to lower your voice just a tad. Yes, spies. This experiment was attracting attention."

CHAPTER 16

DAY THREE, LOS ANGELES, STANTON HOME, SEPTEMBER 10, 2008

While Nicola was calling to check in on Grace, Ben had a moment.

"Oh shit!" Ben slapped his head. "I forgot all about that woman."

"What woman?" Charlie perked up. His brother didn't have so many women in his life that he forgot them.

"The woman looking into the old Vento Internment Camp outside of town."

"What did she want?"

"She said she's writing a book about the internment camps in Arizona during the war."

"Do you have some reason to think she won't write a book?"

"Let's just say I didn't get a feeling that she's really a researcher. Just a gut feeling."

"Well, if she's not writing a book, why is she asking about the Camp?"

"Well, now I wonder too. I've had other people audit my History of Arizona class, but none were as focused on this one topic."

"And you're concerned about this now because? She didn't flirt with you so you think something's off with her? She didn't like the homework you gave out. Or your Spidey sense lit up? Come on, big brother. Spill." Charlie enjoyed giving Ben a hard time. He didn't get the chance very often.

"Because of Nick, dumb shit. Everything is suspicious now. I'm trying to recall her questions. She sent me an e-mail with a few of them. Let me see if I can find it."

Ben having remembered his laptop, opened it and clicked on the e-mail icon. In a minute a tone told them it was active, and he had mail.

"I knew I should have been suspicious. No one her age is named Sedona. Only children of hippies are called Sedona, and she's not quite the right age for that. I think it's a pen name or worse."

"What's worse than being named Sedona?" Charlie was shaking his head.

"When it's a made-up name because you're looking for information about a missing scientist."

"Nah, you don't think that's possible, do you? How long ago did she reach out to you?"

"About six weeks ago. Long before Nick appeared. But the coincidence isn't comfortable. We'll have to tell the others."

"Tell them what? A woman with a funky name e-mailed you to see about sitting in on your Arizona history class because of her interest in the Vento Internment Camp?"

"I think I'm recalling some of her details. She was interested in a young scientist who had been pulled from the camp. She had tried finding families still living who had been at Vento."

"OK, that could be bad. We need to find out if Grace heard from her. And if so, what did she ask, what did she know, and what do we do?"

Charlie motioned to Nicola to stay on the phone. Ben moved over to share the mouthpiece. "Grace, hi, this is Ben Grant. Hey, I've got a question for you. Has a woman named Sedona contacted you about the Vento Camp?"

Nicola looked baffled. Charlie put a finger to his lips and raised his eyebrows.

"She did? How long ago? What did you tell her, do you remember? OK, that's good. We'll see you soon and bring you up to speed. If she calls again, please tell her you haven't remembered anything else."

He gave the phone back to Nicola, who continued her conversation.

Ben shared, "Yes, Sedona contacted her, but Grace didn't tell her much about Nick, just that he had been with them and then soldiers came one day, and he was gone. And then one day, soldiers came to tell them he was dead."

Charlie was serious. "We have to tell the others."

"Tell the others what?" This was their dad.

"That we have another potential problem in the Keep Nick a Secret Club." Charlie wasn't exactly being funny.

"KNASC? Not a catchy acronym." This was Dick.

"No, but it sounds like the government. Let's keep it." Jane was smiling.

"Well, we may have something like a spy, but her name is Sedona." Ben began to sit to share the tale of Sedona Searsy and the history of the Vento Internment Camp.

Jane was constructing a sequence in her mind and spoke out loud. "Ben, you got an e-mail from a woman wanting to attend your class. She came with a very specific interest. She attended your class about Arizona WWII history then left, and you haven't heard anything more. She found Grace Nishimura Acevedo, asked questions, and didn't learn any more than what *Wikipedia* has. Is this about right?"

"It doesn't sound as bad as my gut feels." Ben grimaced.

"Why do you think your gut is twisting?" Jane had learned to trust "the gut."

"I've been teaching for almost ten years. I've learned to read students. This one didn't read as telling the truth. At the time I didn't spend any time trying to figure it out. No reason to. Now I wonder what she was really up to." Ben was serious.

"Let's Google her," Charlie suggested. "Maybe we can find out something helpful." Nicola popped open her tablet and typed in *Sedona Searsy* and waited. Her face fell.

"Your gut is right. Sedona Searsy is the pen name of a reporter who works for one of the national scandal papers. But what the

102

hell kind of story could she be working on? The apology for the Internment was already made. What other scandal could there be?"

Jane was thoughtful, "There have always been rumors about spies around Los Alamos. But that's not new."

Rick suggested, "Perhaps it's time to check in with The Institute and see what the latest is. And to see if our security people know anything about this Sedona Searsy."

"It's definitely late and the staff at The Institute is great, but I don't expect them to be on e-mail at this time of the evening. Let's call it a night and start again in the morning." Jane was being practical. "It's been a very big few days for all of us, especially Nick. We need some time to let all of this sift through our brains. I'll make breakfast here tomorrow. See you at seven o'clock?"

The gang began to move toward the door. Nick was staying with Rick and Jane and Dick. Ben, Charlie, Nicola, and Don were heading for the nearby Holiday Inn Express. The stress of the day had just begun to show as they trudged to the SUV.

As they reached the door of the SUV, Nicola turned to thank their hostess. "Thanks again, Jane. This was much more than I could have asked for. I look forward to tomorrow."

Ben drove. Charlie and Nicola climbed in the back seat. Don took shotgun. It wasn't far to the hotel, and they were all now wearier than they had realized. They agreed to meet in the lobby at six forty-five the next morning.

At the Stanton house, Dick and his long-lost friend had begun to chatter as only old friends can. Jane didn't want to interrupt, but she thought they all needed to catch up on the news of the day, the news of the outside world that is. As the late news began the headline summary, Nick was glued to the screen.

"Did they just say that negro was a candidate for president?"

Dick smiled. "We've come a long way from the camps and segregation. Yes, that man is the Democratic candidate for president. And the Republicans have nominated a former Vietnam prisoner of war."

"So a war hero and a negro man are running for president?" Nick was amazed.

"You should have seen it when Ronald Reagan ran for president! Oh, and since the sixties, we say 'black,' not 'negro.'"

"Who's Ronald Reagan? Why black? I have *a lot* to catch up on."

"And Reagan won. Two terms, after he was governor of California. And he was an actor before being governor."

"And you think it's amazing that I'm here? What you're telling me is way beyond what I could have imagined could happen in the future." Nick was shaking his head.

Jane sat near them. "And there's so much more. We're going to have to think about the context for bringing you up to today. There's society, politics, art, science, finance, the state of the world. I think I have a colleague who can help, but we have to have your back story first."

"Back story?" Nick was unsure what she meant.

"Today, every child gets a social security number at the same time they get their birth certificate. It's all one application, I think. Most kids get a driver's license as soon as they turn sixteen. You have neither, or if you did, they belong to a dead guy."

Nick's sense of humor rose. "I guess so. I'm a dead guy, and I also can't be a dead guy. And if people find out about me…"

Rick spoke. "You'll be the lead story of every news show and your life won't be your own, ever again."

Jane picked up the thread. "So we'll call Grace tomorrow and get her started on your identity. It sounds like she has some skills in this area. We also must decide where you've been for the past few years, where you studied. The best stories are mostly real. You could certainly have done work on your own, perhaps after being home-schooled. You had gotten so far with your studies and realized you needed to engage with a larger community."

Rick suggested, "Let's see what Grace comes up with before we start spinning a tale. And who's going to be asking anyway. It's your Institute, Jane. You get to accept him and bring him onboard to do research. Maybe the less you say, the better."

"Of course, you're right. And you know people will ask. Nick will need a way to deflect."

Dick smiled. "What if he's been sick, was in isolation for a long time. Cured now and returned to society."

"Where was I in isolation? A desert island?" Nick was enjoying this.

"Well, the island of Molokai in Hawaii was a leper colony for many years—very much isolated," Rick volunteered.

"Indonesia has thousands of remote islands. Perhaps this is a story line worth pursuing?" Dick was perking up.

"OK, you two delinquents. Enough of spinning tall tales tonight. I think we all need some rest before we face the morning. Nick, do you have what you need?"

"The Grants were very generous, and I have a change of clothes and a shaving kit, so I guess I'm good."

"Soon, you'll need to go shopping for more clothes and hygiene stuff for you. The shopping will probably be another cultural assault." Jane was shaking her head.

Dick raised an eyebrow. "Maybe back in Indio with Grace?"

"Indio, definitely. Otherwise, he can always go with Charlie when they come back. It'll be less suspicious, and I don't want to be tempted to act like his mother."

Day Three, Nick's Notes

I had not thought about what the people who stayed behind would think or feel after I "left." Theresa had been so confident, in her quiet way, that I would be back. She never said so in so many words, but I felt it from her. I can't put it any more definitely. Certainly not scientifically. Her timing appears to be a bit off. Dick thought he had killed me. He never put any trust in Theresa's gift.

I think it's possible I will be staying in this time. Dick and his son and our old friend Mac kept looking all these years. Yet here I am.

Grace did well for herself and has two famous and talented children and of course Nicola. Nicola, my namesake?

Dick said he had visited Theresa to tell her what happened. He said she was calm. She had told me I would be leaving, and her spirits watched over me. Her "sight" did not have a timetable. He says she's still alive.

I need more modern clothes. They tell me I need to blend in. I have so much to learn and much to prepare in order to stay in this time.

CHAPTER 17

DAY FOUR, LOS ANGELES, THE
NEXT MORNING AT THE STANTON
HOME, SEPTEMBER 11, 2008

It was a glorious California morning, even on the coast. A little fog with the sun promising to break through when Feynman began to bark and wag his tail. The SUV pulled into the drive and the rested travelers climbed out.

They knew the drill today and trooped out to the patio to spread out. Charlie and Nicola went to the kitchen to see how they could help Jane. Feynman went nosing for friendly head pats and someone to throw his frisbee.

Jane had eggs, scones, bacon and coffee ready for delivery to the patio. Charlie grabbed a stack of plates, while Nicola snagged napkins and silverware.

Jane brought out platters, while Rick balanced the coffee pot and a tray of mugs. Once coffee was poured, the conversation started in earnest.

Nicola started, "I think I need to get back to Indio. Abuelita Grace will need some help, and I want to keep her in the loop. I don't think she would go rogue, but she's very independent."

Nick stopped chewing. "You got that right. She's still spunky, that Grace. And I want to spend some more time with her."

Don lifted his mug. "And she's taking care of Sam. That's a lot to ask."

Jane stopped eating. "Sam?"

"Our miniature Australian Shepherd. Short for Samantha."

"Oh, of course. I should have guessed."

"How could you. You just took in a bunch of strays with crazy stories. You couldn't have known."

"Maybe, but I've run The Institute since dad stepped down and I wrangle scientists, rogues and refugees, literally all the time."

Charlie was smiling broadly. "I'm going to fit right in."

Ben wanted to know, "Which one are you?"

"Maybe all of them. At least I like that thought. Rogue sounds kind of rakish and romantic."

Jane nodded. "I've had my share of rogues in residence. They don't last Charlie. Be wary of that role."

"OK. I want to last. The Institute sounds like a great place and I sure haven't been able to find a home for my research."

Don spoke again. "So did you guys decide anything last night?"

"After thinking that perhaps Nick had been on an Indonesian island with a rare disease and that's why he hasn't been around much, we decided to wait to see what kind of identity Grace's resources would come up with. We can create his back story after we have that to start with." Dick sounded sensible.

Jane spoke. "That's practical. Before you head back to Indio, do you want a tour of The Institute? We also have living quarters. We added them about ten years ago when we started hosting scientists in residence for more than a week at a time. I'll check and see when we'll have space for Charlie and Nicola to move in."

Don looked at Charlie. "What's your commitment to NAU?"

"I'm an at-will-adjunct. Almost disposable. I can give them a week's notice and offer to complete my responsibilities for the independent student section remotely and call it good."

"What about the classes you teach?" Ben was concerned.

"I don't have classes, really. I have eight students doing independent study. I can monitor them with e-mail and Skype. I can still get their grades in at the end of the semester."

Don remembered, "What are you going to tell your aunt?"

"I'll tell her that the call I got from you guys was to tell me about an opportunity in California. She'll be excited for me and probably happy to get her guestroom back in time for the holidays."

Don smiled. "I can't argue with that. You know her so well."

Ben was making mental notes. "So, Nick, Dad, Nicola, Charlie, and I are heading back to Indio. Dad, Charlie, and I will pick up Sam and head back to Arizona. Nicola and Nick will stay with Grace while the identity piece is sorted out. Once that's in place, Nick and Nicola will head back here, Nicola to start residing at The Institute and Nick with the Stantons. Do I have it about right? Oh, and Charlie. We can't forget Charlie."

"The only thing that will change that sequence is if our investigative people have found out anything hinky about that Sedona woman." Jane was getting her things ready to head out.

Rick looked at the bunch. "I've got the cleanup handled here. You all need to get to The Institute and find out if your next step is what Ben laid out. Let me know if you need Dad and I as backup. We're here for you."

Jane leaned over to kiss him. "I know, honey, and I appreciate you. I can take someone with me. SUV driver, you follow the red Prius."

Charlie chuckled. "Nick, why don't you go with Jane in her hybrid? She can tell you all about the technology on the drive."

Nick raised his eyebrows. "Hybrid. Sounds like I have even more to catch up on."

Stanton Home, Los Angeles, California, September 11, 2008

Rick and his Dad watched the two-car convoy head out. They spoke almost in tandem. "Nick's gonna need to break out."

Then they laughed. Dick said, "He's still a twenty-four-year-old guy. We can't cage him again."

"I had the same thought. Do you think Charlie would be a good influence or should we ask Nicola?" Rick wondered.

"I think they'll both have his back. They'll be at The Institute together. Charlie and Nicola both have the science piece to share. I think Nick will stay here for a short while and then join them living there. Charlie has the 'guy' piece covered. We may have really lucked out when Nick appeared near Vento Junction, Arizona. We have Don Grant to thank for rescuing a lost soul and believing him."

"Do you think it takes a vet to recognize another one? Nick did serve, didn't he?" Rick really didn't know.

"When they pulled him from the internment camp in 1943, they knew they wanted him and weren't sure what to do with him. They didn't really know what to do with any of us, the scientists. Oppie and a few of the other older guys figured out the best way for us to do our work as scientists was NOT to be military. Then we wouldn't have to obey orders. We could follow the science. So we were civilians at Los Alamos." Dick was smiling softly. "We all wanted so badly to serve. If this was the way to do it, we would do our part. If doing research to help the war effort was it, then we were all in. At least until we began to hear about the radiation."

"What did you hear?"

"We heard about a couple of accidents. Guys getting badly burned, dying."

Rick nodded. "Knowing what we know now, I'm amazed there weren't more deaths during the research phase."

"It was a different time. We were all about fighting the enemy and winning the war, on both fronts. It was just luck for the Germans that they lost before we could drop the bomb on them."

"Was that in the plans?" Rick's eyes were big.

"Let's just say that there was a lot of talk over cocktails. I never saw any plans."

"What makes you think it could have happened?"

Dick paused. "Now that you mention it. That rumor came from Simon Constantine, the Greek."

"Who?"

"He was one of the ones that Mac thought was a spy. At least he had figured out he wasn't a very good scientist. I heard he was disgraced after the war. Maybe Jane has more on him from her sources."

"Let's not forget about that thread. Not when he spent time around Nick." Rick was a little concerned to have that name come up again.

In the Prius Heading for The Institute

Once Nick had his seatbelt fastened, he gazed at the dashboard of Jane's car. She gave him a rudimentary explanation of the hybrid as they pulled away from the driveway and into the neighborhood.

"This is so amazing and yet so sensible. Why didn't we do this all along? And it's a Japanese company?" Nick was shaking his head. "So much is different. I don't know if I can ever fit in."

Jane smiled. "You're smart and good-looking. You'll do fine. I think Charlie and Nicola will be great companions for you as you navigate this *brave new world*. And The Institute will be a haven as you try your wings. There are a lot of visiting scientists, many from other countries. They all feel their foreign-ness when they arrive. In fact, they'll undoubtedly have suggestions for you regarding assimilating."

"Assimilating? That sounds ominous."

"Well, given your unique circumstance, assimilation will keep you safe until, and if, you ever decide to go public with the truth." Jane was serious but not somber.

"I need to visit my mom and dad's graves. Maybe that will help me accept that they're gone." Nick was somber.

"Of course. I'll mention it to Nicola. Where do you think they're buried, Indio? You know, though, even seeing their graves, well, they'll always be with you Nick. Gone begins to mean something different for all of us as our parents grow older." Jane turned into a parking lot next to a sprawling glass building.

"We never talked about it. They were in their forties when I last saw them. Even though death was all around us because of the war, we never talked about any of us dying or where anyone would be buried. For that matter, I wonder where I'm buried. Now that will be a strange visit. Seeing my name on a headstone." Nick almost found the humor in his last thought.

Jane announced, "We're here. And, Nick, until we have your backstory figured out, let's stick with Brown rather than Nishimura. Agreed?" She went on to explain more about this place where they had stopped. "It's close to home, by design. The building was dedicated only about ten years ago. It was state-of-the-art then and we invest frequently to stay up to date. We named it for Mom and Dad right before Dad stepped down. It seemed like it was time to put their permanent stamp on what they started so long ago."

Carved into the wall above the glass expanse of doors at the entry was Patrick "Mac" and Martha MacLane Institute. The building was only three stories tall but extended for a full block.

At The Institute

Jane explained, "The building has several stories below ground level, so it's bigger than it looks."

Nick was looking around. "It looks plenty big to me. Remember, a few days ago, I was in New Mexico looking at Quonset huts and old log school buildings."

"When you put it that way, it must look palatial," Jane grinned.

The others caught up with them. After suitable oohing and ahhing, Jane led them through the entryway. At the reception desk, Nick noticed there were a lot of things that looked different from the reception desks he was used to, but rather than ask, he kept quiet.

Jane said to the receptionist, "Gerald, these are three new hires and two family members along for a tour." He handed her a tablet, so she could fill in their names and reason for being on site. When she handed it back with a couple of taps, he was able to print name badges for the visitors. Jane thanked him and asked, "Would you let Mitchell know we're here? I'd like him to meet our new hires and visitors."

"Certainly, Dr. MacLane."

Jane explained, "Mitchell Stans is our head of Security. I'd like you all to get off on the right foot by meeting him today."

"You have a head of security?" Nick was a little baffled.

"Many corporations do, especially when research and intellectual property are concerned. The Institute has a number of valuable patents as well as people and we take security very seriously. It was something Dad started in the earliest days of The Institute. I think his experience at Los Alamos taught him that you can never be too paranoid." Jane was distracted as a large dark-skinned man walked toward her.

She grinned as the giant enveloped her in a hug. "New hires, huh? What have you been up to Mom?"

The group was more than curious. Jane explained, "Our son Mitchell was a talented football player for UCLA while taking advanced computer classes. When the time came for the NFL draft, we offered him an alternative. Oh, and we had adopted him when he was in high school."

"Mitch, this is Nick Brown, Nicola Acevedo, and Charlie, Ben, and Don Grant. Nick and Charlie have their PhDs and Nicola is being advised by Rick, so hers is coming. Ben and his dad came out to see where Charlie was going to be hanging out. Ben teaches in Arizona, and Don is enjoying being with all of us. So that's a quick snapshot. There will be a lot more to follow, but not today."

Nicola was the first to speak. "I think I may have more questions now than before your explanation. I'm part of the introduction and even I want to know what else is coming! Although I do know that we are doing some very interesting research, very interesting. And that your Mom thinks that The Institute is the right place for us to do our work."

Mitch was chuckling. "She loves to do that. Spring me on people. I got her this time. I was first to the surprise."

"So this is a gauntlet for newbies?" Charlie was getting into it. "OK, I'll bite. Any more kids we should meet?"

"Not so much a gauntlet as a way to check out your ability to absorb conflicting input and keep on going." Jane was smiling broadly. "And there *are* a few more family members to meet."

The group had been walking down a long hall and stopped at the foot of a broad staircase. On one side was a chair elevator. Nick pointed. "And this?"

"We meet all of the requirements of the ADA and then some." Mitchell was proud.

Charlie leaned in to Nick's ear and whispered, "Americans with Disabilities Act. I'll explain later. It's a good thing."

As they were standing at the foot of the stairs a young woman in a motorized wheelchair zoomed up. "Dr. Mac, Dr. Mac, you're here. I had a breakthrough. You gotta come see."

"Suzanne, I have three new colleagues for you to meet and two visitors. Meet Nick Brown, Nicola Acevedo, and Charlie Grant. Along with them for today are Ben and Don Grant. Suzanne is working on accommodations for people with motor skill deficiencies. So watcha got, Suzanne?"

"Oh, not here, you gotta come to the lab to see." Suzanne was grinning and zooming toward the elevator. "See you there."

As the elevator doors closed, Jane explained, "Suzanne Brown had a skateboarding accident when she was fifteen. Afterward, she was a paraplegic. She's thirty now and a graduate of Cal Tech. She graduated in biomedical engineering. We're thrilled to have her."

Nick repeated, "Biomedical engineering?"

Charlie said, "Add it to your list, Nick. I'll explain it all after the tour."

As they climbed the stairs, Jane explained, "We do more than physics here. Biomedical engineering, prosthetic development, alternative fuels, genetic research, cybersecurity. We've got our hands in a lot of pots."

Mitch chuckled. "That's one way to put it. If it does good and makes money it happens here. And if it does good and doesn't make money, we make *sure* it happens here."

When they reached the top of the stairs, Mitch wished them well and engulfed each of their outstretched hands with his massive ones. They continued down the hall to reach Suzanne's lab. The door opened when Jane peered into a small window.

Charlie leaned into Nick. "Retinal scan. Add it to the list."

Suzanne had a robotic hand on a table and electrodes on her forehead. "Watch this." The hand moved its fingers one by one.

Jane grinned, "You did it. You got the thoughts translated to electronic impulses."

"You bet your butt I did. It was a bitch, but I got it to work."

"She still sounds like the skateboarder that she was. But her science is brilliant." Jane was proud.

Suzanne turned to the new hires. "So what's your deal?"

"You mean what are we working on?" Nick spoke. "Well, I can't speak for the others, but I'm looking into teleportation and time travel. Want to try it?"

"Sign me up. I want to go to a time where I can have an exoskeleton and walk." Suzanne was laughing.

Charlie jumped in. "Don't we have those now?"

"Not like Iron Man. Oh no. Lightweight ones that look good and move naturally."

"And that's your next project, yes?" Jane started to guide the troop to their next stop.

Charlie tapped Nick on the shoulder. "Dude, I'll use my phone to start a list of stuff you need to know, so we won't lose track. This is the stuff that will alert people that you're not from these parts, if you get my drift."

Nick looked quizzical. "Dude?"

"A colloquial greeting used by young men of a certain ilk," Ben weighed in as the older brother.

Charlie took umbrage. "A certain ilk? I am no ilk, sir."

"No, but you are of a certain…"

Don raised his voice. "All right, you two, this is your father asking you to straighten up and fly right."

"Now that's a phrase I think I recognize." Nick grinned.

Jane had guided them to a balcony overlooking an atrium. "We try to let in as much natural light as possible. All the plants are native species, and we have a garden on the roof. We have a couple of dieticians working on hunger issues, and the garden is their baby. We study sustainable agriculture, and of course, everyone loves the fresh produce we serve in the dining room."

"Dining room?" Nicola was curious.

"Fresh produce?" Nick and Charlie spoke in unison.

"Have we signed on the dotted line yet?" Charlie was pulling a pen from his shirt pocket.

Don spoke to Jane. "It sounds like my boy will be in good hands here."

Ben asked, "Any guest quarters if I want to check on the youngsters?"

Jane smiled at the Grant family. "Plenty of guest quarters. I'll take you there after I show you this next lab."

To enter this room, she needed a card with a magnetic stripe.

Nick looked at Charlie. "On the list, right?"

As they entered and looked around, it was plain-looking. Each wall had several white boards and a ceiling mounted projector. "So what's cool in here?" Jane teased. "Each board is a computer screen. We can hold world-wide meetings in this room. Scientists and researchers skype in, in real time. Cuts down travel costs and time."

"List?" Nick looked at Charlie, who replied to Jane, "Way, way cool. Maybe I can finally see some of the guys I've been chatting with over the years."

Nick looked at him. "Add it to the list, dude."

"There's a schedule to sign up to use the room, as well as a schedule of meetings in case you want to drop in. It's on the Intranet." Jane filled them in.

Charlie nodded at Nick. "Done, dude."

Nick thought that this list was going to be long just by the time they finished the tour, and he didn't see Charlie writing anything down, although he was tapping on a small metal rectangle in his hand. More questions.

Jane pointed across the atrium to a colorful section of the building. "That's housing. So many researchers come for a short time that it made sense to have temporary quarters for them. Some stay as long as a year, some only a week or two. Their time is precious, and more of it can be spent in the lab or with colleagues this way."

Nicola nodded. "Smart and cost effective. And increases the opportunity for collegiality."

"Let's go check out one of the apartments." Jane pointed the way. They curved around the hallway and soon found themselves greeted by a large heavy door. "Convenient and secure. You'll each get a magnetic key with your own code. We'll know if you're in this area or not. Not really big brother, just a way to be able to reach you if we need you."

She swiped her card and pushed the door open. They were greeted by murmurs. "There's a common area and lots of folks like to gather almost any time of day. There's coffee and snacks at all times."

"I'm in heaven." Charlie pretended to swoon.

Nick looked at him. "Dude…"

Charlie's eyes got big and he started to laugh. "Quick study here."

They all moved toward the common area, and Jane stepped closer to a small gathering to better make introductions to the few people on hand.

Don checked his watch and looked at Jane. "Thank you much for the tour, but I think we better hit the road so we can be at Grace's before dinner."

"Of course. It was great to meet you, Don, Ben. We'll take good care of Charlie for you when he starts here." Jane shook their hands.

The gang of five headed toward the elevator. They looked around to make sure no one was zooming by, but it was all quiet.

They turned in their badges and said goodbye. Walking toward the parking lot, Nick was the first to say, "Nothing's going to be the same, is it?"

"And I say again, what was your first clue? 2008?" Nicola was only half joking. "But you're right. Nothing's going to be the same for any of us. You have the biggest changes to handle, but we all just made life-changing choices. Good choices but life-changing nonetheless."

Don put his arm around her shoulder. "I think you've just made some damn good choices. These are fine people, and they'll treat you right and respect your work. Just watch out for Charlie." And he winked at her.

Ben was staring into space. "Man, I want a room like the one with all the big screens. For my classroom. Think of the places we could visit just from our room? My students would get so much out of it."

"You never know. Maybe we can have a satellite site for The Institute in Arizona," Charlie was serious.

"I'd like that," Don said. "Maybe I'd see more of both of my sons."

CHAPTER 18

STANTON HOME, 2008

Dick, Betsy, and Rick sat quietly around the sunny kitchen table absorbing events of the previous day…or was it only a few hours? Feynman rested near their feet. He was tired out from all the people and excitement.

Rick gazed at his folks. "This whole whatever it was that just happened sheds a lot of light on some fuzzy history that you two share. I always appreciated your interest in research and Skyridge, but I see them differently now."

Betsy smiled. "There were so many good reasons to start the school that we didn't really need to share the actual origin story. The time your dad and I spent at Oak Ridge is all true. How he came to be there—well, it was the war and people were sent lots of places to do lots of jobs. And you know Suzanna and George. After the war ended, we all decided that California was where we would build our lives."

Dick continued, "It was easy to get a loan as a GI and I found the property for the ranch pretty soon after getting a teaching job at UCLA. You can't picture what it was like in 1946. Open land as far as you could see. Granted the roads left a lot to be desired."

Betsy laughed at him. "How can you even say that after living in mud city that year? The roads here were dusty, but I'll take dust any day over all that mud. And Susanna and George felt the same way."

Dick was remembering, and he had a thousand-mile gaze as he spoke. "It was quite the trip bringing them and their kids out that first time. That truck should never have made it, but by God it did. George was a wizard at making that thing run. That and every other piece of equipment we ever had out there. He really transformed those old buildings. First the house, then the barn as a schoolhouse. That didn't last long as I recall."

"No." Betsy smiled. "We needed more room and a bunkhouse really soon. Word of our school for girls spread quickly when you told your friends at UCLA."

"When did you ask Aunt Blackie and Aunt Trudy to come out?" Rick wanted to hear the familiar story.

"Oh, they were watching our progress." Betsy nodded. "I got regular telegrams from them wanting to know how things were progressing. It didn't take much for the two of them to take the train West in February 1947. As I recall, it was a cold time in Boston, and they kept asking how warm and sunny it was here."

Dick was warming to the familiar tale. "And when they did get here, my buddies at the University were the first to ask them out. It wasn't long before both had serious suitors."

"And that 'suited' them just fine." Betsy laughed at the memory of those dates. "Our little ranch school had teachers, students, buildings, and the best caretakers anyone could ask for. We've been so lucky."

Rick jumped in. "How are they all? I haven't seen Susanna in a few months. I know George is having trouble walking. How's that Assisted Living place working out?"

"As soon as they let Susanna in the kitchen, everyone was happier." Betsy was rueful. "It's a good thing it's a small place. Susanna in the kitchen wouldn't have worked otherwise."

Dick smiled, "How about we go there when the time comes, honey? It would be like old times with Susanna's cooking. I know they only have twelve units, but we could put our names on the list."

Rick grinned. "I can't even tell you how happy it makes me to hear you say that. I put your names on the waiting list the last time

I visited Susanna and George. I got a call a few weeks ago. A unit should be available by the end of the year. What do you think?"

Betsy leaned over to take Dick's hand. "I'd feel a lot safer if the two of us were there, dear. I worry about falling. When you decide to do yard work, I find myself standing at the window watching to make sure you're all right."

Dick responded to her by squeezing her hand and holding it to his heart. "If I make you worried, that was not my intent. And if it would put you at ease, then we can move. Good thing it's not far from campus. I'd hate to give up my visits to the Department."

"I'd drive all day to pick you up, old man. Any time you want to visit my class or just hang around, I'll make sure you're picked up and safely delivered." Rick was visibly relieved that this conversation had been easier than he and Jane had expected.

CHAPTER 19

THE INSTITUTE, LOS ANGELES, CALIFORNIA, JUNE 3, 2000

Dick Stanton appreciated the fact that Mac kept in touch—even after the war. The box with artifacts from the New Mexico site was an odd "gift." But as he watched his contemporaries over the years, he and Mac and a couple of others seemed to fare quite well. He had asked Mac about the "gift box" once. His response was his usual vague nothing, but at the end, he let slip something about "weird rocks." Well, why the hell not have a box of weird New Mexico rocks in his basement? He also had Nick's notebooks. He had never let anyone know he had them, and no one had ever asked.

Every so often in the early years after the war, he and Mac had met up. They were both in Southern California, Dick at UCLA and Mac and Martha at The Institute, a think tank he and his wife founded soon after the end of the War. It was funded by "anonymous patrons of science." Dick was pretty sure it was family money from Mac's side, maybe even to assuage some post-war guilt, but he couldn't prove it, and what did it matter anyway? They did good work. Great work in many cases.

By the 1970s, Dick was leading annual seminars at The Institute. It was the easiest and most discrete way to pursue the science behind Nick's disappearance. UCLA was not a big proponent of molecular transference or anything remotely related to "teleportation." But no one had an explanation of Nick's experiment nor where he may have gone.

The staff at The Institute followed the careers of the students who attended Dick's annual symposia. They often made quiet offers to the best of the young researchers. It was gratifying for Dick to know that his pursuit of answers would not end with him. It was also a continued demonstration by Mac that he really did want to find Nick or learn what happened to him.

When the level of engagement on Mac's part began to diminish, Dick was concerned for his friend and for what would happen with The Institute. So when Mac asked him to meet, he was anxious.

"I know you've heard the rumors." Mac was seated on the couch in his office. The windows to his left opened to the courtyard of the three-story building. It was misleading, of course. There were more floors below street level that housed the more sensitive research labs from prying eyes.

"If we didn't respect and care about you…" Dick started.

"Yeah, yeah. Thanks, but that's not why you're here."

"OK, why am I here?"

"Because I want you to know what's ahead for The Institute. Jane's going to take over." At this Mac grinned. His daughter was a brilliant scientist in her own right and Dick's daughter-in-law.

"I'm pleased and not at all surprised. It's a wise move, both for continuity and for quality." Dick was sincere.

"Martha and I talked about it. It wasn't a long conversation. We both agreed that Jane's the best choice. She's got a way about her that disarms people, and those scientists with almost no social skills open up to her. That's really important with some of the sensitive stuff that happens here."

"Have you told Jane about the plan?" Dick wondered how much was known and by whom in the small circle of people who had known Nick.

Mac sobered, "We talked to her and Rick last night. They're both still absorbing my diagnosis, and we wanted to allay their fears about the future of this place. They were very gracious, but I know they were also relieved to know what the future would hold."

"Tell me about that diagnosis, now that you mentioned it."

"I have early stage dementia. I'm not dangerous to myself or anyone else, yet. But what's ahead is uncertain. Hence the hand-off to Jane."

"I'm sad to hear that, but I admit that I'm relieved to know that The Institute will continue. I'll continue with my annual symposium, and more if they want it. I can't thank you enough for what you've made happen for all these years. We may not know what happened to Nick, but we do know more about the science. And that's not nothing." Dick was utterly sincere.

"Well, Nick was Martha's star student. I couldn't let his disappearance go, and neither could she."

"Speaking of Martha, how she's doing with all this?" Dick had a special relationship with Martha that went back to his student days. And for many years, he and Mac and Martha had been colleagues in the work of The Institute. While on the surface this sounded like it was a husband-to-husband kind of question, it was a lot more. And as he asked the question, he wondered how his Betsy would react in a similar circumstance.

"She's got that Irish streak that finds humor in the darkest hours, but she's troubled. It's comforting to know that Jane and The Institute will be a distraction for her when I'm gone." Mac looked into the distance.

Dick was startled. "Where are you, Mac?"

Mac seemed to focus. "I was back in New Mexico—back with the team."

"OK," Dick waited to see where this was going.

Mac grew sober as he bored into Dick's eyes, "Dick, I'm losing today. That's why Jane is stepping up now."

Dick leaned forward. "Jeez, Mac, it's got to be hard. What can I do?"

Mac was sheepish. "Martha's a trooper. Always has been. Reading a lot. Finding new drugs or treatments."

Dick leaned back a little. "So what's the next step? For all of us?"

Mac was back in charge. "Life at The Institute will go on under Jane's steady hand. You may have noticed that she's had more responsibility in the last few years." This was a tongue-in-cheek admission of what they both were keenly aware. Dick was close to his son Rick, Jane's husband, so he didn't miss much that went on at The Institute.

Dick looked away. "And that felt natural. I'm Emeritus now at UCLA. Gotta make room for the next generation. What about the future?"

Mac leaned back in his chair. "It's hard to even think about the future for me. But Martha has found a place in Oregon with a fine memory program. We'll live there away from any person or place that my memories could hurt."

Now Dick was confused. "Hurt? How do you think your memories—oh, the project—all *those* secrets."

Mac smiled a knowing smile. "Indeed, all those secrets. Even more than you knew. I want to be somewhere far from here. What we've been learning is that early memories are the last to go. And there may come a point, I don't know when, perhaps even Los Alamos will be my reality."

Dick leaned forward again, "Holy…so this place in Oregon will be safe? For you and what you know?"

Mac sat straighter. "And Martha can be with me. I can't imagine life without her, Dick. She's been through almost all of it."

Now Dick became curious. "So how did you find this place, and are you sure it's as good as you think?"

Mac grinned. "I called a few people. Turns out old spies can get dementia like everybody else. And they know things that shouldn't be told."

Dick was thinking out loud. "I guess that makes sense. So when do you leave? What about the house?"

Mac leaned his forearms on his knees. "We're about at the end of the science season, as we call it. Every year—well, you've watched it. The ones finishing their time here, the alumni, are packing up to head home. The new 'recruits' arrive. It's a good time to slip away. The new ones won't even meet me. I'll just be a photo on the wall. Jane's dad."

Dick spoke softly. "And so much more. You'll let me know how to reach you. Betsy will want to come visit."

Mac started to rise. "Martha will like that."

Dick stopped short. "How are Jane and Rick doing with the news?"

Mac sat back. "Jane's trying to decide whether or not to be tested, and even if she wants to know, I'm eighty-two now. I really don't know when the onset was. It's so small, so incremental. We also don't know how long I have until—"

Dick stood up. "You're doing the right thing, for everyone. As you always do."

The silence hung in the air. The two longtime colleagues and friends didn't need words.

Mac and Martha moved to Oregon just weeks after that conversation. Dick and Betsy traveled to see them a couple of months later.

As they were leaving their driveway to start their drive north, Betsy began to weep silent tears. "It's really going to end for them, isn't it?"

Dick gripped the wheel of the car and stared at the road. "I don't see any other end, but Mac made the right choice for him. Not sure about Martha, but he always did want to have a say in the way things happened."

Shortly after he and Betsy returned from their trip to see Mac and Martha, Dick got a message from Jane. She and Rick needed to see him and Betsy.

Rick and Jane arrived promptly at six and were greeted by Dick and Betsy. Betsy pulled Jane into a moist hug. Then Jane said, "Thanks for that, but we're here because of a different matter." She pulled out a note and video from Mac.

Patrick MacLane Confession

This is Patrick MacLane. It's time for me to share something that I've been carrying since the War. I led a group of amazing young scientists in the desert of New Mexico. Everyone's heard of Los Alamos and Oppenheimer. There was more, a lot more.

While those guys worked on the bomb, we worked on something called molecular transference. The closest thing to it was fiction created by a guy named Rodenberry when he came up with "Beam me up, Scotty." We, or at least those brilliant young men, were all working on moving molecules across distance. We had hoped across great distance. For the war effort. We weren't trying to kill the enemy. We wanted to save our guys. If we could get supplies and medical equipment to hard-to-reach places, soldiers would live.

Or so we told ourselves.

Anyway, it all went wrong. We thought we were ready to try an experiment moving a person. We had been moving small stuff, across a room, across the base. Turns out a box of bandages is different than a man.

The young scientist who volunteered for the trip was Nicholas "Nick" Nishimura, a physicist we grabbed from the internment camp in Arizona. I still can't believe we put our American citizens, our friends and neighbors, into prison camps.

Anyway, Nick volunteered. He hoped if the experiment succeeded, the war would end sooner, and he could get his family out of the Camp. I am ashamed when I remember that time.

Anyway, Nick was the guy. What we didn't know was that there were enemy spies on the base. We just thought they were like the other scientists sent along by the brass in DC. Well, he was sent by DC all right, but they hadn't done their homework.

So I find out afterward, too late, that there are spies among us.

Back to Nick. So he steps into the chamber. We close the door and power up the machine they've been working on for more than a year. The lights dim, and the machine stops. Dick Stanton, Nick's best friend, reaches the chamber. The power has made the door hot. He grabs a rag to pull the door open. Nick's gone like we expected, but he's not across the room. We called over to where the bandages showed up. They got nothing.

It hit us. We don't know where Nick is. Or how to track him.

That afternoon, there was a massive electrical storm. Rains washed out the roads. It was an emergency for everyone. After a few weeks, things were back to what resembled normal. The work on the gadget was making progress. We were going to try the Trick, what they called it, again. But the power drain was vetoed. Then I get the news that the War Department was shifting money to the bomb. We had to shut down our operations. I was angry and afraid. We all wanted to find out what had happened to Nick, where he could have gone. The guys didn't think he was dead. For whatever reason, they didn't think that happened. But they needed time and a lab to try to figure it out.

The War Department said no. It said more than no. They broke up the team that we called the Tricksters. I had to give the order to each of the guys and send them to new posts. It was only after I sent everyone but one that I got the wire about "the spies." They wanted me to come up with a reason to sit on the two of them until they could send an escort for them.

And then it was just me in a Quonset hut in New Mexico. I'd been told to destroy the files. I didn't. I kept them. I also didn't identify the box as New Mexico experiment. You'll find the box in the basement with the kids' baby pictures. I called it Early Years: Family 1948.

If you're reading this, then I'm not at The Institute, and you need to get the box to Dick Stanton, Rick's Dad. He's teaching, probably UCLA. He's a physicist, as you know, and part of our visiting science staff for summer symposia. He was Nick's best friend. He should have had these things all along.

Just know I tried to do the right thing. It was a different time. Now I'm a different man and might have done things differently.

After they watched it, no one spoke. The silence hung heavy in the room.

"So, you have questions." It was a statement not a question from Dick.

"No shit we have questions, Dad." Rick almost exploded from his seat. "All these years you kept a secret like this?"

"Well, yes. We did. There didn't seem to be anything else useful to do. With Mac and Martha's help a lot of science has been supported at The Institute that has a direct impact on our secret, but no answers yet."

Jane continued in a more measured tone, "I think I would have done the same thing, although it would have been nice if Dad had felt he could confide in us."

Dick shook his head, and Betsy held his hand. "We talked about it over the years, particularly as The Institute became such a serious site for cutting edge-research, but there was never a right time to say, 'Oh, by the way, we disappeared a colleague in 1944 and have been looking for him ever since.' So no, we never found the right time to tell you."

Rick had settled down. "So nothing really changes then. We go on as we have before."

Dick tilted his head. "Not quite. Now you have the full context for The Institute's support of some of the projects, and you may find young scientists in the future who will forward our search for answers. And of course, you have a much better appreciation for why Mac wanted to be somewhere his secrets couldn't compromise us if or when they come out."

CHAPTER 20

DAY FOUR (STILL), INTERSTATE 10, HEADING EAST FROM LOS ANGELES, SEPTEMBER 11, 2008

With Don at the wheel, the SUV hummed on cruise control like white noise as it sped east toward Indio and a very different future than what had been ahead just a few days before. Nick spoke first. "I just want to thank you all. It's amazing to me that you all have come along on this wild ride. When I stepped in the chamber, I had no idea that so many unknowns would be added to my life. That I could or would lose so much. Lose that life."

Nicola sitting next to him reached for his hand. "I can't imagine doing anything less. You're family. Granted, it's gonna be weird in the family tree when we try to add you in. You mentioned Theresa when we were in Rick's living room. Is she part of the family tree?"

"We have a family tree?" This was another new thing for Nick.

"Dude, you have so much more to learn. Ever since DNA testing, people have been finding out their real roots and the whole genealogy thing has become huge." Charlie warmed to the topic.

Nick continued to be baffled. "DNA? And Theresa was a friend. She was our maid at Los Alamos. One of the local Indian girls. She comes from a family of healers and spirit people."

Charlie perked up. "Was there something going on between you two? Should we be trying to find her?"

Nick shook his head slowly. "Dick said she's still alive, I should find her. Because she was right. The spirits have been watching me. As a scientist, I can't explain how I met the right people almost immediately after my time shifted."

Ben chimed in, "I know something about the tribes in the Southwest. They have a long history of healing and shamanism. If your Theresa comes from that kind of people, it will be valuable to track her down. As a history teacher, I can tell you DNA has been a big help to bring history to life for some of my students. If they know they have a family member who was in the Spanish and Indian War, they have a reason to read about it. And lots of people are finding that they have native blood in their veins."

Don kept his eyes on the road and added, "Watson and Crick were the ones who discovered DNA. It was quite the breakthrough. We'll pull info from the Internet when we get you to a WIFI hot spot."

"Do you think I can learn it all?" Nick was almost serious.

"Dude, it's only sixty-four years. You're brilliant. I give you until Thanksgiving to do it all." Charlie grinned. "Ben and I will draft a curriculum for you. Right, Ben?"

"No test, though, right, Ben?" Nick was half serious.

Ben assured him, "No tests. We know you have a lot at stake here. To be taken seriously as a scientist and, more importantly, not to raise suspicions."

"So, Ben, what was that plan you started to explain?" Nicola prompted.

Don jumped in. "I take you and Nick back to Indio. Grace creates a backstory for Nick and gets him identification, a medical checkup, and a supportable back story to explain who he is and why he may not be current with, well, everything we take for granted."

Ben continued, "Dad and Charlie and I pick up Sam and head back to Vento Junction. Charlie picks up his car, gracefully exits his relationship with NAU, picks up his stuff in V. Junction, and heads back to Indio to pick you up, I imagine. How long do you think you guys will be in Indio?"

"If Mother and Father are buried there, I'd like to visit their graves. And of course, I want to spend time with Grace. I probably ought to learn about my new life before I have to talk about it with strangers." Nick was serious.

Nicola said softly, "You might also want or need to see your headstone. It's in a section of the cemetery reserved for World War II heroes."

Charlie was serious when he asked, "It doesn't have his picture, does it?"

"Gah, I can't remember. I hope not. If it does, maybe we can have it removed for cleaning or something." Nicola sound a little panicked.

Don said, "I'm sure Grace is ahead of all of us on this. She's really pretty amazing."

The miles flew by, and before they knew it, they were on the exit for Indio and passing the Wal-Mart. As they pulled into the quiet street where Grace lived, they saw a large motorhome next to Don's truck.

"I should have known," Nicola muttered.

"Known what?" the guys all asked together.

"Aunt Vic is here."

"What do you mean, Vic is here? Victory the actress?" Ben asked.

"One and the same. My Tia Vic has a sixth sense about her mom. She probably called and heard something in Abuelita's voice. And here she is. And that means my dad won't be far behind."

"Both of them?" Nick was uncertain.

"Oh yeah, both of them. They check in on their mom every day. I should have known this would happen."

There was nothing for it but to pull in beside the impressive rolling metal home. Nicola was out first, followed by Charlie, Ben, and lastly, Don and Nick. "We'll just take it slow, son," Don advised. "We don't know yet what Grace has told them. For all we know, she was waiting for your return to say anything."

At the opening of the door, the Samantha fur ball launched herself first at Charlie, then Ben, then Don, and finally, Nick, her new family member. She was a wiggle storm of happiness and a good distraction. The group traipsed into the small living room to greet Tia Vic.

Grace hugged Nick and Nicola and introduced the others to her daughter.

The actress took over. "So my mother has been very, very close-mouthed about what's going on. Who wants to tell me what's up?"

Nicola looked at Grace. "What have you told her, Abuelita?"

"Just that you and some friends went to California to see your advisor," Grace said primly.

"That's the tone she uses when she's helping someone get papers to stay one step ahead of La Migra." Vic was having none of this.

"Well, you're not too far off the mark," Nicola admitted. "Abuelita, this is as much your story as anyone's. I think you should go ahead."

Before she began, Grace asked if anyone needed anything. No one was moving. No bathroom or beer would come in between them and this drama.

"You remember stories about my brother, your Uncle Nick, the scientist who was killed in the War? Well, we never really knew what happened to him. We never had a body to bury, no details. A nice young captain brought us a box of things that belonged to him, but your grandparents never opened it. They wanted to move past the war and the camp."

"I remember they were fragile when I was small. That experience robbed them of something I could never put a name on. It wasn't just losing a son. It was more. They loved us like grandparents do, but we felt more precious somehow. As small children, we had no language to describe it, but we knew their love was special."

"You're a sensitive one, *hija*. They did lose more. Even though Daddy was able to teach again, he was never the same. He and Mommy kind of faded. I think they died too soon from the fading." Grace was far away in her memories.

"Here's the note from his box of effects. I couldn't show it to them."

If you're reading this, then I haven't come back.

We are so close to proving the science of our work that I knew it had to be me to take the risk. Of course, I didn't think there was a risk. I guess the joke's on me if I didn't come back. I guess there was more risk than I thought.

Anyway, I'm sorry it didn't work. It was going to be such a help to the war effort. In my heart, I thought that if the war could end sooner, you all, the people I love most, would be out of the camps and home, where you should be.

I love you all and am so sorry not to see you and tell you in person how much I love you all.

The men I worked with here are great, and if one of them is bringing you this note, please share stories about me with him. Don't be sad. I did this willingly. I'm a scientist and a researcher after all. While part of me is afraid, part of me is eager to learn what happens with the experiment. Forgive me.

Love,
Nick

The room was utterly silent. Nick was visibly uncomfortable with the memory of writing that note, which for him was just a few days ago.

Vic brought them back to the room. "And…now. Do you know more because of these people?"

Nick spoke. "You could say that."

Grace smiled. "We have to trust her, Nicky. She's my daughter and you're her uncle."

"Uncle? I don't have an uncle. At least I never have had an uncle. What do you mean, *uncle*?" Vic was trying to follow the improbable implication.

"My name is Nicholas Nishimura. My father and mother were Henry and Sunny Nishimura. I was born in 1920 and…"

"Wait just a damn minute here. You were what?" Victory Acevedo was on her feet and not having any of this. "You're scamming my mother, and *you*"—she turned on Nicola—"are going along with it. Whatever this is."

"No, Tia. We have proof. That's why we went to California."

"Proof. What in the world kind of proof could there be for this outrageous story?"

"My best friend is a scientist named Richard Stanton. He's ninety now and an Emeritus professor at UCLA." Nick spoke softly. "We were working on an experiment to help military intelligence in 1944. I volunteered to be the one to go."

"Go where?" Vic backed down a little.

"Apparently here," Grace said. "At least this year. He arrived in Arizona first and these nice people brought him here."

"What do you mean *this year*?" Victory turned to the group.

Charlie spoke. "I'm Dr. Charles Grant, and this is my dad and brother. I've studied your uncle's work for years. What his papers from Stanford showed was a way to transfer molecules through space, teleportation, and now we know, also time."

"So you think my uncle just beamed himself here from 1944? You're smoking something really powerful and certainly illegal." Vic was on the offensive again.

Nick spoke softly at first. "I know it's hard to believe. How do you think I feel? The experiment was never meant to do this. We wanted to help spies send messages for the war effort. We never expected it to be time travel!" The more he thought about the situation, he became exasperated. "But with everything I've seen in the last few days, how can you *not* believe it's possible? Cell phones, Internet, hybrid cars."

"Well, when you put it that way, I suppose you have a point. It's just that all of those happened incrementally. You just popped in." Vic grimaced.

Don decided to give her more context. "I saw him at a stoplight. I was watching the intersection as I headed to lunch." Don's voice softened as he thought back to the scene just days ago. "He was wearing a sharp suit and a fedora. You don't see that anymore. When he came into the restaurant, I watched him. He seemed a little lost. After he sat down, I asked if I could join him."

"I've been wondering about that. Why would you do that?" Nicola asked.

"I taught high school science for almost thirty years. I had more than a few lost kids come into my office and even into my home. I know the signs." Don sighed.

Ben stared at his dad. "I hadn't even connected that. Of course you would have seen that in Nick. Just like all my friends from school and all the kids I saw you with over the years."

Don smiled. "It wasn't hard to see he needed a friend."

Grace reached over to touch Don's arm. "Thank you for seeing that my brother needed you."

"Your brother. Your…brother. Your brother?" Victory was putting the pieces together.

A heavy vehicle joined the others in the driveway. Sam barked happily and wagged her tail.

"Oh, you didn't. You couldn't have waited?" Nicola was upset. "I thought we'd have more time."

Victory was defensive. "Of course I did. I thought my mother was being scammed and your father is the best lawyer I know."

Daniel Acevedo was about to make an entrance.

CHAPTER 21

STILL DAY FOUR, INDIO, CALIFORNIA, GRACE ACEVEDO'S HOME, SEPTEMBER 11, 2008

Hurricane Daniel was a sight to behold. While he wouldn't be described as tall, he was fit and trim with an athletic build. He wore an expensive suit and carried himself like a field marshal. That's just what it felt like—a battle ground shaping up. He stepped from his vehicle, straightened his shoulders, and faced the house. The house he and his sister had helped their parents to add onto as the years brought more kids. No grandkids. But he had hopes.

Grace met him at the door. "Stop, *hijo*. It's OK. These people are friends. More than friends. Family! And your daughter doesn't trust easily. Something she learned from you. So just sit and listen." She turned to the group gathered in her front room to ask, "Who wants to fill him in?"

"Please breathe, Dad. You know how you can get. Sit down. It's OK." Nicola was earnest with her plea. "Let me introduce you to our friends and family." She began pointing around the room. "This is Don Grant. He's the one who first met my Great-Uncle Nick. His sons, Ben and Charlie. Ben teaches history, and Charlie is a PhD physicist teaching at Northern Arizona University. And this guy who kind of looks like Abuelita, this is your Uncle Nick."

Daniel opened and then shut his mouth, gathering steam. Nicola continued, "We got a call four days ago asking if we knew what had happened to Great-Uncle Nick. All we knew was that he was a war hero. But then it turned out there was more. We exchanged e-mail, and the Grants drove here from Arizona with Great-Uncle Nick."

Daniel spoke harshly. "But how do you know it's really him?"

Nick spoke, "We went to California and spoke with my best friend from school and the War. He hadn't seen me since 1944. He's ninety now. Of course, I had seen him, the young him, less than a week ago. But he knew me. This was the research we were doing for the war effort. And it worked. Kind of."

Looking right at Nick, Daniel held up his hand. "And who are you?"

Don spoke up and stepped closer to Nick. "I'm Don Grant. This young man, Nick, appeared kind of suddenly in Vento Junction, Arizona. I thought he needed some help. So I offered him a place to stay." He pointed at Ben. "My son Ben is a teacher at the local community college. And a skeptic like you. It turns out my other son Charlie (pointing) has studied your uncle's work."

Charlie jumped in "I'm a physicist with a doctorate. I've been studying Nick's work for the better part of my research career."

Don continued, "We looked up Nick's immediate family online to see if anyone was still living. That's how we found Grace and, of course, Nicola. We called Charlie to quiz him about Nick. When he heard what was happening, he drove down from Flagstaff to meet us. We rented that SUV in the driveway. We thought it might be safer than taking a truck registered to me. The four of us drove over so Nick and Grace could see each other."

Nicola took over. "When they got here, we didn't meet at the house at first, Dad. It was a neutral place, the car show. I thought maybe the vintage cars would help. But when Abuelita saw her brother, I knew it must be him. We didn't want to have a family reunion in the Wal-Mart parking lot, so we all came here for dinner. Abuelita mentioned that she had the box of Nick's stuff that came from the army after he died. The lid of the box had the name of the person who brought it to the family, Dr. Richard Stanton. Dad, he's the father of my advisor at UCLA. So I e-mailed my Dr. Stanton to see if his Dad was still around. We had checked *Wikipedia* and knew he was still alive and that he had a distinguished career at UCLA. Rick said his dad was visiting, so we drove over there to see him."

Nick spoke softly. "My friend Dick thought he had killed me. I hadn't thought about what it would be like for the people left behind. Of course, it's been less than a week for me to even think about those things. I thought I'd be going right back or be dead."

Daniel spoke almost to himself. "So a military experiment from 1944 brought my not-actually-dead uncle to Arizona in 2008. He met profoundly trusting people with uniquely perfect skill sets for just this situation, and here we are."

"There's more." Nicola hesitated. "The colonel who led their project in New Mexico started a Think Tank after the War. You may have heard of The Institute. The Colonel's daughter married Dr. Rick, my advisor. Nick and I and Charlie have been invited to continue his research at The Institute."

Grace stepped in. "That's all good to know, but while you were gone, I found something you're going to want to know about." She had everyone's attention. "I decided to look through the box of your things from the war. There are some tapes. Did you make any recordings, Nicky?"

He looked puzzled as she pulled out two manila envelopes that said War Department. "These aren't mine. In fact, I don't recognize much of anything in this box." As he looked into the box with the tape in his hands, his eyes widened. "We heard that there was German recording equipment on the base, but no one said anything about recording our group."

Vic spoke up. "How would German anything be on your base?"

Nick gazed. "I think it was from an engineer who defected. He went to London first and then over here. That's how a lot of the guys ended up working on our projects."

Ben held out his hand, "Let's have a look at them."

Grace handed the oversized envelopes to him.

Ben was rueful as he examined the return address. "War Department. Before the days of the Pentagon or the DOD." He opened the first envelope and pulled out a large shallow square box. It had a German name on it.

Vic was excited. "I've got guys with skills in LA who can safely transfer whatever's on these things."

Daniel stared at her. "Can you trust them? It may be potentially risky to even know what's on them."

"Sure." She grinned. "When I tell them it's not porn, they'll just run the tapes through their process."

"Carefully." Nick and Ben spoke at the same time.

Ben continued, "Tape can be finicky, and we may only get one chance to do the transfer."

"I'll hand deliver them when I go back to LA tomorrow or the next day. I can tell them it's old family stuff." Vic was embracing her role in the mystery of Nick and the tapes.

Charlie added, "Maybe we should let Jane know. She's got her fingers in lots of things, and whatever's on these tapes may help her find out what happened with the spies in New Mexico."

Daniel's look pierced Charlie. "What kind of Think Tank is this?"

Don weighed in, "Mac MacLane was the CO of the Project at Los Alamos. When he mustered out, he ended up in San Francisco trying to track information on Nick and his friend Dick Stanton. He ended up meeting their physics teacher from Stanford, married her, and started the Think Tank, and their daughter Jane runs it. It's called The Institute."

Charlie jumped in, "They do amazing work in all kinds of cool research. Scientists from all over the world go there."

Nicola added, "And of course, since Mac was military intelligence, they follow chatter."

Daniel put his hands on his knees, getting ready to rise. But Grace stepped in. "First, everybody eats. Boys, you clean up, so you can help carry things to the back yard. Don, you put Sam on her leash and take her for a short walk. Nicola and Victory, in the kitchen to help me."

Daniel smiled at his mother. "And what is my job?"

Grace's hands were on her hips. "You set up tables and chairs. Our group keeps growing. Maybe we should invite Father Joe to join us. We're going to need his skills with ID very soon."

Nick had been heading to wash his hands but stopped to speak to Grace. "I'm told I need a backstory. What is that, and can you get me one?"

Grace smiled. "Hold that question while you get ready for supper and I call Father Joe."

Nick didn't move. "Father Joe?"

Grace shooed him toward the sink. "All in good time."

Nick was as confused as he had been since his arrival. Father Joe sounded Catholic. The last he knew the Nishimura's were Methodists, but things had changed—a lot. He was amazed at the ease with which his new friends had accepted him. His nephew Daniel's response was more like what he had expected, even if he hadn't time traveled. Just arriving without a train or bus would have alerted people in 1944. He decided that he liked this year. People seemed smart, tolerant, funny. He liked the ones he had met so far. And he wanted to read more in that book that Don gave him, the one about bodies. He had begun to hope he could use it. He liked the way women were in 2008, a lot.

While the group was preparing for supper Grace called her long-time friend and co-conspirator Father Joe Perez. Together they had helped immigrants with new identification for many years. Father Joe had come to Mexico from Spain in the fifties. He had been transferred to California by the church in the sixties when Indio's parish was struggling.

Our Lady of Victory was losing the battle for parishioners when Father Joe had arrived. It was his energy and passion that brought it back to life. This, however, could be his greatest challenge.

Grace had been vague when she asked the priest to come over. Of course, he loved Victory and Daniel and it was a treat to see them both.

It wasn't long before the sound of a small motor sounded near the house. Daniel had chairs under his arms when he saw the spry priest through the front window. He opened the door to greet him.

"Father, it's great to see you. What have you been up to? No calls to my office, that makes me suspicious. When I'm not hearing from you about trouble, I think you and my mother are creating it."

"Ah, Daniel, border crossings are fewer in September at the end of the season. They'll pick up when the temperatures cool off. Are you needing business?"

Daniel had turned back to his task. Looking over his shoulder, he smiled indulgently. "I'll always take your calls, Father."

Grace was holding a dishcloth with two hands as she came out to greet her friend. "Joseph, thank you for joining us. I have some new friends for you to meet and a family member you've never met."

They continued through the kitchen to the backyard. Samantha came up to sniff the new person. Father Joe raised both eyebrows. "A dog? You?"

Don smiled and snapped his fingers for Sam to come back. "No, she's mine, or I should say ours, my sons Ben and Charlie."

Nicola came around the corner and launched herself at the priest. "Father Joe! I'm so glad Abuelita called you. We have so much to tell you, and we need your help."

Vic spoke up. "This one's a tricky one, *hija*. He'll need the chance to choose if he can help or not."

Daniel shared his sister's thinking. "She's not wrong there, Father. This is one is the likes of which I've never come across."

Grace joined them with Nick in tow. "Father Joe Perez, this is my brother Nicholas Nishimura."

Nick held out his hand. Father Joe automatically took it then paused. "Madre de Dios. Did I hear Grace say you're her brother? Like a close friend, so close she thinks of you as a brother?"

"No, Father. I'm really her brother. We share parents and the internment camp in Vento, Arizona. Nicola just took us over to meet her PhD advisor. His dad is my best friend. He's ninety now."

Daniel had a cold bottle in his hand when he turned to the priest. "Father, I think you can use this about now."

Father Joe took the beer, sat down, and stared at Nick. "And the rest of you are in on this. I don't think it's funny. I'll see you at confession tomorrow."

"*Amigo mio*," Grace began, "it is much to take in, but science brought my brother to us from 1944. Nicky, help us out."

Nick took the beer Daniel handed him and sat next to Father Joe. "The army pulled me out of the camp in 1943 and sent me to Los Alamos to work on a military project. An intelligence project, not the bomb."

"We all know about the Manhattan Project."

"This was a different one. In Los Alamos, but not a weapon. Our research was to help get information over distance safely and quickly. My work at Stanford was on molecular transference, teleportation."

"Like 'Beam me up, Scotty'?"

Nick looked at Charlie. "Add it to the list?"

Charlie spoke, "Yeah, dude. Add beaming and Scotty to the list. And Father, it's a yes-and-no answer. Nick's work was not interstellar, but you've got the general idea."

Nicola joined the explanation. "My work mirrors Uncle Nick's. My advisor, Dr. Rick Stanton, was intrigued by it and very support-ive when others weren't. Now I may know why. His father is Nick's best friend and saw him disappear on September 8, 1944, not to be seen or heard from again until a few days ago. All these years, he thought he had killed his best friend."

"So this is not a practical joke you're playing on me?" Father Joe spoke slowly.

"There is no joke here, Father. I'm here, and from what we've been able to learn, probably staying here. We have some concerns about that, but according to Dick, no effort was ever made to bring me back." Nick was serious now.

"Who knows about this?" Father Joe was starting to appreciate the issues at hand.

Nicola said, "The people in this room, Rick and Dick Stanton and Jane MacLane Stanton. Everyone else has met Nick Brown, a friend from Arizona. And that's why we need you and Abuelita to help us give him an identity to keep him from being a sensation. And taken by the government."

Daniel swallowed and offered, "I can't even begin to think what laws might be involved. He's an American citizen, but he was declared dead. A war hero in fact. So none of the identity documents he has can be used. Not even his name, really. It could alert someone."

Ben said, "We've already had a suspicious reporter sniffing around the old camp, but it was about six weeks ago, so I hope Nick's arrival and her interest aren't related."

Grace interrupted, "The food is on the table. We can talk and eat. Brains need food, and we'll need all our brains."

Grace turned to Daniel. "Do you remember your Uncle Greg? The one who went to Colorado to a camp there. I think he may have stayed in that area after the camps. And I think he may have had children."

"I'll look into that. You're thinking that being from Colorado could be the cover for an adult needing identification documents and shifting the focus away from Arizona?"

"Colorado's not a bad thought." Father Joe was filling his plate. "They have a lot of survivalists who live off the grid and are just established enough not to raise suspicions. I have some contacts up there. Any idea what part of Colorado your brother moved to, Grace?"

"He was partial to the southwest, coming from California. I would start in the four corners area. The last I heard from him was when our parents died. He didn't come. He wanted nothing to do with us who seemed to just forgive this government that imprisoned him because of his nationality. If he had ever asked, we would have told him that forgiving is not forgetting."

Father Joe grinned. "I have fellow priests who minister to the native tribes around there. I think I can come up with something workable."

Ben spoke up. "Speaking of graves, kind of, does Nick's headstone have his photo?"

Grace shook her head. "The marker the army provided had no picture and we were too wrapped up in starting new lives after the war to spend money on your grave, Nicky."

"That's okay, Grace. I wouldn't have expected it. Times were hard, and now that I'm back, a fancy stone could be a problem."

Vic was the last to sit down. She chose the place next to Don. Then she spoke. "Once we figure out who Nick is going to be in today's world, we'll need to create a few profiles for him, yes?" As heads nodded around the table, she suggested, "My publicist knows how to plant stories." As the guys recoiled, she continued, "Hear me out. The best approach is to get ahead of any potential story. We can have enough provable information to put any reporter off his scent. Nicola, did you say something about The Institute helping?"

Nicola wiped her mouth. "In fact, both Charlie and I are going to join Nick and finish his research there. I can finish my dissertation. Charlie can work without having to grade papers, and Nick can be in a safe place."

Vic liked this plan. "You'll be closer to me. I like it. They can do a press release announcing new hires, and Nick is just another new hire. And you said they have scientists from all over the world? A scientist from Colorado wouldn't raise any red flags. This is sounding like a plan, folks."

As the group settled into the enchilada casserole and handed out a new round of Coronas, Don decided to get over his shyness.

"I can't believe I'm sitting next to a movie star."

Vic smiled at him. "Once maybe. Now I do more teaching than starring. Roles for women, especially Latin/Asian women, are rare. And when my agent finds one, they just aren't interesting. This is the most interesting story I've heard in a long time."

He nodded, "I have to agree with you there. So far it has drama, suspense, great characters. Can you see it on the big screen?"

"It's a story I may just write, but not right away."

"I've been thinking the same thing, but from the science side. I was a high school science teacher. This has a lot to offer youngsters."

Vic tipped her beer to him and asked, "Have you ever written a script?"

"Lots of other things, but not a script," he replied with chagrin.

"Then maybe we could work on it together. Especially since you were the first one to meet him from this time."

"I think I'd like that. When I get over being starstruck." They clicked beer bottles.

"Oh, I can help you get over that, and my mother will certainly help with it."

"I like your mom. She's quite a character. She took all of this in stride. And your niece! She's a handful, but in a good way. She'll be good for my Charlie." Don was smiling ruefully.

Vic shared an insider smile with him. "The family has always been full of characters. I wish you could have met my dad, Hector. He loved mom so much. They went through a lot during the war. I think the way he was treated and mom's people really forged a bond."

While Don and Vic were making friends, Charlie and Nicola were watching out for Nick. Ben was chatting with Daniel and Father Joe. Grace looked on and beamed at her expanded family.

Ben and Daniel looked over at Grace. Daniel asked, "What happens tomorrow?"

Ben took the bait. "The Grants, including Samantha Jane, here, head back to Arizona." Hearing her name, the happy dog came over to see Ben for a pat. He continued, "Charlie goes up to Flagstaff to wrap up his teaching gig. I e-mail Sedona the reporter, and Dad, not sure. Dad, what are you planning to do?"

"Hard to say. I'll help in whatever way I can."

Daniel picked up the thread. "Nick here needs identification documents. Tomorrow, we'll call Jane at The Institute and see what she has to say. If she wants to leave it to us, Mamacita, and I and Father Joe will get to work on an identity for Nick Brown."

Nicola jumped in. "What about me?"

Her father looked at her. "You, my dear daughter, will pack up your things and get ready to move into The Institute, where you will finally finish your dissertation and get your degree, making your father very proud."

Charlie asked her, "Wanna drive over together? I'll have my car when I get back from Flagstaff, and the three of us could go back to LA together."

Ben suggested, "We'll need to get Nick a cell phone so he can call for help. He may need it if you two are leading the pack."

As the evening wound down and energy levels dropped, the group began their good-nights. Nick would be staying at Grace's until Charlie returned to collect him for their new positions at The Institute. Daniel would stay at Father Joe's and continue to catch up.

Nicola would spend the night with her Mom in the fancy motor-home. Since she had driven her vehicle, she would help her Mother hitch the car behind the motorhome to get it back to Los Angeles.

Nick gravitated toward Grace's side. "It's a lot to take in, but it feels right. It feels like I belong."

She put her arm around his waist and leaned on his shoulder. "I'm not sure who has more to absorb, me because you're alive or you because you've appeared in an unimaginable future. And of course, you belong. You're family. You're just the newest member, that's all."

"There is that." Nick slowly shook his head. "In my wildest dreams, I didn't imagine moving across both space *and* time. I suppose it was always a remote possibility, but we were so focused on what needed to be done to help the war effort…"

They heard the front door close. "I didn't even hear anyone say good night." Grace slumped a little.

"I think they saw we were deep in thought together and wanted to give us some time."

"Yes. It's not as much for them to take in. They didn't live it like we did. The war is something in movies and books. Family photos, what few we have. But for you and me, it happened to us. It changed us. It made my whole future possible." Grace was lost in her memories.

"And for me, it was just a few days ago. To have seen my best friend as an old man. The war is over and there have been even more. Mother and Father are dead. Just so much to take in. Not to mention your son and daughter and a granddaughter! And she's a scientist! It's all so wonderful it's hard to be sad for what I've lost." Nick had tears in his eyes.

"Oh, Nicky. I'm so sorry and yet I'm so happy that you're here and you have made such wonderful friends. I don't know how it happened, but I'm easy with the Grants, and I do like their dog. Maybe I should get a dog…" Grace had moved on from the past and was back in her kitchen.

"I think you should sleep on that." Nick grinned at her. "Where shall I bed down?"

Grace began to walk back to the living room. "The couch is a sleeper sofa. Let me get you a blanket and a couple of towels."

Day Four, Nick's Notes

Everyone seems to believe I did not go back, or anywhere but here. I wish I shared their confidence. The science, such as it is, remains murky. Until I know what happened, I can't rest easy here.

Charlie and Nicola will be good research team members. They may be as current as I am with the experiment.

And Grace helps immigrants. Of course, she would.

I'm eager to get to work, but I also need to spend time with my family. I owe it to them and to myself.

Amazed and *overwhelmed* come to mind. Jane, Mac's daughter and Dick's daughter-in-law, took us to tour The Institute. Again, luck is at hand. It is the ideal place to continue my work safely and without drawing attention.

We returned to Indio to find my niece and nephew in battle mode to protect their mother from what they presumed to be a fraud, if we had not just come from the Stantons, and if Nicola's respected advisor was not my best friend's son, they might not—no, could not—believe who I am.

And Grace's friend Joe, the priest. Her life has taken many strange turns after the camp. But I think all of my friends and family will be needed to help me.

CHAPTER 22

Day Five, Interstate 10, Driving East to Vento Junction, Arizona, September 12, 2008

Breakfast had been loud and fast at Grace's home. Sam was eager to get in the car, which made leaving a bit easier. That and knowing that Charlie would be back very soon. The ride back to Arizona alternated between flashes of conversation, shared concerns about the future, and deep silences. Each member of the Grant family had their own thoughts to ponder.

Charlie broke the silence. "I'm trying to imagine a day at The Institute. I can't even wrap my head around the thought of being surrounded by science and scientists. It's too good to be true, isn't it? Tell me it's not a fantasy."

Ben spoke quickly. "I'm relieved that you'll be there, not just for the research but so you can keep an eye on Nick. I kind of grew protective of him in just the short time he's been ours to watch over."

"I know what you mean," their dad said. "He needs more than just his family to find his way. I think both of you boys will be taking on new roles, in our family and the Acevedos as well."

"I know the first thing I'm going to do when I get home." Ben had both hands on the wheel and was looking to the flat horizon in the east. "I'm getting in touch with that Sedona woman, or whatever her real name is. I have to make sure she's not a threat to Nick."

"Be careful." Charlie warned. "It's totally not clear what she's up to and how much she knows. Do you want to wait until Nick is safely at The Institute before you contact her?"

"How soon will that be?" Ben glanced at Charlie.

"We get home today. I'm in Flagstaff tomorrow. I'm back to you guys the next day and to Indio the day after that. Maybe four days before Nick and Nicola and I are at The Institute."

"I can work with that." Ben smiled. "I'll send her an e-mail and find out where she is. I'll stall her on meeting until after you guys are in LA and safe."

Don look at his son the scientist. "Do you really think Nick is here to stay? If I were in his shoes, I'd be pretty nervous."

Charlie shrugged. "None of my research tells me he goes back, or that any attempt was made to get him back. Whatever components were around at the time Nick left weren't there afterward. I'm hoping Dick Stanton can shed some light where none has been available from other sources."

Ben weighed in. "Do you think others have tried to contact Dick about what he knows—or doesn't know?"

Don was thoughtful. "They may have tried, but as one who went through a war, you don't readily revisit those memories and certainly not with someone you don't know and with questionable bona fides."

Charlie winced. "You think some of the people who believe in time travel are crackpots, right?"

Don chuckled. "Not all of them are as grounded in real science, agreed on that. Dick is a respected academic with a lengthy career. I can't see him investing time when the inquiry wasn't from a peer."

Ben cocked one eyebrow. "Dad makes a good point. You have to agree, some of the people who post on your list serves are tinfoil hat types."

Charlie winced. "Yeah, but they believe there's more that we don't know. Sadly, they are also paranoid conspiracy theorists."

Don showed his palms. "Like I said, crackpots."

Charlie didn't give up. "OK, OK, but for Nick's sake, I want to find answers."

Meanwhile, Back in Indio at Grace's Home

Grace looked at Nick with a combination of love and sadness. "We only have a few days before you go back to LA. What shall we do?"

Nick cocked his head. "Well, I'd like to know more about what I missed."

Daniel mimicked having a pad and pencil. "All sixty-four years? Maybe just the highlights. Politics? Sports? Arts, Science? What kind of science did you follow back then? If you like space, we have lots of great photos of galaxies, ours and many others. Maybe we should put on Sagan's *Cosmos*."

Nick looked quizzically at his nephew. "I was a new PhD when I was sent to the camp. You know I studied molecules and how they could be moved from place to place. Are there scientists working in that field today?"

Daniel got serious. "Not sure, but we can find some scholarly societies and see what the journals are publishing."

Vic got interested. "Even science fiction could be helpful. Gene Rodenberry was way ahead of his time."

Nicola got up to head down the hall. "So I should get my Star Trek DVDs is what you're saying?"

Daniel grinned at his smarty pants daughter. "While I do the other research, or my assistant does, that's not a bad idea. Besides, the culture of today has adopted a lot of phrases and concepts from that show."

Vic looked at Grace. "Mom, you have that DVD player I gave you, yes?"

Grace paused. "I think it's in the closet in your old room."

Nicola was on her way. "I'll go get it and hook it up to the TV."

Nick looked dazed. "I'm lost. Anyone want to translate?"

Day Five, Nick's Notes

Grace asked if I wanted to see where Mother and Father and I are buried. How strange to say that. To even think that. They were alive just a few days ago, and I am still, we hope, alive. It was emotional. I had not considered what this experiment might cost me. Of course, I considered that I might die, but this is, was, war and so many are giving their lives. But my family. They never knew what happened. What really happened. Just that I died a hero.

Grace assures me that Mother and Father had a good life after the camp and were surrounded by love and respect. That is good to hear, good to know. Given my brief time with Grace's extended family, I believe her.

Seeing my "final resting place" is surreal. And reinforces how complicated my existence is.

Grace is so resourceful. We went thrift shopping for clothes for me. The items are used but good quality. Grace says these clothes support my back story. I like the prices. Things are very expensive today.

If only we had such stores in 1937 when I was preparing for Stanford. I would have taken no new clothes and saved so much money. I remember Mother mentioned the Goodwill store, but that was where she gave old clothes. Maybe things have changed. What am I saying, of course things have changed! I just don't know what changed exactly. I can ask Nicola. She is much like Grace, although I did not get to know Grace at that age. She is what I imagine Grace was like at twenty-five.

Day Six, Nick's Notes

After the whirlwind trip to Los Angeles, I'm back at Grace's house. I have a few days to be with her and Nicola before Charlie is back. I'm looking forward to everything that's ahead and I'm also sad.

I've missed so much. Our group of Tricksters never considered what else could happen when the Trick worked. I don't think my decision would have been any different, because the circumstances were the same. Family in the camp. Hoping the Trick would speed up the end of the war. How could we know?

Grace will help me grieve the losses. She says I must do this in order to move on. Haven't I moved on too much?

Having Nicola—that is what she prefers to be called—around helps. She smiles all the time. The war took our smiles away. I want mine back.

I'm not sure when, or if, things will start to slow down. It may be that life is lived faster in 2008. Between cell phones, Internet, and fast cars that run on electricity I don't know when people have time to think here.

I think it's Saturday. If it was Los Alamos, I'd be meeting Theresa at Edith Warner's house. Then I'd go back to join Dick at one of the cocktail parties that we used to let off steam.

Grace is a remarkable woman and so are her children. She is so capable and ordered. I am not anxious about anything they plan on my behalf. Monday Grace will take me to a doctor who will check me out. As a family, I do not recall seeing a doctor very much at all when we were growing up. As a nurse, Grace is more familiar with medicine and advances. She says he's accustomed to seeing people with no medical records. I really hadn't thought about what might happen to my body during the experiment. I feel all right, I think. When I stop to think about it my brain is what stops me and not my body. I find myself standing or sitting, motionless, for minutes at a time. How is a body supposed to be after jumping forward in time sixty-four years? Getting a checkup is a good idea.

Daniel is researching my legal status in case I'm revealed at any point. He thinks there is precedent with soldiers who went missing during recent wars.

CHAPTER 23

GRACE'S HOME

Nick and Grace had talked late into each evening so that he could begin to follow all the threads of the lives he had both left behind and was now just getting to know. The story of Nicola touched him when Grace had filled him in.

"Nicky, you should know about our Nicola, the girl named after you." Grace reached for his hand as they sat at the kitchen table, her favorite spot he now knew. "Victory was busy acting and Daniel was dating many women after his first divorce. Yes, he's had more than one."

Nick squeezed her hand. "You don't have to if you don't want to. I'm thinking that bringing up all these stories from the past has been hard on you."

Grace shook her head slowly. "Not all of them. Nicola's story is sweet, sad, and still going."

"OK then. If it's not too much for you." Nick was relieved. He did want to know about his great niece with the beautiful face and bright brain.

"Victory was filming a movie in India. When it finished, she and some of her new friends came back to California. One her new friends, an Indian actress, was a particular favorite of ours. When Daniel met her, he was head over heels for her. But she was not so sure. Daniel had a reputation, not the legal one. He was known for dating actresses and then breaking things off. He broke some hearts out in Hollywood. His sister took him aside and let him know in no uncertain terms that her friend was not going to put up with his games. And that if he thought he could treat her like the others she was going to put a stop to it. That got his attention. He did treat Priya differently. Soon a baby was on the way. Father Joe married them quietly here at his little chapel."

"So when do I get to meet her?" Nick was eager for more family.

"This is part of the sad. Nicola was born, and they were all so happy. They were living in the Hollywood hills. One day, when Priya had gone to an audition, there was a terrible accident on the Freeway. Fortunately, Nicola was with the nanny. When Priya didn't come home, Daniel was frantic. It was about that time that a California Highway Patrolman rang the doorbell. Priya had been killed instantly in a head-on collision. It was a truck that had lost control. Priya was not the only death, but it was the only one that mattered to Daniel. He was devastated. Hector and I came to help. We all decided it would be better for Nicola to come with us and spend some time in Indio while her daddy coped with grief. Nicola was three. She has some memories of her mommy but mostly when she looks at photographs."

"So how long did she stay with you?" Nick was beginning to understand how the bond between Nicola and her grandmother had become so close.

"She just stayed with us. Daniel buried his grief in his work. He would come out often at first, but as Nicola seemed to adapt here his visits became fewer. Until it got to be holidays, and graduations." Grace was a mix of happy and sad.

Nick was confused. "So he had a daughter and abandoned her?"

"No, no, Nicky. It wasn't like that. Both Daniel and Victory love Nicola. They just couldn't give her the kind of home they had when they were growing up. And he wanted that for her. He didn't want her being followed by photographers. And some of Daniel's cases have gained national attention and with that has come threats. He couldn't do what he does and worry about his daughter."

Nick was nodding. "OK. I think I understand. And I think I would have loved to have grown up here. I wish I had known your husband. Someday you can tell me more stories about him. Right now, I think we're both a little tired." Nick got up and gave Grace a hug as he headed off to bed.

Day Seven, Nick's Notes, September 14

Nicola wants to show me things so that I won't reveal my lack of knowledge of the day-to-day activities and expectations of people. I'm so glad Grace filled me in on some of her background. It doesn't explain everything, but it helps a lot. She's such a happy person. It doesn't seem possible that she could have had such sadness in her life and be this way. Maybe someday I can ask her. But not now.

Grace and Father Joe have an identity for me that should be a good cover for what I don't know. They had to explain about survivalists. What a notion. Why anyone would reject all these modern inventions is a mystery to me. But I must remember that I am a scientist and we often do not fear what is unknown. Apparently, after my war, the trust we all had in the government began to erode. Of course, it was lost in our family early on.

Nicola took me to the high school that she attended and where father taught. It felt hollow to me. And yet I felt something when I was there. In a place where he had been alive and happy and respected. Better than in the cemetery.

I do like the food here. The Mexican dishes are tasty. They remind me of Theresa and her pueblo. I hope she has had a good life.

CHAPTER 24

DAY EIGHT, VENTO JUNCTION, ARIZONA, APARTMENT OF BEN GRANT, SEPTEMBER 15, 2008

Ben couldn't procrastinate. He knew the wait until Charlie, Nick, and Nicola would be at The Institute wasn't long, but too much was at stake for Nick. He had to find out what was behind Sedona Scarsy and the sooner the better. He pulled out the class roster and found her e-mail. He wondered why he hadn't been at least a little suspicious, sedonasearsy51@aol.com. Fifty-one? Really. He thought carefully about what to say to entice her to meet him without suspicion.

> To: <u>sedonasearsy51@aol.com</u>
> From: <u>Ben.Grant@vjcc.us.az.edu</u>
> Monday, September 15, 2008
> Re: Follow up to your interest in
> Vento Internment Camp
>
> Hi, Sedona,
>
> I've wanted to reach out to you and see if there is any further help I might provide in your search regarding the Vento internment camp. I have personal research that I don't usually share with the class as it takes additional time that the

syllabus does not allow for. If you would like to meet I'd be happy to discuss my research.

Ben Grant

It didn't take long for him to receive a response. It was later that day.

To: Ben.Grant@vjcc.us.az.edu
From: sedonasearsy51@aol.com
Re: Follow up to your interest in
the Vento Internment Camp

Hi Ben,

I'm very pleased to hear from you and intrigued by your additional research. I'm living in Tempe right now. Could we meet somewhere in between? There's a great truck stop on the Interstate outside Eloy. The Triple T. Do you know it? What does your schedule look like next week?

SS

Ben arranged to meet her at 1:30 the following Thursday, September 18. Nick would be safely at The Institute by then.

Day Ten, September 17, 2008, Nick's Notes

Charlie arrived midday. Nicola and I climbed into his jalopy. He likes that word. Says it's old-fashioned. I guess I'm old-fashioned—for now.

I have a backpack—I called it a rucksack—and my new old clothes. Charlie thought the thrift store was a brilliant way for me to show a rural (read poor) background—not at all fashionable or current. Maybe the thrift stores will be different in LA. I think I look a little rustic right now.

I may not have paid much attention to fashion, but I always looked professional in school and at Los Alamos. We all wore suits. And ties! Things are very casual now. Perhaps it's better this way. Maybe when I start at The Institute, I will find a different way to dress. I'll ask Nicola. She'll know. I like Charlie, but I trust Nicola to help me fit in.

We are all excited to be returning to Los Angeles. I'll stay with Dick's family for a while. I want to meet his wife Betsy. And he and I can begin to structure the re-creation of the 1944 experiment. And face it, he's old. I want to spend time with him while he's still alive. That sounds grim. I don't feel grim. Just realistic. That's funny. Realistic when my best friend is now ninety while I'm about to turn twenty-five.

Dick and Betsy don't have a dog. They have a cat. The presence of pets in this time is such a change. Maybe it was the Depression, but the only animals I knew about had lived on farms, and they worked or were food.

CHAPTER 25

DAY THIRTEEN, VIC AND DON EXCHANGE E-MAIL SEPTEMBER 20, 2008–OCTOBER 2, 2008

Date: September 20, 2008
From: DSGrant@vjhs.k12.az.edu
To: VRA@pwp.org
Re: What's new here

Hi there,

I have to warn you. My correspondence skills are pretty lean. My students complained about my cryptic notes on their homework.

The last time I really wrote letters was during Vietnam. I sent letters, real paper letters to Ruth. We were newlyweds then. She wrote me every day. I wasn't so good, but we were in-country a lot and it wasn't possible to write.

We got home from Indio just fine. Charlie went north with almost no break from the drive. He's so eager to start at The Institute. The whole mystery/adventure is just pulling him like a magnet.

Ben has sent an e-mail to that Sedona person to start figuring out if she's a risk.

Samantha Jane and I are looking forward to a walk after dinner.

Thinking of you,

D

Date: September 23, 2008
From: VRA@pwp.org
To: DSGrant@vjhs.k12.az.edu
Re: Update from the coast

Hi Don,

Like you, letters are a lost art for me. I think I stopped getting fan letters more than 20 years ago. But that could be a reflection of my waning popularity too. These are facts. I do have a website and that draws some attention.

The truth is, I'm relieved. I like to spend more time behind the camera or helping youngsters start in the business.

But speaking of "the business," my tape guys sent me a CD of what they were able to get from those old tapes we found in the box of Nick's effects. They were pretty funny about it. Told me if it was a script to save my money and that the actors had no talent. I'm going to send the CD to Jane so she can share it.

I hope it will be revealing. Jane and I think we should all be together when we first hear it. What do you think?

Until I know more, or maybe tomorrow,

V

Date: September 25, 2008
From: DSGrant@vjhs.k12.az.edu
To: VRA@pwp.org
Re: the tapes

Hi, V. Do you want me to call you V, Vic?

Like you, I hope the tapes will be interesting. Perhaps there will be new players that will help our scientists figure out why the experiment worked back then. Ben is looking into the War years at Los Alamos. Most of the women were wives at Los Alamos, although his research is finding that a few of the wives had careers before Los Alamos interrupted them. Could cause some resentment. Maybe enough to be a spy?

Based on the arrival of the tapes, I imagine a meeting at The institute will be soon. I'm hoping we can try the video capabilities to save time driving. Not that I don't want to see you again.

Ben has been able to set a time to meet in person with Sedona. Once we have a better idea of who and what she is as a risk, we can plan more.

D

Date: September 27, 2008
To: VRA@pwp.org
From: DSGrant@vjhs.k12.az.edu
Re: Risks and rewards

Hi D,

And yes, you can abbreviate to V. Victory had its uses when I performed, but it has quite a lot of baggage.

Jane will be working on the voices on the tape and trying to compare with lists and profiles of the scientists and other civilians on site in 1944. To the best of her ability, she has narrowed the time to June or July 1944. Some of that will come from sounds caught on tape, birds, vehicles. That kind of stuff.

I hope Ben is comfortable in his role meeting Sedona. He's a nice man, and honest. This could be hard for him to play a role.

I have asked my research assistant—yes, I have one—to look into the Internment Camps and what happened to the young men who went. If there were other scientists or engineers scooped up and scattered it could be good to know.

Looking forward to the next time.

V

Date: September 29, 2008
From: DSGrant@vjhs.k12.az.edu
To: VRA@pwp.org
Re: Ben and his new role

Hi V,

Ben is comfortable with his role. He has been a Chautauqua performer for quite a while. Early Arizona historical figures mostly. We worked on his back story a bit so that he had a rational reason to want to follow up with Sedona.

I miss the early pace of meeting Nick and finding all of you, but I guess we couldn't keep that up.

Other than meeting Nick, meeting you has been the highlight for me.

I look forward to hearing from you and sharing what's happening here.

Samantha misses your Mom,

D

Date: October 1, 2008
To: DSGrant@vjhs.k12.az.edu
From: VRAS@pwp.org
Re: curious

Hi D,

I've been wondering. You said your wife died a few years ago. Is it too sad to talk about?

I've had some sad relationships, but not because of death, more disappointment. I think I've always been looking for what my parents had. It's unfair, but there it is. From great injustice came great love. I know it moved slowly, but what I watched was so profound between them—the connection ran so deep. I don't know if I can ever do that or have that.

So there it is. The source of my singleness is all their fault. Don't believe it. I know that I'm part of all my failed relationships, but there's a kernel of truth in the part about watching my folks.

Thinking of you,

V

Date: October 1, 2008
To: VRA@pwp.org
From: DSGrant@vjhs.k12.az.edu
Re: curious no more

Hi V,

I like that you want what Grace and Hector had. What they had sounded real and grounded in shared hardships. Those hardships can't be duplicated, and that's a good thing. Vietnam was the hardship I shared with Ruth. We met in college. I got drafted. We married when I came home from basic training. There was a lot of uncertainty ahead of us and we decided not to wait. Being in love and getting married was our way to defy uncertainty. Not real smart, but we were lucky.

I saw a lot of awful things that I can't unsee, but with her letters I somehow stayed the person she knew at the U of A. When I got home, we started anew. She had watched other couples have troubles and didn't want that to be us. So we went to a new town and got new jobs. She was smart that way. Being around people who didn't know us from before turned out to be the key to our success. People only knew Don and Ruth from 1971 on. When Ben and Charlie came along, we built on that and didn't look back. We didn't keep the boys from their grandparents, but we were picky about when we saw them and under what circumstances.

And so we survived together. I don't know if it was the love that Grace and Hector had, but it was good, solid, lasting, trusting. I miss her friendship most of all. I see her in the boys.

But just like we did after our war, I'm not going to look back. I need to be in a new place, maybe not geographically this time but certainly emotionally.

Does that help you?

D

Date: October 2, 2008
To: DSGrant@vjhs.k12.az.edu
From: VRA@pwp.org
Re: finding a new place together

D,

Thank you so much for opening your heart. I have a very clear picture now and know that I can trust who you are and what you say to me.

Perhaps it's meeting my Great-Uncle, but life's temporary nature is very real for me and I think I don't want to wait. Because, really, I don't know what I'd be waiting for.

Maybe I've been waiting for you. My life had gotten safe, predictable, kind of sad without being sad, if you know what I mean.

I'd like to see what our friendship can find for us.

What do you think?

V

Date: October 2, 2008
To: VRA@pwp.org
From: DSGrant@vjhs.k12.az.edu
Re: Friendship

V, my answer is yes.

Ben and Michelle, Sedona's real name, will probably be driving out to LA soon. I'd like to tag along.

Will you be around?

D

Date: October 2, 2008
To: DSGrant@vjhs.k12.az.edu
From: VRA@pwp.org
Re: finding a new place together

D, my answer is also yes.

V

Day Twelve, Nick's Notes

Charlie got a call from his brother Ben. He spoke to the woman reporter he was worried about. Nothing definite yet. Charlie says that Ben is a smooth operator and will be fine. We had reporters who tried to get into Los Alamos. They always wanted to know what we were working on. I think they were more interested in Oppie. He is quite a character or was. He's dead they say. No one ever spoke to me. I think they kept me kind of hidden. How would you have explained someone looking like me at a top-secret place?

It will be interesting to hear what Ben learns. I know he'll let Charlie know. Watching them together and even at a distance makes me wonder what it would have been like to have a brother. I never thought to ask why it was just Grace and me. We didn't ask those things then.

Nick's Notes, September 24, 2008

I'm going to stop counting the days. Nicola thinks it will help me be "in the now" as she puts it. She has a point. Counting the days has stopped being helpful. It was great to spend time with Dick and meet Betsy, and then it was time to leave. They were so gracious, and so was their son Rick. It was his house, after all. We just kind of invaded for a week. All of them being parents themselves, hard to believe, they knew before I did that I was ready to move on to The Institute. It was time to be with my new contemporaries and get back to science. Like Nicola says, be in the now.

I arrived in time for movie night, a weekly event. Jane explained that for visiting scientists, especially from other cultures, movies are a rapid way to share the American cultural shorthand incorporated in much of our daily conversation.

Tonight's movie was *The Godfather*. The original. I'm told there are others. I think one is enough for me for now. The subculture of the Italian mafia was curious. Italian-American, I should specify. I didn't care for the violence. But having the context for "an offer he can't refuse." Could be useful.

Nick's Notes, Wednesday, October 1, 2008

I've been in this time for a little over three weeks, and I am feeling more at ease. That is undoubtedly due to living in the semi-closed environment of The Institute. I would be lost without this place and the people who rescued me, I am now beginning to appreciate how risky my arrival was.

Tonight's movie is a modern classic according to Charlie, Nicola, and everyone else I see. *Star Wars* is popular science fiction. H. G. Wells was popular when I was in school. Some even believed his fiction predicted the future. I thought it was fun to read, but I didn't let it influence my research. Despite not being "real," they tell me that the movie has become part of the fabric of modern culture. Perhaps like a fairy tale. Now when I hear someone say, "May the Force be with you," it makes sense, more sense anyway. It's a story of good and evil, heroes and villains, war and peace. I like it. I hear there are more.

The movies are all in color now. And the pace is so fast. I'm used to stories that take more time to unfold. Maybe it's the scientist in me. Life doesn't happen fast. Okay, what am I thinking? I get it, I sped up my life by sixty-four years. Maybe I need to pick up the pace to belong faster.

CHAPTER 26

NEAR ELOY, ARIZONA, DAY 26, FRIDAY, OCTOBER 3, 2008

The original meeting with "Sedona" had not worked out. Ben's school duties had interrupted his focus on the situation at hand. But they had finally found a time to meet. He arrived early. He didn't want to miss this. When she arrived, he did a double take. Gone was the ponytail and faded jeans. This woman had bobbed her hair, had blue-rimmed glasses, and wore tailored slacks with a crisp white shirt. She had originally reminded him a little of Diane Keaton in *Annie Hall*. A bit ditzy. The woman he was looking at now was more Diane Keaton of later films.

He stood to wave her to him. She smiled widely and walked quickly to his table.

"Wow, you look different. Great, but different." Ben decided to be forthcoming from the start.

She blushed a little. "This is a newer look for me. And a more familiar self."

"How so, if you don't mind my asking?"

"I was originally a journalism student. I was at the Cronkite School at ASU. But then my dad got sick and I had to drop out to help my mom with the bills."

"I'm sorry to hear that. It's never easy to give up a great school, or any school for that matter."

"No, but I'm glad I was able to help. And it made a big difference for my mom. I got a writing gig with an online magazine. Not a great one, but it paid well. It was a startup, so they were willing to hire a J-school drop out."

"Is that who you were writing for when you came to my class?"

"After a few years of it, that was my final assignment with them. I had gotten tired of chasing rumors and myths made up by conspiracy nuts and internet crazies."

"So how do Japanese internment camps fit into that scenario?"

"Oh, there's been a rumor since WWII ended that a Japanese-American scientist was at Los Alamos working on some experiment. The rumor just won't seem to die. The story goes that a Greek scientist was part of a team working on a separate project from the bomb. The Greek wasn't very good at science, but after the war, he went to the Soviet Union and tried to parlay what he had seen into a job for himself."

"That's a heckuva rumor. Have you had any luck with your sleuthing?"

"As my Hispanic friends would say, *nada*. I think it's smoke and mirrors. The Soviets were never able to get anything out of the Greek, and I think it ended a few years later."

"How can you be sure?"

"Is it important?" Her eyebrows raised.

Ben looked across at her face and got serious. "A lot of things are important. Like your real name."

"Oh, I really like this name. It's one of my favorites. You don't like it?" She was trying to be light.

"Oh, it's fine for a writer working for an online conspiracy rag, but I don't think that's who you really are. Before we go any further, I need to know who you really are. I think Sedona Searsy is a pen name. Who am I talking with?"

Ben continued to look in her green eyes across the table. "I want to trust you. I'd like to trust you. Help me here."

"I'm going to need some black coffee if we're speaking truth here." She got the waitress's attention and ordered coffee. Ben asked for a refill.

"It was easier to work for that awful rag under an assumed name. I didn't ever want my future journalism career to be tainted, so I adopted a pen name. My real name is Michelle Matthews. I'm originally from Chicago. I did my undergraduate work at the university there and then decided to get away from the winters. And my folks had moved out here, so when Dad got sick, it made sense to stay out here."

"Wow. I expected to hear that you were using a phony name, but the rest is refreshingly forthcoming."

"OK. Now you. What do you know, or was this just a come-on?"

Ben smiled, a little chagrined. "I admit I wanted to out you as a phony or at least hiding behind a phony name. But I didn't expect all of this. I do have more research. A lot more. I'll have to make a phone call before I can read you in, but your assignment was not all smoke and mirrors."

The woman who now looked more like Michelle than Sedona put her hands flat on the table and looked at him somewhat stunned. "You're not kidding, are you? There's something there?"

Ben sat back. "As I say, I need to make a call. Wait here. I'll be right back." As he walked to the parking lot, he pulled out his cell phone and dialed The Institute and asked for Jane.

Jane picked up on the second ring. "So how'd it go?"

"It's still going. She's inside waiting for me while I make this call. Although she doesn't know I'm calling you. I just said that I had to make a call. I think she's OK. I don't think we're at risk, and she's smart, with integrity. I'm surprised to hear myself even say that." Ben was energized.

"What's your gut say about the next step?" Jane trusted Ben's instincts.

"I think I'd like to bring her to The Institute. Not to meet Nick but to share how all the threads that began at Los Alamos have woven into this amazing thing." Ben was surprising himself.

"Do you think she'll be satisfied with that?" Jane pushed him.

"There are a lot of threads. Your dad, Rick's dad, Betsy's school. A lot of good came from the research in New Mexico that no one

173

really knows about. And some of it they could know about." Ben was thinking out loud.

"Have you thought about how you link that to the Vento Camp?"

"Not quite, although she's already spoken with Grace, so I can tell her the truth that Nick was in the Camp, went to Los Alamos and did research. All true."

"It's indeed all true, and will she be satisfied with a dead war hero with no remains?"

"She'll have to be, for now. It's all anyone had until a month ago."

"When you put it that way, it sounds less risky." Jane spoke deliberately. "Just in case, I'll have my security people run a background check on her. See if you can put her off a day or two."

"I can do that. If her background is good, we come to see you. If not, I take her to an internment camp in Colorado. If she's willing to suspend her investigative journalism, then I'll see if she's available for a road trip." Ben had a smile in his voice.

Jane said, "We need to know what she knows. You can talk about The Institute and mention Charlie as your connection. Don't give Nick away quite yet. We need to know more. Good work, Ben."

As he walked back to the table, he saw that Michelle had her reporter's notebook out and was scribbling rapidly.

"Writing a new article?"

"And what if I am?"

"I can tell you that my brother Charlie, Dr. Charles Grant, noted research physicist, is now working at a Think Tank in Los Angeles. Much of his academic career has focused on the area you were pointed at, but from a very different angle. He never followed a rumor. He followed research."

Michelle leaned in. "All they had was the name of this Greek guy who said he was there, Los Alamos. His name was Constantine. I don't know if that's first or last."

"If I go further with you, you're going to have to agree to end your work with the online magazine."

"And why would I do that?"

"Because I think you're a serious journalist at heart."

"And if I am a serious journalist, why shouldn't I pursue what you have?"

"You'll have to trust me and your instincts. Check out my brother, Charles Grant. Dr. Charles Grant. You'll learn his research is kind of fringy but interesting. If you want to change direction with your career, this is a chance. I have to get back to the college to teach class this afternoon. Let me know what you decide."

"All I have is your e-mail. Can I have your cell number?"

"Sure." He gave her his card. "I do hope I hear from you."

As he walked away, she thought she'd be crazy not to take him up on the offer. Smart, looks like a young Redford, and has a story that doesn't seem to quit. Oh yeah. She'd be calling him.

Later Friday, October 3, 2008

Michelle dialed the number Ben had given her. A female voice answered. "Benjamin Grant's office. May I help you?"

Michelle smiled. The voice sounded student-like. Ben had given her his office phone.

"Yes, is Mr. Grant available?"

"Whom may I ask is calling?"

"Tell him Michelle Matthews. I think he'll take the call."

The next voice she heard had a smile in it. "Glad you called. I think I can help you connect the dots on the story, but I have a request."

"And what might that be?"

Ben was hoping this would work. "Join me on a road trip."

"And what road trip might that be?"

Ben thought maybe, just maybe, this was working. "The one I'm offering to you now."

Michelle knew better than to get in cars with strangers, even a handsome one who worked at a community college and taught history. "Just us?"

Ben spoke quickly. "No, no. My dad and our dog will be along."

"To chaperone?"

Ben thought he had her. "Far from it. He has his own interest in LA."

Michelle was definitely interested. "And when might this road trip take place?"

"Next weekend, the tenth to the twelfth, if you can make it."

Michelle was working out the details in her head. "I think my mom can feed my cat. Count me in."

"Great. We'll leave from my dad's place in VJ right after breakfast on Friday. We need to be in Indio by lunch. Oh, and you're not allergic to dogs, are you?"

"I thought you said LA, and I love dogs. The cat has a long story. Perfect for a road trip."

Ben filled in the gap. "Indio is part of the story."

"OK, I'm all in now. What's the dress code?"

"Nothing fancy. Aim for comfort on the drive and casual in the city."

Michelle was making notes. "E-mail me the address. I'll be there at 7:45 a.m. on Friday next."

Ben put down the phone then grabbed his cell and dialed his dad. "Dad, you'll be happy to hear Michelle is up for a road trip. We're leaving from your house for Indio and then LA next Friday after breakfast. And you can bring Samantha."

"So I'm coming too? You rascal. You know I've been wanting a reason to go out again. And I know Grace wants to see Samantha."

Ben explained his thinking. "We're stopping in Indio first. I want Michelle to meet Grace. After all, they've spoken. And Grace and Hector's story is so compelling. It deserves to be told."

Don nodded to the phone. "You'll get no argument from me. How are you making the connection sans Nick?"

"I think our very own Charlie connects a few dots. His study of Nick's work led him to research the family...didn't it?"

"That could work."

"And The Institute is all Dick and Mac, then Jane. It all connects."

"That it does. Clever work. Let's hope when your Michelle put the pieces together, she forgives you the pieces you left out."

Nick's Notes, October 8, 2008

Nicola and Jane took me shopping today. Apparently, my thrift store duds have served their purpose to maintain my "back story," as Vic calls it, and it's time to keep moving into present day and today's clothing. I will say that the casual clothing worn now is much better than what we had. No suits, no ties, no starched shirts, and oh my god, tennis shoes! Or trainers or running shoes—all of them so comfortable! Why did it take so long to invent them? I recall tennis shoes, literally for playing tennis. But no one made comfortable shoes for everyday wear. For that matter most clothes were uncomfortable, too. The new fabrics are soft. Amazing.

Tonight, we all watched a WWII baseball movie, *A League of Their Own*. The women's baseball league was something I vaguely recall. But watching how those gals worked and played hard made me cringe for all the women I knew during those years. They wanted to help and were not allowed. And that line, "There's no crying in baseball." Brilliant. Perhaps there should have been. I know I had tears when at the end of the movie, they showed the real women, still alive today, who played for that team. I'm happy that some of these stories are being told. There was more than war happening during the war years. Of course, the stories I'm thinking of were not big screen stories. But maybe they could be on TV. Lots of things are on TV now. So much to learn, so many years to make up for.

CHAPTER 27

VENTO JUNCTION, ARIZONA, FRIDAY, OCTOBER 10, 2008

Ben was up early to pick up the rented SUV for the road trip to California. After that first trip it was understood that he and his dad would not use their personal vehicles for trips to "see Charlie." That had become their shorthand.

Just before seven-thirty, a small car pulled up in front of Don's house. Samantha began to wag her tail and bark. Ben opened the door to greet Michelle. "And this is Samantha Jane. She approves of you, so come on in. Meet Dad and take a breath before we head out."

"Thanks, it's good to stand. I've been on the road from Phoenix since six. Traffic is...well, it's Phoenix." Michelle knelt to pet Samantha creating great doggie delight.

As she continued to rub Sam's belly, she asked, "Did I understand you to say that she's coming with us?"

Ben nodded, smiling at this connection between the two females in the house.

"Then she can sit with me. I love her already."

A deeper male voice spoke nearby. "Then you're OK in my book no matter what my son says."

Michelle looked up to see an older version of Ben smiling at her.

"I can see where Ben gets his good looks."

"And she's tactful too. Good job, son."

"All right, you two." Ben was chuckling. "Dad, is the vehicle loaded? Sam's stuff, your stuff, the care package for Charlie?"

"All loaded and ready. Michelle is this your only bag?" Don pointed to her backpack.

"It is. I learned to pack light a while back. Long story."

Ben looked at her to ask, "Do you need a minute? Once we start, we won't have a place to stop until Yuma."

She thought briefly, and Ben pointed down the hallway. "Smart move. There's nary a bush between here and Yuma."

She looked over her shoulder as she headed for relief. "Nary? Did I hear you say *nary*?"

"You did. I read books. Just because I live in a small town…"

Her voice came from behind the door. "Point taken. I won't underestimate you again."

Once they were on the road, gratefully heading away from the morning sun as they pointed west, Michelle addressed Don in the passenger seat.

"So, Mr. Grant, how did you come to be in Vento Junction?"

Don shifted in his seat to look back at the attractive young woman his son wanted to trust. "You can call me Don, and my late wife and I moved there to take teaching jobs."

"So you're a teacher too?"

"High school rather than college like my boys. And I retired when my wife became ill."

"I'm so sorry."

"Thank you. It's been a few years now."

"What did you teach?"

"I taught science. Not the most popular class but certainly useful. We added robotics and technology before I retired."

Michelle was filling in gaps. "So your other son Charlie took after you?"

"He's much more of a researcher. Teaching was just a way for him to be paid to be near labs for his work. Me, I loved the students."

"Am I going to get to meet Charlie?"

Ben smiled as he looked ahead to the long straight stretch of Interstate. "Oh yeah. You'll meet Charlie. Just know he's not like Dad and I."

Now Michelle was curious. "In what way?"

Ben cocked his head to one side. "I guess I'd say Charlie is more of a rogue element."

"Well, that's an intriguing way to describe a brother."

Don stepped into the conversational breach. "*Rogue* is an interesting word. I suppose I would call him an explorer. He likes to pursue the unknown and make it known."

Michelle nodded, "Kind of like an investigative journalist."

Don agreed. "Yes, but his agenda is his own."

Michelle took the bait. "And you think mine isn't?"

Ben stepped in. "I think you started with someone else's agenda and have found and chosen a better path."

Michelle relaxed. "I like the way that sounds, and I agree. I'll always have a nose for a story, but I'd rather see where it takes me than point in any predetermined direction."

Don also relaxed. "Then we'll get along just fine. I think you'll find what we have to share pretty unusual."

Ben glanced over at his dad. "I think you're getting ahead of yourself, Dad. Let's just start at the beginning."

Don half-closed his eyes and let his mind drift. "I think for me it starts with Charlie. His interest in science went to physics early on. And of course, he read a lot of sci-fi."

Ben offered some direction. "And what does that have to do with an internment camp, you might ask? We have a few more steps before we get there."

"I'm all ears," she said as she rubbed Samantha's.

Don continued. "Charlie's work caught the attention of the head of The Institute in LA."

Michelle semi-frowned. "The Think Tank?"

Ben confirmed proudly, "One and the same. They had been following Charlie's work for some time."

"But why? What was he working on?"

Don looked back at her. "You ever watch *Star Trek*?"

180

Michelle was not quite following, "Yeah..."

Don grinned. "Beam me up, Scotty?"

Michelle's mouth began to drop open. "You're kidding. That's real?"

Don nodded. "Our Charlie would like it to be. So his work is of interest to The Institute."

Michelle needed to make sure. "You mean they think it could be real?"

Ben nodded. "They're willing to back Charlie's research."

Michelle kept rubbing Sam's ears as she took it all in. "I did not see that one coming."

Ben spoke evenly. "That's good. It's supposed to be on the down low."

"OK, so we have Charlie and The Institute. I still have a gap."

Don again shifted to look at the back seat. "The guy who started the Institute was inspired to do so after being at Los Alamos in 1943."

"But they worked on the bomb."

Ben added. "We think that's not all they worked on."

The reporter kicked in. "You think? You don't know?"

Ben smiled. "We may find out more on this trip. The call I made when you and I met at the Truck Stop was to the daughter of The Institute's Founder. She runs it now."

"Why her?"

Don was getting into the swing of the reveal. "Why does she run it or why did Ben call her?"

Michelle shrugged. "Both, I guess."

Ben continued. "She runs it because her dad and mom retired. I called her because there may be a connection to your search."

Michelle reviewed for them. "I was researching a Japanese-American scientist who went missing from the Vento Camp and then was declared dead and a war hero."

Ben nodded. "Un-huh."

Michelle continued, "He didn't go missing?"

Ben hesitated. "Not exactly."

Michelle was in full investigation mode. "OK you can't be a little bit missing. He was or he wasn't."

Don spoke. "Well, some people did know where he was. And it was a secret."

Michelle probed. "Secret. Like Los Alamos secret?"

Ben nodded. "Like Los Alamos secret."

Michelle had to absorb this. Her mouth opened and shut a couple of times as she kept stroking Sam's ears. The flat desert streamed by as she tried to sort out what she had just been told.

"OK. So John Doe scientist is in the Vento Internment Camp. Somebody finds out he's there and sends someone to go and to get him?"

Don was matter of fact. "Not quite. And not just someone. Robert Oppenheimer scoured universities here and abroad for the best engineers and physicists. The army went where he pointed them."

"Right. So our John Doe is tracked down and taken to Los Alamos. To do what?"

Don smiled. "Remember Charlie?"

"Beam me up, Charlie?" Michelle tried to follow.

Ben was nodding. "That's the one. Charlie has studied an obscure Stanford grad."

"Let me guess. Our John Doe scientist?"

Don confirmed. "Our John Doe."

"OK, but where do I come in?"

Ben said. "When you called Grace Nishimura Acevedo a few flags were raised."

Michelle spoke deliberately. "So John Doe scientist was her dead war hero brother?"

Ben nodded. "Yup. And The Institute wanted any interest in that work to stay quiet."

Michelle was baffled. "But it's the stuff of science fiction."

Ben agreed. "Today it is."

Michelle was shaking her head. "Well, you guys sure know how to spin a mystery."

Don rubbed his hands together. "It's about to get better."

"Better than teleportation?"

Don shrugged. "Maybe."

Michelle said, "OK, I've come this far. Like what?"

Don was enjoying this. "Like the missing scientist's niece is an actress who just had some vintage tapes transferred to CD and we'll be hearing them at The Institute."

Michelle was nonplussed. "Holy mystery science theater, Batman."

Ben shrugged. "Yeah, it's kind of like that when Charlie's your brother."

Don continued, "And you'll be dropping me at Grace's house in Indio, so I can drive to LA with Victory."

Michelle raised her hand to slap Don's shoulder. "No way. Victory, the actress?"

Ben added, "And Grace's daughter."

"Grace that I spoke to?"

Ben replied. "The same."

Michelle rolled her eyes. "What have I gotten myself into?"

Ben chuckled. "Too late now, Dorothy. You're not in Kansas anymore."

"But which one of you is the man behind the curtain?"

Don warmed to the reference. "Neither of us, and it may be a woman behind the curtain."

Michelle leaned forward to grab both men's shoulders. "I'm all in. And it's a lot to take in."

Ben reached across his chest to grip her hand on his shoulder. "Imagine how we feel?"

The weary trio pulled into Indio shortly after noon. Samantha was on all four paws and wagging her whole body. She knew this house. Ben pulled into the driveway of the tidy house with the fenced front yard.

Don opened his door and let the wildly happy Sam out to bound up to the smiling older Asian woman at the open door. Grace waved hello and reached down to rub the wiggling dog. After Sam sniffed the perimeter of the yard, she followed her people into the house.

Ben introduced Michelle to Grace. His father had disappeared. Grace Nishimura Acevedo shook Michelle's hand. "I'm pleased to meet you and to know that you have been welcomed by my friends Ben and Don Grant."

Ben looked around. "Where did Dad go?"

Grace pointed to the backyard. Ben grinned widely at the scene unfolding there. His dad was holding hands with Grace's daughter Victory, who was smiling shyly. Michelle leaned down a little to speak softly to the diminutive older woman. "Can you fill me in here? I think I've lost my two guides."

Grace supplied some information. "When their Charlie was here, he met my granddaughter Nicola. Like Charlie, she's been invited to continue her research at The Institute. Her father and my daughter needed to check out this prospect. That's when Charlie's dad met my daughter. I think they may have more than the scientists in common."

Michelle was putting things together. "So your daughter is Victory, the actress?"

Grace nodded yes.

"Is your son famous too?"

Grace smiled. "Yes, but not in the same way."

Michelle was trying to process this new information. "I'll bite. In what way is he famous?"

Grace replied simply, "He helps people with their problems."

Michelle had to pursue this. "That's pretty vague. Can you be more specific?"

Grace said, "His name is Daniel."

Michelle halted a step. "Your son is Daniel Acevedo, and he helps people. Daniel Acevedo the lawyer who fights for social justice. That kind of helping people?"

Grace just smiled and nodded.

Michelle looked to the backyard. "Is he here too?"

Grace shook her head. "He's ahead of you and back in Los Angeles now."

Michelle just dropped down into a nearby chair and tried to shut the mouth she knew had fallen open at this last news. After a minute, she spoke mostly to herself. "A famous actress and a fearless social justice lawyer are part of a mystery surrounding a Japanese-American scientist who went missing in 1943."

"Actually, we think he went missing in 1944." Ben was speaking to her. "He was found in the Vento Camp in 1943 and taken to Los Alamos. We have a scientist who knew him then. You'll meet him at The Institute."

Michelle was still reeling. "You're not on something are you? This is real?"

Ben smiled. "Remember when I said I could help you connect the dots?"

At that moment, the backdoor opened and Don and Vic entered the kitchen. Vic held out her hand to Michelle. "You must be Michelle. I'm Vic, Grace's daughter."

Michelle shook her hand. "And a bit more."

Vic smiled. "Today, I'm just Grace's daughter, and I'm part of this mystery."

Don reached for her hand. "Are you ready to head to L.A.?"

Grace looked at Don. "I'm dog-sitting, I hope?"

He handed her the leash and a bag with food and chewies. "I certainly I hope so. She loves her time with you, and I think we're going to be kind of busy."

Ben and Michelle made their necessary stops and followed Don and Vic out the front door. Grace waved goodbye as she held Samantha's leash.

Nick's Notes, October 10, 2008

Charlie and Nicola told me that the families would be arriving today. It seems a lot of interest has been generated around the tapes we found in the box of "my effects." I admit I'm interested too. I wonder if hearing voices will be painful. It's still so recent for me, and yet now as I'm here, it begins to seem far away. How can a person become part of a new time if they are reminded too often of a different one? I struggle with this.

I'm looking forward to seeing Ben and Don, and of course, my niece Victory. Such a concept. My niece. I need to ask for one of her movies on movie night.

Thinking about those days on the Hill, it's starting to seem longer ago. But the talk of spies is alarming. I was the one people looked at with questions. I wonder if my being different made it easier for a spy to hide. Too many people were looking at me. Maybe we'll find out.

CHAPTER 28

IN THE SUV WITH MICHELLE AND BEN HEADING TO LA FROM INDIO

"I told you it would be interesting." Ben glanced over at his passenger.

"I think you said it wouldn't be boring."

"And which was it? Interesting or not boring?"

"Both. I have connections between some pieces of the puzzle, but now I have more puzzle pieces, too." The was a little frustration in Michelle's voice.

Ben nodded. "From what Charlie says about the universe, that it's expanding, we shouldn't be surprised that anything a physicist works on would be expanding."

"You're cute. But really, how much more can there be?"

"You'll get a chance to make up your mind in a couple of hours. We're going to meet up with Dad, Vic, and the others at The Institute."

So, we're heading for THE place, the actual Institute?"

"One and the same. I don't know who all will be there, but there are more puzzle pieces in our future. Oh, and we'll be staying there in the guest quarters, in case you were wondering."

Michelle shook her head slowly and sat back in her seat to enjoy the next part of the mystery tour.

In the SUV, Heading to LA with Vic at the Wheel and Don in the Passenger Seat

Don enjoyed the stretch of highway ahead as Vic sped up to merge onto West I-10. "How is your mom doing?"

"Pretty darn good, all things considered. Having Nick spend a few days with her was so good for both of them. And they visited the grave sites."

Don raised his eyebrows. "That must have been both surreal and sad for both of them."

"For Mom, she got to share more about what my grandparents' lives had been like. Nick was sad. Not like tragic sad, just a realization of missing out kind of sad. When he left Los Alamos, he said that he thought he would be the one dying. Kind of a macabre trip when you really think about it."

"You were with them?

"No. This is from what Mom told me they talked about."

"I know something about that surreal feeling. It can also be called survivor's guilt. A lot of us had it after Vietnam."

"I hadn't thought about it in those terms, but you're right. He did survive. No one then knew it, but they also didn't know to expect him back. They all mourned and grieved long ago."

Don glanced her way. "But now it's fresh. I get that. I've been to the Memorial in DC. It's hard to walk it. Like a punch to the solar plexus every time. And any time I even see a photo of it, I'm right there."

Vic took her right hand off the wheel to grasp his. "Speaking of war, kind of, I sent the CD with the conversations rescued from those old Los Alamos tapes to Jane. We should get to listen to them when we get there."

"What do you think is on them? Or do you already know?"

"I actually resisted the temptation and had a courier take it to Jane, so I'm curious like you. I can tell you that the guys who did the copying told me that the actors on the tape had no talent and not to hire them."

They both chuckled. "I hope we hear something that will help Nick. I think he still feels some uncertainty."

Vic shrugged. "Well, uncertainty is the stuff of life, yes?"

"Yes, but most of us are pretty sure of what era we will be in when we wake up." Don gazed at the horizon.

"Point taken. But between Nick's friend Dick and Jane's mom and dad, it doesn't seem like they were ever able to even try and get him back."

Don grew grim. "But the spies are out there. What did they have or think they had? Did they ever try an experiment, and if so where?"

Vic agreed, "The mystery isn't solved by a long shot."

Don was thinking about their time together. "Other than our visit to The Institute, do you have anything in mind that you want to do?"

"I say keep it simple. Dinner at my house tonight, and you're my guest. It's a big place. No need for you to stay at The Institute with the youngsters. My brother is in town, and he'll be joining us. I think he's bringing a date. It's always interesting when Daniel is around."

"I'm sure it is. He's pretty intense."

"You got that, huh? Yeah, he is that and he's witty and goofy too."

"That side I look forward to seeing."

They turned off the freeway and began to negotiate surface streets. As Vic drove into a curving drive Don prepared himself to see something a Hollywood star would live in. Big, lavish, big... What he saw when she stopped the car was a white stucco ranch with a classic red tile roof and terra cotta pots of bright geraniums ringing the entry. It was perfect. He reached for her hand, kissed her knuckles, and it all felt right.

"Nice start. You can keep going." She smiled at him.

He leaned over to cup her chin. When they kissed, he felt like he might stop breathing. It took a few seconds to pull back to see her face. From his vast experience with women, it appeared she felt it too.

"You're not just some small-town guy." She shook her head slightly. "Maybe I can trust my gut again."

"What does your gut say?" Don wasn't sure he wanted to know.

"My gut says keep going."

"Well, if we do that right now, we won't meet the kids and hear what was on those tapes."

She frowned. "And I do want to hear. So let's get you in the house and settled so we can head over there and then get back here."

Dan was smiling at her. "I like the way you think, ma'am." And they opened their doors to enter Vic's tidy *casa*.

As they approached the front door, it opened to reveal Daniel, extending two bottles of cold beer. "You've had a long dry drive. Come in and cool off. We still have a few minutes before we head to The Institute."

"Much appreciated." Don accepted the cold bottle with relief.

"Have you heard anything?" Vic wondered if Daniel's daughter was into sharing.

"Not a word, not an e-mail, not a text. Nada. Situation normal."

"Charlie has been equally chatty, and also, situation normal." Don added.

Vic grinned. "So no one's hair is on fire. I like it. Probably won't stay that way. What do you want to bet?"

Don set his backpack down and looked around the spacious living room. Loaded with folk art, leather sofas, and one not-too-large TV.

"No bets on a sure thing." Daniel was chuckling. "Finished with those beers? It's time to hit the road and see if we can start the next chapter of Nick's mystery life." Daniel wasn't really joking.

Don shook his head. "Hard to believe it was what? Five weeks ago, when this all started?"

Vic added, "We've accepted it all pretty easily. I keep waiting to hear something that stops me cold. So far, the situation has been 'out there,' but there's just enough history in the books that I can go along. And of course, there's Jane and her dad."

CHAPTER 29

THE INSTITUTE, LOS ANGELES, CALIFORNIA, OCTOBER 10, 2008

It was always a bit of a surprise to pull up at The Institute. The building blended into the surrounding hilly residential area seamlessly, and yet it was at least three stories tall. Ben pulled into Visitor Parking. The entry door to the building opened when they approached. Mitch greeted them.

"Great to see you again, Ben. Charlie's been looking forward to your visit. And you must be Michelle. I'm Mitch, head of security, here." His large brown hand engulfed hers. Ben just smiled at the scene. Mitch was impressive on lots of levels but definitely in regard to his size. As Michelle tried to absorb both Mitch and the modern glass lobby, Charlie appeared from a side hallway.

"Whoa, dude, you didn't say anything about her being so pretty—just way smart." Charlie almost blushed but caught himself.

"Let me guess, Charlie Grant? Dr. Charlie Grant?" Michelle decided this would be fun.

"At your service, Ms. Matthews." Charlie had recovered. "Nicola was right behind me, I thought. Where's Dad? Not with you?"

"Do you want to fill him in or shall I?" Michelle was grinning at Ben like a co-conspirator.

"Oh, you go ahead," Ben chuckled.

"Your dad drove over from Indio with Victory Acevedo."

"Nah, Dad and Vic? Really?"

"Really," Ben and Michelle replied in tandem.

"This I gotta see." Charlie rubbed his hands together gleefully.

Mitch raised his hand. "Um, you mean not-quite-Dr. Nicola's guest is a famous person?"

"And her dad's coming too. And he's famous too." Charlie's glee knew no bounds. Rubbing it in, he said, "You mean your mom didn't read you in?"

"She just said two VIPs were coming. All visiting scientists are VIPs here. But they're not scientists?"

"Oh, no." Nicola had arrived. "You thought the VIPs were scientists. I'm so sorry. No such luck. An actress, my aunt, and a lawyer, my Dad."

"Not just any lawyer." Ben joined the act. "Daniel Acevedo, the crusading social justice lawyer."

"So my dear mother did not think to tell me, to make mention, to hint, that we would be welcoming Victory and Daniel Acevedo?"

"Right now, in fact." Jane had appeared just in time to pat Mitch on his shoulder and greet Don, Vic, and Daniel.

Mitch muttered, "You all keep it interesting."

Name badges were printed and hung around the necks of the five visitors while Michelle met Daniel and greetings were shared all around. And then it was time to head to the multimedia recording studio where they would be able to listen to what had been rescued from the sixty-four-year-old magnetic recording tapes. Nick would join them at the studio. He'd been on an intercontinental video link with some German physicists.

When they were all seated in the baffled room, Jane set the stage and introduced Rick and his dad, who had slipped in with Nick. "This room is more often used for radio astronomy and other sensitive audio research, but it seemed like the best place for us all to hear together. Vic, do you want to take it from here?"

Vic spoke seriously. "When we finally opened the box of Nick's effects, that his friend Dick delivered to the Nishimuras in 1945, we found two old reels of quarter inch magnetic tape in envelopes labeled 'War Department.' Through my work in the film industry, I have contacts who restore old film and audio recordings. My audio colleague was not told the source of the recordings. Just that they were old and fragile. When he called to tell me they were ready, my buddy, the engineer told me not to invest in the script and that the actors had no talent."

With that said as an introduction, Jane let them know that there would be four different conversations, clicked Play, and a woman's voice began to speak. A few of the listeners took notes. Michelle was listening intently but looking at Nick and Dick.

Conversation Number One

Woman: Do you think they can do it?
Man 1: It's not looking good.
Man 2: (British accent) Let's not underestimate them. That Jap is smart.
Man 1: He's hard to read, that one.
Woman: You're not helping me here.
Man 2: What are you looking for?
Woman: Likelihood of success.
Man 1: I think this damn war will end before their Trick is even tried.
Man 2: I wouldn't be so sure, mate. Their talk is getting more specific.
Woman: What does that mean and what does it mean that Groves put MacLane in charge, anyway?
Man 1: Not good for MacLane.
Man 2: Not so fast. Could be just the push they need.

Conversation Number Two

Man 1: There's more action over there. Should we do something?
Man 2: Like what?
Woman: You can't be thinking about interfering. You idiots.
Man 1: Why not gum up the works?
Woman: If their Trick works, this will be more important than the Gadget.
Man 2: Indeed. We can write our own ticket to the future.
Man 1: Whaddaya mean?

Woman: If we have their technology, then we can do what they're
      doing.
Man 1: Exploding pencils?
Woman: Tell me again why you're here?
Man 1: I'm maintenance. I can go anywhere without a question.
Man 2: Have you been able to copy anything useful yet?
Man 1: What am I looking for?
Woman: Papers, plans, photos, notebooks, anything that will help us
      repeat their experiment.
Man 1: That Jap scientist is always writing stuff down.
Man 2: Yes, I've seen him. But I don't know where he keeps his notes.
      Anyone?
Woman: He spends time with that Indian girl, his maid. One of you
      go to his quarters when he's gone and search.

Conversation Number Three

Woman: What have you got for me?
Man 1: Damn notebooks aren't in English.
Man 2: So you found them?
Man 1: I found one.
Man 2: Did you use the camera to take pictures?
Man 1: Nah. They can't be read. Why waste film on that?
Woman: We can figure out any language.
Man 1: Shoulda told me that first.
Man 2: You mean you found his notebook and decided it wasn't
      readable by you, so no pictures.
Man 1: Well, yeah.
Woman: Go back and take photos.

Conversation Number Four

Woman: There's a lot of buzz. What happened?
Man 2: They did the Trick. They sent the Jap.
Woman: They put a man in that box?
Man 2: Indeed.

Man 1: Where'd he go? I don't see him around.

Man 2: That's rather the point, mate. No one is seeing him. He's gone.

Woman: So it worked?

Man 2: No one knows.

Man 1: Whaddaya mean, no one knows?

Man 2: My good man, the gentleman who entered the chamber did not exit. His colleagues do not know where or if he made an exit.

Woman: Do we have the notes?

Man 1: Yeah, I got the pictures.

Woman: Well, that's something, anyway. Give me the film.

Man 1: And then what?

Woman: Our real work begins.

Man 1: Whaddaya got in mind?

Man 2: I think your work here is over, my good man. Keep your head down. I'll let you know if you can be of further assistance.

Woman: Bring that film to my house tomorrow between ten and eleven. My child is in school and my husband will be at the testing ground.

When the fourth conversation ended, the room was silent.

Rick spoke. "Dad, who were they? Do you know?"

Dick spoke slowly. "The Brit must have been Fuchs, but the others…not sure. Nick, your memories are more recent. Anything?"

Nick looked angry. "Oh, definitely that jerk Fuchs. I'm trying to place the other two. I don't think she was a scientist, but there were several wives there. Maybe some of the pictures from the parties would help us recall."

Michelle gripped Ben's hand and squeezed hard. He glanced at her long enough to see that her eyebrows were raised.

Jane looked at Rick and his dad and asked, "Do you think Mac might remember if he heard these?"

Dick replied, "That's probably a call to Martha, but it's a good thought. He apparently spends more time in those days than today."

Nick had scrunched his face. "Can you play that last bit again? The dumb one might be coming back to me. There were a lot of maintenance guys at Los Alamos."

After the conversation ended, Nick looked at Dick. "Remember that idiot mechanic who worked on the jeeps? I think that's him."

Dick raised his eyebrows. "That could be. I do remember a dim bulb from the motor pool. In fact, he was my driver that last day, when I left. He had a lot of questions."

"Like what, Dad?" Jane was leaning in.

"Like why was I leaving, was my work done, where was I going, what had I been working on? And of course, the answers were all 'Classified.' Maybe he thought since I was leaving, I'd spill something."

Jane continued, "You just thought he was so dumb he didn't realize you couldn't talk, but he might have been pumping you for information."

Nick said, "Damn, I used to feel sorry for him. Being so dumb. Now I think he's a real creep."

Jane smiled. "The Freedom of Information Act should give us a list of the grunts there. It's been so long, and I'm not asking about scientists, after all."

Dick spoke. "If Mac remembers, that will save us raising a flag to outsiders."

"I'll call Mom. Stay here. I'll be right back." Jane took off at a brisk pace.

Don spoke to Vic. "I see what your engineers meant. That dialogue was lousy, and the plot was pretty murky."

Vic smiled. "It wasn't exactly 'The Gang That Couldn't Shoot Straight.'"

Don replied, "Nope, but they didn't have a great cast. Now I want to see that movie again."

Ben interjected, "All right, you two, focus."

Nick spoke. "The woman sounded like she was in charge, and she didn't have an accent."

Vic said, "Even Americans have accents. We can probably figure out where she was from. Jane may have a linguist she can call."

Charlie raised his hand. "Yes, Dr. Grant. You have something to add?" Nicola teased him.

"Some of the people on my message boards have some wicked skills."

"Wicked?" Don was skeptical.

"Really good, Dad. One of the people who used to post helped people shed their accents."

"That is an interesting skill. Time travelers want to shed accents?" Ben was teasing. "And where might this person be, and might they help us without asking a lot of questions?" Michelle had recovered her investigative sleuth persona.

"I think so. She owes me," Charlie said mysteriously.

Ben batted Charlie's shoulder. "You sly dog. What do you mean she owes you?"

"It's not like that. She's a grandmother in the Bronx. She loves *Star Trek* and time travel and posted for a while. I'll call up the site and see if she's still active. She worked with a lot of actors."

Vic said, "Not Miss Piggy!"

Charlie looked shocked. "You know her?"

"She's the best in the business if you need to lose or acquire an accent for a job."

"And she's still around?" Michelle was focused.

"I haven't referred anyone to her in about a year, but she was pretty active then." Vic was nodding her head in staccato bursts.

"So how will you approach her, Charlie, and how does she owe you?" Vic wanted to know.

"One of her grandkids was working on a project for a science fair. I helped."

"Well, Charlie Grant, wasn't that sweet of you?" Nicola meant it.

"Maybe you didn't fall too far from the tree." Don smiled at his black sheep.

Jane came back in smiling. "I played the conversations for Dad. He nailed the guy. You were right Nick. He was a motor pool mechanic no one trusted. They just called him Bud."

"We think we can figure out what part of the country the woman was from. That could link her to one of the scientists." Vic was proud of this contribution.

"How soon can that happen?" Jane was eager.

Vic said, "I'll get Charlie a number and e-mail. You want to take it from there, Dr. Grant?"

"This will be fun, but how do I explain the source of the tape?"

Vic paused. "How about saying it's an old radio play and we're trying to find the rest of it for a project at the production company."

"The Production Company?" Don was curious.

"She has a production company." Daniel jumped in before his sister could reply. "She's not just another pretty face."

Looking at Nick, Michelle spoke softly. "The more we know, the more there is to know. Like who is Nick, and how does he know you all?" Michelle stopped the room cold.

Jane realized that it was time for damage control. "Michelle, you haven't met my husband, Rick, and his father, Dick, Richard Stanton Sr. They are both physics PhDs. Nick Brown is a member of the research team with Nicola and Charlie. They've been spending a lot of time with my father-in-law and appear to be so steeped in 1944 that he talks like they were there. Now my dad, the founder of this place, was also there in 1944 and corroborates that the second male voice is known."

Everyone but Michelle eased back a little in their seats. Reveal postponed. For now.

Jane stood and held out her hand to her husband. "It's time to invite everyone to the house for dinner."

Rick rose. "Indeed. I started dinner in a slow oven before I left. There's plenty and lots of cold beer."

Charlie looked around to announce, "I'm in." As if anyone doubted that he'd turn down food.

Ben reached for Michelle's hand. "You game for more of these folks?"

Before she could reply, Vic interrupted, "Don and Daniel and I are off to the Casa for our own feast, and to meet one of Daniel's new conquests."

"OK then, we can circle back tomorrow before you all go back to Arizona." Jane turned to Ben and Michelle. "Let me show you to your guest quarters before we head to the house."

They walked down the hall to take the elevator up a couple of floors to the residential wing of The Institute. The handful of guest suites were near the elevators, so it didn't take long to get them situated. Jane left them to unpack and said she'd be back momentarily.

After Michelle put her toiletries in the bathroom and her journal by the bedside, she knocked on Ben's door next to hers. He opened the door to find her pushing him back into his suite.

"Who is he really? I don't quite buy that researcher so steeped in 1944 stuff. When Nick heard those conversations, he reacted like someone who had been there. I mean really been there. And why did Dick say Nick's memories were more recent?"

"I think we all got wrapped up in the conversations. Then Jane talked with her dad, who has dementia by the way, so his memories of 1944 are better that his recollections of breakfast."

"Don't try to distract me. He's Japanese-American and a physicist and bears a strong resemblance to Grace. And he's working on the same project, teleportation, as Nicola and Charlie. And Charlie studied Nicholas Nishimura's work."

"All true, but his backstory explains all of that. You should ask him. Let's find Jane and get over to the house with the gang. You can grill him there."

CHAPTER 30

STILL AT THE INSTITUTE, OCTOBER 10, 2008

Charlie had grabbed Nicola, Nick, and Dick before they left the listening lab. "That was close, and I don't think she's convinced."

"But how or why would anyone leap to the explanation of time travel. Really?" Nicola was trying to remain calm. It had been close.

"It's probably easy enough to chalk it up to an excitable geezer," Dick offered.

Charlie was pacing while glancing at Nick. "Ben will cover, and he's good. But we should be ready with your backstory when we get to dinner."

Jane stuck her head in the door. "I'm going to collect Ben and Michelle. Are you ready to back fill?"

Nick's shoulders slumped. "I guess this is a real test. I've been surrounded by people who know and now I have to be the other Nick, for real."

Nicola declared, "Your back story is excellent. Grace's brother was sent to a camp in Colorado. After he was released, he moved to a remote community, married a native American woman, and lived on the rez. His kids were survivalists, and then you came along. A science geek who read every book in the reservation school library until one of the local missionaries, a friend of Father Joe's, sent you to Jane's school. And now you're here."

Nick started a slow smile. 'It is a good story. Even I believe it, mostly. Also explains why I know so little about present-day culture."

Charlie slapped his head. "Dude, we need to watch more movies with you, maybe every night. It's the fastest way to immerse you. You're what, twenty-five now? You've watched *The Godfather, Star Wars, A League of Their Own*. There's just so much for you to see."

Nick nodded.

"OK, when you were ten years old and if you had not been 'on the rez,' you'd have been watching *Jurassic Park, Groundhog Day, Wayne's World*, stuff like that."

Nicola warmed to the task. "Oh, and he should see *Sleepless in Seattle*, don't you think?"

"Well, it's a decent rom-com."

Nick raised his eyebrows. "Rom-com?"

"Romantic Comedy, dude. Chicks love 'em." Charlie was clearly not a big fan.

"How soon can we start? I need to get up to speed. Sixty-four years is a long time to catch up on." Nick had his notebook out.

"We'll start with movies you would have seen as a twenty-five-year-old of today. Then we can reach back into the years you missed." Charlie was taking a pragmatic approach.

Jane approved of the plan. "Let's go then. We have some of those titles on DVD at the house. It can be running in the background."

Nick turned to her. "How do I play this? She's bound to be suspicious."

"Don't be alone and let her come to you. Charlie and Nicola will be your best buffers. Talk about the research. That's good for a snooze." Jane chuckled.

Rick and Jane had anticipated that the group would need to talk after listening to the tapes, no matter what had been on them and no matter that Nick was in the room with them. Hearing voices from 1944 made the situation more real in some strange way.

Rick looked at Jane as they drove home to lay out dinner. "Tell me why this whole thing feels stranger yet even more real after hearing the tapes?"

Jane shook her head. "I wish I could, and I feel the same way. It was creepy to listen in and to know that a place that was supposed to be so secure had so many traitors."

"I can't imagine what it was like for Nick to hear them. He recognized at least two of the voices. Talk about creepy." Rick slowed the car to pull into the driveway. Sometimes he wished the drive was longer, so he and Jane could enjoy their "car talks." Joyful barking from the back yard greeted them. Rick went to the kitchen, and Jane let poor deprived Feynman in to join them. Rick had completed the prep for the meal before he left. He checked the roast and was pulling it from the oven when he heard Jane open the front door to let the party in.

Multiple cars had arrived. Nick, Charlie, and Nicola peeled out of Charlie's ancient sedan. Ben and Michelle trailed them in the rented SUV. They got out more slowly, continuing an intense conversation. Lastly Rick's dad pulled up in the vintage pickup truck he couldn't part with. He had had to add a step on both the driver's and passenger's side so he and Betsy could still climb up.

Ben and Michelle turned to greet Dick and meet Betsy, slowing their arrival a few minutes to accommodate their senior speed.

The decibel level ratcheted up as the conversations that had started in their car converged at the Stanton house, punctuated by yips and barks. Several of the arrivals offered to help, and Rick put them to work creating a buffet line leading out to the back yard, to Feynman's delight.

The cooler with beer and soft drinks had been opened, and the sounds of bottles and cans releasing trapped carbonation filled the air as well as the savory smell of the slow-cooked roast that Rick was slicing.

Jane greeted everyone at the door pointing the Institutors to the backyard and the beer, allowing the next wave to head toward the couch and take a breath. Dick dropped to the couch with a thump. "Thanks, hon, I'm still processing hearing those voices from so long ago."

Ben held Michelle's hand and with his other he signaled her to let this play out.

Betsy sat next to her husband and volunteered, "What the heck did you hear or not hear on those tapes?"

Ben spoke up. "We didn't hear names. I don't know if they were being careful or just knew each other well enough. Of course, I don't think they were aware they were being recorded. Maybe it's just regular old spy paranoia."

Betsy probed, "You're sure they were spies?"

Dick muttered, "Oh yeah, they were up to no good. We were lucky nothing else went wrong."

Michelle squeezed Ben's hand when she asked. "Nothing else? What did go wrong?"

Dick gave her an incredulous look. "Nick didn't come back. The whole point of the Trick was being able to make a round trip with intelligence. We couldn't get him back."

"And you tried?" Michelle was in reporter mode.

"Not then, then the War Department broke up the team. They decided to focus on the Gadget. They've been focusing on weapons ever since."

Jane reached out to Betsy. "Hey, Mom, you want to toss the salad? I think the natives are probably both restless and hungry. Rick won't be able to hold them off much longer."

They moved toward the kitchen. They met Nicola and Jane whispered, "Better rescue, Dick. Michelle's asking questions."

The young scientist raised her eyebrows and bolted to the living room. "Hey, slowpokes. The beers are cold, and I need you to help me with the troublemakers."

Ben chuckled. "My brother is probably the ringleader, so let's hustle." He reached to help Dick get up from the couch. Michelle joined Nicola heading for the backyard.

Ben spoke in Dick's ear. "Remember, Michelle doesn't know. And for now, we hope to keep it that way."

October 10, 2008, Nick's Notes

I think since I stopped counting the days, time has gone faster. Maybe we should research that!

Victory has the recordings from Los Alamos. The ones that Grace found in the box of my stuff, except a lot of it wasn't my stuff. Maybe Dick wanted to get a few things off the Hill and the box going to my family was a slick way to do it. I'll have to ask him. Anyway, the tapes are ready for us to all hear. Everyone will join us to hear them today. In fact, very soon. I'm not sure what I'll hear, but I'm looking forward to seeing my friends Dan and Ben and to meet Ben's new friend Michelle.

Everyone but Michelle knows who I really am. I've gone over my background story multiple times. Mitch is good practice. His security background means he's tough. He's caught me a couple of times, and I'm grateful for his help. I'm still getting used to thinking of him as black and not negro. Just another change to note.

Ever since Dick gave me back my notebooks, we've been going over and over them. He and I keep circling the question of why the Trick worked on September 8 and not since. What was different on that day or in that place?

I'm still amazed that Dick kept the box of stuff from our room. It's hard to imagine that he lugged it on the train from Los Alamos to Tennessee and then California. It's a little worse for wear. Things rattle in it. I need to ask him what's broken and making that rattling.

Later on…

Today was a true test of my new identity. Listening to the recordings of the three spies made me so angry. I nearly—I hope nearly—revealed my true self. Ben's friend Michelle was in the room. She's the only one who doesn't know, and it could have been a problem. Good thing I had rehearsed my story. She tried to corner me at dinner at Rick's; Charlie had my back. I don't think she's satisfied, but she also stopped pressing.

Being in this time and being who I am is a problem, and not one I can solve by myself.

I'm glad I moved into The Institute. I liked being around Dick even though it was hard to see him at ninety years old. But we all realized that if I'm going to have a chance at living my life in this time I have to be surrounded by today and not yesterday.

Nick's Notes, Wednesday, October 15, 2008

Been here more than a month and a new lifetime. Learning how to use the internet is exciting. Hell, learning everything is exciting. Everywhere I turn, I'm amazed by something. Even food! So many different kinds of food and different ways to prepare it. How did we never think about doing interesting things with food? I must admit, though, pizza is my new favorite. Along with new beers. Just amazing. Charlie is right about food and beer. He's a bit eager on the science, but his instincts on pizza and beer are excellent.

Still can't understand why teleportation and even time travel is considered science fiction. Especially when I know it's not. Has research been co-opted by corporate interests as Nicola and Charlie say? But even if it has been, then wouldn't a corporation want to have the corner on the market of teleportation?

The movie tonight was a very sweet story called *E. T. The Extraterrestrial*. I choked up when the creature wanted to "phone home". I know the feeling. What I wouldn't give to talk to Mother and Father again. I also gained an appreciation for what Don, Charlie, and Ben were concerned about when I first arrived. When the military swooped in to try to take him away it was frightening. If my friends are protecting me from such a thing, then I am even luckier than I thought. I am no one's science experiment.

CHAPTER 31

NEAR THE INSTITUTE, LOS ANGELES, OCTOBER 17, 2008

Irish scientist Nicholas G. Fabian III presented a sturdy figure, black Irish with blue eyes. And brilliant. And big. Both tall and sturdy. Built for the outdoors of coastal Ireland. He was invited to travel from Sligo when his work at University began to outpace his professors. He was profoundly gifted at solving puzzles. When given intro cryptography challenges, he blew through them and was ready for more. He knew all about Alan Turing and the Enigma machine. He planned to be the man who solved the next Enigma.

His current enigma was the new hire at The Institute, Nick Brown. Certainly an alias. And what was with Charlie Grant and Nicola Acevedo sticking so closely to him? And Jane MacLane was in on it too.

His first task was to get Nick alone, but the only time he was alone was when he ran, and Nicholas G. Fabian III did *not* run.

Charlie and Nicola were watching Fabian, as they called him. He was way too interested in Nick. Jane was watching too. But Fabian was gifted in cryptography and cybersecurity. And they would be needing him, probably soon. Chatter was beginning to give up enough details to stitch things together. The questions grew daily, and the details were from Ukraine, Romania, Poland, China, Japan. This was turning out to have more twists and turns than a drunk trying to line dance.

Charlie and Nicola were in the Park waiting for Nick to finish his run. Once he had been introduced to modern running shoes, there was no stopping his dawn runs. But it was also great time to be uninterrupted. Few scientists at The Institute were up, unless they hadn't slept—and they didn't care about anyone else's life. Except Fabian.

Charlie posed a possibility. "You know, if we bring everybody in on it, we could crowdsource the research and make more progress."

Nicola thought about that before responding. "That makes some sense. It would be a hard sell to the family, and I mean the family outside The Institute. They're terrified about his secret getting out. But I like your crowdsourcing idea. We have a lot on our— whatever we want to use as a metaphor—plate, screen, trough, to solve. And that Irish oaf is too damn good at what he does not to uncover something soon."

Charlie mused, "Is it time to bring in the big gun?"

Nicola raised her eyebrow. "And that would be?"

"Why, Jane, of course."

"In my family, that means my dad."

Charlie grinned wickedly. "Oh, I like that idea a lot. A top immigration lawyer could put the fear of God, and ICE, into that Irish oaf."

About then they saw their very own silver steak heading toward them from the east. "Let's see what his nibs thinks." Nicola smiled.

He was only slightly sweating. It was the advantage of running at this early hour. In addition to being left alone, the temp was cooler. As he bent over to hold his thighs and catch his breath, he grinned. "What have you two been hatching? I can see it in the aura around you."

Charlie jumped on the current culture reference. "Aura? Dude, what do you mean *aura*? Am I pink or something?"

Nicola weighed in, "Oh, much more lavender, I think."

"No, you guys have a conspiratorial look about you when I come back from my runs. It happens all the time."

"Busted." Charlie held his palms up to the sky.

"Okay. We were discussing the possible advantage of crowd-sourcing our research by telling the scientists at The Institute the truth," Nicola said softly.

Nick sat on the bench next to them. "Tell me again about crowdsourcing and why you think it could work."

Charlie warmed to the topic. "It's a way to put lots of brains on one problem. Ostensibly using the Internet so you have a distributed group of smart people applying themselves. In our case, rather than being distributed geographically, we are distributed among disciplines. I think it could really work and save a lot of time."

Nick nodded. "It makes sense. What does Jane think?"

Charlie and Nicola spoke simultaneously. "We haven't asked her."

Nick moved rapidly to his feet. "Then we don't have any time to waste. Let's go see her."

The three of them walked purposefully toward Charlie's heap of a car. It still worked, and they were quite sure no one in SoCal would steal it. For now, it worked for their purposes.

Nicola got out her cell phone and speed-dialed Jane's number.

A smile in her voice, Jane answered on the first ring. "Up with the runner?"

"Don't you know it," they answered to the speaker phone. "We have an idea that we need to discuss with you. When will you be in the office? Or maybe we should come to the house because Rick will want to weigh in on this."

"We're all up, and coffee's ready. Come on over."

A few minutes later, Jane opened the door, and the trio poured in. They looked at each other, and Charlie started to speak.

"We have an idea. It could solve a few problems and buy us some time."

Rick handed out coffee and mugs. "I'm listening."

"Fabian is getting pushier with his questions about our work, our team…" Nicola started to sip and pace. "If we have to spend time and energy distracting him, it interferes with our research."

Rick sipped and said, "Tell me again who he is and why he's a problem."

Nicola frowned. "He's that great Irish oaf with a specialty in solving cyber puzzles, and he's decided Nick is a puzzle he wants to solve."

Jane agreed. "And he's really good at what he does. You have a solution?"

Charlie grimaced. "Not so much a solution to Fabian but a layer around the work. We think we could crowdsource some of the stuff we're stuck on. We need his cyber skills to keep out hackers and it might buy us some time. And it brings him in, kind of."

"I like it, I think. What do you think, hon?" Jane looked at Rick.

He considered it. "It has merit. And we could get some useful science help. How do you want to start? Does The Institute have an existing platform for this kind of idea sharing?"

Jane replied. "We usually keep our crowd small and internal. That said, Fabian could help us build a safe space open to approved participants."

Nicola stopped pacing. "That would be perfect. He'd be busy and in the middle of things. He likes that."

Charlie looked at her. "How do you know that?"

"I've been watching him."

Nick nodded. "She's right. He likes to be in the thick of it. At Los Alamos, we had regular sessions where all the scientists would come together and hash out where we were stuck. It was quite useful. Oppie had to fight for it for us. It was not a military thing to do at all. This sounds like that, just maybe not all in the same room."

"Exactly. You and Dad and Nicola and I can work on the scenario/hypothesis to put out there." Rick had become enthusiastic. "Charlie, do you want to tackle Fabian?"

Nicola squinted. "I think he'll take it better from me. I don't think he sees me as competition, but all you PhD alpha males…"

Nick was confused. "Alpha males?"

Rick laughed. "Males who dominate their packs."

"We're not like that, are we?" Nick was almost concerned.

"Some of it lies in the perception of others." Jane saw a teachable moment. "If you're looking for it, you'll find it."

It was in the conversation about crowdsourcing that the crazy idea surfaced. Charlie mused aloud, "What if someone else from 1944 could be part of the conversation?"

Jane reminded him, "Nick's best friend Dick is already involved."

"But what about your dad? What I read about memory loss is that the long-ago memories are the last to go. Any chance he could recall something that neither Nick nor Dick could?"

"That's an interesting thought. Everything Mom has been told agrees with you. In fact, when he begins talking as if he's back during the war, she just goes along with it." Jane was pensive.

Charlie was growing excited. "He thinks he's back there, some of the time?"

"According to Mom, it's more and more often now." Jane's voice was a mix of sadness and excitement.

Nicola spoke up. "Do you think if he saw Nick that would spark some memories?"

"I think I need to call my mother and see what she thinks. The more details we have, the better our crowdsourced results will be." Jane rose to head to the phone.

When she was out of earshot, Nick leaned in to speak softly to Nicola and Charlie. "Do you recall the talk of spies in the Tech Area?"

Charlie grimaced. "Yeah. That was not encouraging to hear. Why did you think of that now?"

Nicola was thinking out loud. "What if visiting Mac brings that up and upsets him? We could lose him. Dementia is a tricky thing."

Nick cocked his head. "Tricky in what way?"

"Well, memories are tricky. One can trigger another and so on, but the person may not be able to reel themselves back in, if you get my drift."

"Not really."

"Their brains don't have the flexibility ours do, so if you stretch it one way, it may not come back to the same place."

"Oh, so you think if what we want is Mac thinking about answers to the problem, bringing up spies will take his memories in a different direction?"

"Exactly."

Charlie was confused. "And why would we introduce spies into the crowdsourcing mix?"

"Perhaps something for our cyber-man to be aware of. If any of the spy networks are still lurking, an opportunity to weigh in on this research could bring them out, and we want to be able to find and follow them."

Charlie grinned. "OK, that I like, and so will Fabian."

Nick's Notes, Wednesday, October 29, 2008

Halloween was not a big thing when I was growing up. Maybe it's cultural or maybe it was the Depression, but costumes, candy, and tricks are new to me.

There's going to be a costume party here, and I'm told I *will* be going. Maybe I could go as a time traveler? Not likely. My secret is still closely guarded, and I'm grateful. Especially when I remember what was going to happen to ET.

So tonight, we watched a movie about science and something (again) that happened in real life. *Apollo 13*. I admire those men. The space program was not even a glimmer in 1944. Those guys were and are pure explorers. I went on my voyage to save my family. They were on a mission of discovery. And now I know where yet another phrase comes from and why. "Houston, we have a problem." I've heard that one more than a few times around here. And now, again, thank you Jane. It makes sense.

When I think about those pilots, fresh from the war and ready to explore, it makes me wonder where some of the other guys from our group went. I think I'll ask Jane if she and her staff might track them down. We were all at the beginning of such promising careers. I hope they all did something with themselves after the war.

CHAPTER 32

SOMEWHERE ON THE OREGON COAST, OCTOBER 30, 2008

This cocktail party was either a brilliant idea or a new kind of crazy they didn't yet have a name for. But Nick was excited. Jane sat next to him in the backseat of the SUV. Her husband, Rick, was at the wheel with his WWII vet Dad next to him.

"Are you nervous?" Jane was sincere.

Nick shrugged. "Well, he might know me, and he might not. I've got a 50/50 chance, right?"

Dick chimed in, "Maybe less. We don't know where his mind is at these days. Though Martha sounded pretty positive. But then that's her way."

Nick grinned. "I remember that from class. She always believed we could learn anything, do anything, be anything. We always liked that about her, if I recall correctly."

Dick nodded. "You do. You do. It was just simpler times then and easier to believe the impossible in the face of the improbable."

Rick began to turn the wheel. "OK you two, save your reminiscing. We're almost there. I can see Martha waving from the porch. Open your windows and smell the trees. These evergreens are amazing."

Nick dropped his jaw. "This looks like Fuller Lodge."

Dick turned around to grin at him. "It does, doesn't it? I think that's why Martha is so positive. The stage is set for our memories to flow back."

"Hey, it was just a few weeks ago for me. I can still taste the dust."

"Speaking of taste,"—Dick opened his door to exit the SUV—"I can taste the Old Crow as we speak."

Nick stopped in his tracks. "It was a faster drunk than that awful homemade beer."

Dick looked at him with a sly smile. "But what about the rum? That was tasty stuff."

Jane tried to move the group toward the porch and away from the vehicle. "OK, OK, save it for the party."

As Dick finished getting up from his seat and gripped the door, Rick moved around the parked car on the narrow driveway to help him negotiate the tricky path to the steps. "Slow up there, Dad. You may be remembering young, but the body isn't keeping up."

Martha's eyes hadn't left Nick from the time she saw him through the SUV's open windows. As he opened the door and stood next to the car, she cried out, "They said it was you, but I couldn't believe it, couldn't even accept it. But you're here. You're here. Just like you were." And she began to sob softly. Jane reached her first and, with an arm around her, guided her to a cushioned wicker bench. "It was so, so long ago…"

Jane loved that her mother's Irish roots still warmed her speech as she squeezed her slightly. "And yet for Nick, not so long ago, just a couple of weeks since he saw Dad."

Martha looked up, and her arms went out to Nick. He stepped to her, took both her hands in his, and dropped down to embrace her. After a few seconds, Martha straightened her shoulders and dabbed at her eyes. "I can't let him see me like this. He'll worry."

They all knew she meant Mac, her husband of more than sixty years. Jane smiled at her mother. "No worries today. Just some Old Crow on the rocks and some stories."

Martha stood resolutely. "Well then, let's get this party started." She led the way into a casually furnished front room. The bar, along the far wall, was set with an ice bucket and glasses. Dick held up a brown paper bag holding the ever-so-important bottle with the ever-so-familiar name, and announced, "Look what I've got." They all laughed when he unsheathed the trusty Old Crow.

The laughter had drawn a late arrival to the doorway of the kitchen.

"Well, Marty, who've you got here for me?" Mac seemed to have energy today.

"Some old friends from the army, dear." She was setting the stage.

Mac looked around the room. "Well, some of you look familiar, and the old guy—well, thanks for the booze, but..." His gaze stopped at Nick. "But this one I know."

He walked slowly over to Nick to look him in the face. "Where did you go that day, son? We all waited, but you didn't come back."

Nick lifted his shoulder as if to shrug. "Well, I didn't quite go where we thought I would, and it took a while for me to find my way back."

Mac straightened. "Oh. OK. Are you OK, hurt? How was the trip?"

Sly glances revealed that the room had relaxed. This was going to be all right. Mac might have been back in the forties, but he was accepting what he heard.

Nick continued in the vein he had begun. "It was fast. Kind of felt queasy when I arrived. But not too bad."

Prior to their arrival, the others had gone over some of the possible responses with Nick, deciding that the whole truth would not be helpful, if the point of their visit was to learn what Mac knew about their time on the Hill and what happened after Nick left and the research was shut down.

Nick continued, "I'm sorry I couldn't get word to you. It was hard to know who to trust."

The plan was to plant that thought with Mac to see if he might divulge more details from those days in the fall of '44.

"We sure found that out, didn't we?" Mac scowled. "No, you wouldn't have known. After you left that day, some information came to light. We had to shut things down, pronto."

Nick continued this line of thinking. "Shut things down? Was that why you were hard to reach?"

Mac nodded. "I stuck around for almost two months before they shipped me back to DC. The rest of the team was split up then to protect them."

"Protect them? Why would they need protection?" Nick was genuinely curious.

Mac was grim. "Spies. Goddam spies. At Los Alamos in the Goddam desert. Oppie was fit to be…they had given him such a hard time with His being a Communist and all and then to have to find out that their precious security clearance process had some big holes in it. But they had to continue work on the Gadget. They were so close."

Nick brought the conversation back to a point they all wanted to know more about. "You said spies, more than one?"

Mac had sat and was sipping his drink. "We had been suspicious of that Constantine guy, but he turned out to be more of an opportunist, a con man. Just not a great scientist."

Nick cocked his head. "Could have told you that. Did, in fact, tell you that several times. Couldn't figure out what Oppie saw in him."

"We were just so desperate for your brains to help with these projects. Oppie had known him at Cal Tech as a foreign exchange student, and when the war started, it was too dangerous to go home."

Nick was not happy to hear that. "Oh. Me they give the third degree since I came from the camp. Him from the classroom sails in. Figures."

Mac shook his head. "That was a bad deal, son. Never should've happened. Glad we got you out. And you're here now. Let's drink to that."

While the two men had been talking, their bartender had been busy. Rick and Jane had been handing out the drinks. After starting with Mac and Nick, they all lifted their glasses.

Martha moved closer to Mac. "This truly is a treat, honey. I can't recall the last time we had a cocktail like this."

Mac grinned. "Well, we have friends here to join us. The days are long and dusty here." He was there, she realized.

Nick played into it. "Man, that dust. Never saw or felt dust like that. Not in California."

Mac leaned in slightly, holding his drink with both gnarled hands. "No, these mountains in New Mexico are hard country. Bad roads if there are roads. Hard on us all, especially the families. Damn roads never did get any better. State of New Mexico tried with that gravel, but it all washed away in the big storm the day you left. Couldn't get them to come back either. We just had lumpy mud for roads until the end of the war. Some of the Indians complained that the gravel went all the way to their village. Never could prove that. Didn't have time to go check it out. The Gadget was taking all of everyone's time."

Nick perked up. "Did you ever find out where that gravel came from? We thought it might have been important."

Mac raised his head. "The gravel. I do remember that. I talked with someone. Not sure they knew. Why?"

Nick stared into space. "Still trying to figure out why it worked that time and not the others. I guess we just didn't have enough time, enough power, enough brains—enough everything. There were some sleepless nights. The cocktails helped many of those nights."

Mac nodded. "We had sleepless nights after you left. Tried to figure out who knew what. Damn Fuchs was one of the spies. We still aren't sure what he knows. He was interrogated but kept his mouth shut. Our worry was that he and the others had sabotaged the experiment. Did they?"

Nick was serious. "Still not sure. I've kept working on it at my new place. Still not sure. Who got into the lab?"

Mac stilled. "We think Fuchs got in but didn't get enough to matter. But we never knew. And your friend here said that you kept notebooks. Never could find them. That was a worry. There were some other characters we wanted to investigate, but the clock was ticking, and the gadget got all the attention. Shame that. There were some people we should have really looked into."

Nick reassured him, "My notebooks were just for me, and my handwriting is lousy. And not even full sentences. Just enough to remind me of things I wanted to remember. Did I work with any of those characters?"

Dick began to speak, but Rick stopped him with a hand on his forearm. Dick muttered to Rick, "No wonder I could never figure them out. I have them all."

Martha distracted Mac by addressing Nick, "I remember you keeping notes in class. In little black notebooks. I looked over your shoulder sometimes in labs and couldn't figure out a thing."

Nick smiled at her. "Well, maybe that was a good thing. No one could cheat by looking at my class notes."

Mac was drifting. "You would have been one of those characters if you hadn't gone missing. There were stories that floated after you left and after the bomb. Stories that the Russians had the technology. We knew they had the bomb but could never track down the other."

Nick looked quizzical. "Why do you think the Russians got in?"

Mac sharpened. "Just chatter in DC. They knew we'd been working on something. They liked to test us with false information planted by their guys here."

Nick wanted to follow up on this. "What kind of false information?"

Mac smiled. "That it was actually a time machine you were working on and not transferring from place to place."

Nick was curious and alarmed. "When did they say that?"

Mac shook his head. "I can't quite recall." Mac stared at his drink and took a sip. "Sure is good, Old Crow."

Nick wanted to know more. "Could they ever prove any of the stuff they said? The Russians?"

Mac smiled. "No, but they sure stayed busy for a while. After the war when we weren't friends anymore. It's kind of fuzzy. There were new names for countries. My memory's not what it used to be."

Martha and Jane could tell he was tiring. Nick had one more question. "Colonel, what did Oppie say after I left?"

Mac paused. "Didn't say much at all. Mostly cussing over losing you and the goddamn spies."

Nick mused, "I guess that's nice to know. That he noticed and he cared."

Mac looked at him. "Oh, he cared, but everything moved on. Goddamn war."

Martha kissed his forehead. "And on that note, I think the party's over."

Jane began to hum the song that phrase recalled. The younger ones collected the glasses while Nick joined Martha and Mac to say goodbye.

Nick shook Mac's hand. "Colonel, I'd sure like to do this again."

Mac tried to focus. "What? Oh yes, sure, son. Martha will set things up."

Martha stepped toward the two men. "That would be nice. I'll let you know what our schedule is like."

Jane leaned over to kiss her father. "I love you, Dad."

"Janie, have you been here all the time?"

She hugged him and smiled. Behind Mac, Martha kind of lifted her shoulders in a small, uncertain shrug.

Nick smiled. "Then I'll wait to hear from you."

"That's a plan." Martha smiled with her voice as sad eyes watched Mac walk slowly down the hall and into his own world.

Nick and his oldest friend, Dick, looked at her. "If he says anything else at all, please let us know."

Martha's eyes were hooded. "Of course, but don't get your hopes up. I heard more today than I've heard in a while. We just don't know what's going to happen."

Jane embraced her mother. "I don't know how you do it."

Martha smiled a tired smile. "I love him. It's all I can do and all I want to do. But I did just think of something. When your father rambles, I sometimes take notes. The doctors want to know. So I take notes. After hearing what we did today, I'll look at those notes with new eyes."

Nick's Notes, October 31, 2008

Yesterday was surreal. We flew on a private jet to Oregon to have a cocktail party with Mac and his wife, Martha, my former prof at Stanford. Seeing them was bittersweet. Martha is still the same, so beautiful and so smart, just older. Mac now spends most of his days back in the war years. He recognized me and for a minute *I* felt like I was back there, too. I don't recall any talk of dementia in my time, my former time. Maybe we died before we could lose our minds? Maybe it was called something else. But I don't remember knowing any older people with what Mac has, I mean the way he is.

I think we learned some new information. I hope so. It even jogged my memory to be with him talking about that time. Even I could tell that Mac is fragile now. I hope I get to see him again.

And I hope Jane can find some of the other guys. If anyone who was there remembers anything, anything at all to fill in the gaps. Thinking about those guys makes me hope nobody else has dementia. And if they do, could anything at the site have contributed? What an awful thought. I'll ask Grace. She's a nurse and might know.

CHAPTER 33

THE INSTITUTE, NOVEMBER 1, 2008

Only a couple of days after the 1944 cocktail party at the Oregon home for wayward spies, as Martha called it, Jane got a call.

"You were right. Your father began to remember more. He was talking to himself. It was about the road. He talked about the workmen complaining about where they had to go for the stuff. He kept talking about 'white sand.' The only thing that makes any sense is that they had to go south to the white sands area of New Mexico. I hope this is helpful." Martha sounded tired.

Jane assured her mother it was a big help. Now she had to assemble her team. They gathered eagerly, and she brought them current.

Nicola started, "OK. We know there was some kind of road surface applied in July 1944."

"And it washed away on that day two months later, so it probably was loose," Charlie added.

Nick was thoughtful. "Where is that box of stuff Mac sent to Dick? He said it had some rocks in it."

Charlie had the laptop open. "What was happening at White Sands around 1944? The testing was in the future, yes. But maybe something else happened." They began their searches. Nicola sent e-mail to a geologist friend. Jane began to write on one of the ever-present white boards. Because it was a "smart" board, they were able to Skype Ben into the conversation.

"Okay. I like your approach. I can see where we might go with this direction and thinking." Ben was at ease with the technology and fully engaged.

- White Sands?
- 1944 summer
- Loose material
- Geology
- Activity
- Major rainstorm
- Where did it wash away to?
- Is it still there?
- Are Dick's rocks samples of the stuff?
- Did this make the difference in the experiment?

"That's really the question, isn't it?" Charlie summarized.

Ben was thinking and reminiscing out loud and on the screen. "Charlie, remember that crazy song on the CD Dad has from that group in Tucson. What was their name? Anyway, remember that line 'God is gravel'? I just keep playing that over and over in my head."

"Oh my god, how could I not have remembered that? He loved that CD, and that line was so crazy. Yeah, God is gravel. What are you thinking big brother?"

"Well, your list has 'loose material' on it. Do you mean gravel? Are you thinking that the road surface could be the anomaly?"

Ben blurted out, "Thunderhead North."

Charlie laughed. "Yeah, that was the name of the group. Pretty crazy. I think it was in the early nineties when Dad brought that CD home from one of his trips to Tucson."

"And the other line was 'Pink flamingos are living in my underwear' if memory serves."

"That it does, big brother. Not sure why Dad loved that CD so much, but he played it *a lot*." Charlie was thinking and remembering.

Ben got back to the topic at hand. "Do you think you're on to something with the gravel?"

"How much do we need to know before we take a field trip back to the hill?" Nick posed the question.

"We're going to need to know what Dick's rocks are so we have a source to compare with." Nicola was practical. "Where are they now?"

"Right here." Charlie had gone to the team's work room to get the box.

"There's a geology lab somewhere downstairs, right?"

Jane told them where and reminded them they needed someone to run the tests. "Fabian was a geologist before he found cyber. This could be your opportunity to use his skills to bring him in."

"I know we talked about having his help with crowdsourcing information to try to solve the problem, but still. Gah, the Irish pain in the ass?" Charlie was not a fan.

Ben jumped in. "Hey, you all, this has been fun, but I have to teach a class. Let me know what the next step is. And remember, God is gravel." He laughed and exited the conversation.

Nicola put a hand on Charlie's arm. "Jane's got a great idea and a great point. Fabian's a pain because he's curious. That's what we need to sort this out."

"So who does the deed?" Nick was on board.

"He won't believe any of us," Charlie said grudgingly. "Jane, it's got to be you."

"I agree. And he's here over the holidays. Too far to go home. I'll text him now."

Moments later, the shambling Irishman arrived slightly out of breath. "You need my skills? Are we being hacked again?" He was concerned.

"Not this time," Jane assured him. She slowly waved her hand around the room to acknowledge the group. "You know Charlie, Nicola, and Nick. We need your geology knowledge, but it's time you know more about the situation. You've been curious to the point of being worrisome. So here it is."

Nick said, "I was born Nicholas Nishimura in 1920. After graduating from Stanford with my PhD in December 1941, I was put in an internment camp in Arizona with my family. In 1943, Oppie found me and pulled me out of the camp to go to Los Alamos. Not for the gadget, what you know as the bomb. Something that I had been working on at Stanford. In September 1944, I volunteered to be the first human to try the process. It kind of worked and did more. I traveled from New Mexico to Southern Arizona, but I also arrived in 2008."

Charlie picked up the story. "My dad found him at a diner. He looked lost, so Dad took him home. Nick had been somewhat close-mouthed, but when my brother Ben came home from teaching, they all started to talk. Nick told them his story. Knowing my work, they called me."

Nicola picked it up. "They looked online to see if any of Nick's family was living and they found my Abuela, my grandmother. I was visiting and answered her phone."

Nicholas G. Fabian III had sat down at some point in the telling. His mouth had opened and shut several times. Now they waited for him to speak. "If Dr. Stanton wasn't here, I'd tell you you're all full of it and pretty cruel, albeit creative. But she is here, so…"

Jane stepped in. "My father-in-law was, and is, Nick's best friend. My father, the founder of this place was their CO. It's the truth."

"You're a time traveler!" Fabian grasped it. "Holy Mother of God! Who else knows?"

Jane smiled. "My husband, his father, and my parents. Nick's extended family and one amazing Catholic priest, and of course, Charlie's dad and brother."

"So how long have you been in this time and are you staying?"

Nick answered eagerly, "I got here a little over six weeks ago, and from what we learned from Dick Stanton, I'm staying." Nick was matter of fact.

"So where does geology come in?" Fabian had begun to assess the situation.

Charlie stepped to the white board and began to explain what they were thinking the anomaly could have been that made the experimental process work when it had failed before.

"Take me to the lab. This'll be fun. Let's see what we've got." The Irish oaf was more than onboard and the team all relaxed.

In the Geology Lab at The Institute

Nicholas Fabian worked intently on the rock samples Charlie had gingerly handed over. They carefully marked the glass dishes holding them.

It wasn't long before Fabian looked up at Charlie. "Where did you say these things came from?"

Charlie said, "They were in a box of stuff from New Mexico, left over from research that was being done in 1944."

"Who told you it was from New Mexico?"

"The guy who was there." Charlie was recalling that Dick Stanton said he got the box from Mac.

"Well, these are not from New Mexico. They aren't from anywhere in our known world, Charlie. I say again, where did these come from?"

"You know that Jane's dad founded this place, right?"

Fabian nodded.

"Well, he was the one who put these rocks in a box and sent them to Dick Stanton, Nick's best friend. It was after they left Los Alamos and Nick's project shut down."

"I say again, these rocks are not from New Mexico. Does anyone know where they came from?"

Nicola spoke up. "The team of Tricksters, that's what they called themselves, were trying to find out where the New Mexico Department of Road and Construction or whatever it was called then, got the rock to spread on the dirt roads in July 1944."

"You're telling me this is gravel? Plain old gravel?" Fabian was dumbfounded.

"We now think there's nothing plain about it at all. We think it may be the missing link in Nick's research." Jane had come into the lab.

Jane had been a little late to the party and offered a summary: "Here's what we think we know. The roads leading to Los Alamos had been dirt and very dusty when they weren't mud. In July of 1944, the state of New Mexico finally put a surface on the dirt. Given it was wartime, it would not have been a smooth, hard surface. It's much more likely it was gravel. We also know that the day of Nick's experiment, there was a huge rainstorm with lots of wind, pouring sheets of rain and lightning, and most of the gravel washed away from the roads into the surrounding hillsides and gullies."

"So this is the missing link?" Fabian was putting the pieces together.

"We think so." This was Nick. "We had not been successful for more than a year. Then we began to have success. Then I stepped into the Chamber and walked out into Arizona in 2008. After I left and after the rain ended, as we now know, the experiment could not be replicated."

"Gravel is the anomaly. More specifically, lots and lots of rocks like this handful." Fabian stepped away from the samples. "Well, what the hell do you think they are?"

Charlie began to think out loud, "We may not know what they are, but we think they might be a power source. And maybe just a few can't do it, because there must have been a lot of gravel still in the area, just not right next to the building where the chamber was."

Nick continued, "That makes some sense. Our building was at the end of the complex of buildings, and a couple of roads converged near us, as well as a parking area. So there was a lot of gravel. And since we were at the end of the plateau, the stuff would have washed off down the hills."

He paused, unsure of what he was about to say. "There's something else. Theresa, our maid at the Lodge. She was a healer and much more. She said she could see things."

"What kind of things?" Fabian asked.

"Things about people and about what would happen."

Fabian began to have thoughts of far away. "We have them at home, too, those people. We call 'em Seers. They're for real when they actually have the gift."

Nick was curious. "The gift? What do you mean?"

Fabian shrugged. "The gift of sight."

"Well, she had it. She told me that things were changing around the time of the gravel being spread. Then she told me that the spirits would watch me." Nick spoke softly, drifting back to that memory.

"She thought you'd be back. But not *when*, I take it." Fabian was just a little sarcastic.

Nick shrugged. "Her gift was rarely specific, but she was often right on the basics. I guess this was right too. Those spirits made sure I was okay, even traveling through time."

"Anyone else think this calls for a road trip?" Nicola was ahead of them all.

Fabian wasn't so sure. "Don't you think we should try to find out if anyone knows what this stuff is before we go looking for more?"

Charlie thought he had a point. "Got any ideas who we could call on for help?"

Jane had an idea. "A few years ago, we had some geology wunderkind from Montana. He's not far. In fact, just over at UCLA. We could call him in."

They all nodded. "This is exactly the advantage of The Institute. Talent when we need it." Charlie was excited.

"What's this kid's name?" Fabian was curious.

"You might know him." Jane smiled. "Clary McGonigle."

"Ach, he's a pain in the arse, but he's wicked smart. How old is he now?"

"He's just eighteen. Still not drinking age, even here." Jane was smiling broadly.

"Well then, he can be our designated driver next time. Road trip it is." This time, it was Nicola who spoke. She had followed them into the lab and heard the updates.

She continued their train of thought but with a spur. "Nick, you and Dick mentioned that the local pueblo girls, not just Theresa, were the maids for the complex, right?"

Nick nodded.

"Well, chances are that some of today's tribal elders remember those days. They might be able to fill in some gaps since Mac and Dick were gone pretty soon after you left."

Nick straightened his shoulders. "They might. I recall often meeting with them when the other scientists and I would have dinner at Edith Warner's house. I still remember her chocolate cake. Of course, it wasn't that long ago for me."

CHAPTER 34

THE INSTITUTE, NOVEMBER 3, A FEW
WEEKS BEFORE THANKSGIVING 2008

Thanksgiving was a big holiday at The Institute. It was a break for much more than a meal. Jane continued her mother's tradition of building relationships over food…and drinks. Too often research and researchers siloed themselves. Not as much with the younger crowd, familiar with digital communication. But for them it was a chance to have face-to-face time with colleagues. And it was a time to be grateful. Martha made sure of that. Even now that she was Skyped in. The meal was big, but the weekend was even bigger. Families came. A block of rooms was secured at the nearby hotel when the inhouse quarters filled. So it was that Nick's extended family came to The Institute.

"So how do we explain them all?" Charlie thought he was being practical.

Jane paused. "You don't think the backstory is enough? Colorado survivalists home school their genius and finally send him to shirttail friends and relatives in California and Arizona?"

"I think we better prepare the players. We don't know how much they know. I'm not worried about Victory. She's a pro. Even Grace can handle unexpected situations because of all her refugee work." Charlie was thinking out loud.

Jane thought he had a point. "Do you want to put something together? Maybe a chart?"

"Now I like that approach. I'll have something for you to look at tomorrow."

Jane smiled. "That's none too soon. Guests will start arriving in two weeks. Do they all know the others that are coming?"

Charlie grinned. "Dad and Ben and Michelle know. And Dad's been looking forward to seeing Vic again. I guess they've been burning up the e-mail."

"So Ben and Michelle?" Jane needed to know more.

"Oh yeah. Once we learned who she really was, and they started working together…a lot. I think they're making progress on sourcing that gravel from 1944 with some of Michelle's sources. But she still doesn't know everything."

"Interesting images you're giving me." Jane was the one grinning now. "Do we need extra rooms?"

"I'm not going to enable any romances. My track record sucks." Charlie showed his palms. "How about your side?"

"Well, Rick, certainly. The kids are curious this year, so they'll try to be here. And Dick and Betsy, of course. They wouldn't miss the tradition. And Theresa and her granddaughters will be on hand."

Charlie stepped back. "Whaaa! The Theresa? And what granddaughters?"

Jane smiled broadly. "You'll see. Now get to work. I think a seating chart is just what we need. The tables will be set for five, just like Sunday suppers, and the same rule holds. Sit with new people as much as you can."

Charlie was nodding, warming to the task. "I'm on it. What are the granddaughters' names, or do I just say number one and number two?"

"Elizabeta and Mercedes, if you want to know. And the rest you'll need to learn from them."

Nick's Notes, Wednesday, November 5, 2008

So much to think about. With Mac's mind slipping away, do we move forward trusting his stories? It hasn't been so long since I was there, and I find my memories are starting to be cloudy. We'll trust science and not memories. Perhaps one will inform the other. Maybe I'll check with the doctor on staff here and see if she thinks my unique condition could be affecting my memory. Seeing Mac that way has spooked me.

The guys were all enthused about tonight's movie. A spy flick, they said. Turns out a real spy from the UK wrote the books—imagine that, a British spy… Still, I can see why the guys were eager to watch 007. And these movies were made less than twenty years after my war, so a lot of my contemporaries made them popular. I did get a chuckle out of "A Martini. Shaken, not stirred." Pretty pompous. Reminded me of at least one of the Brits at Los Alamos. They weren't very forthcoming about their research over there. All we knew was that they came to us when they got stuck.

I wonder why this movie spy was so popular. Charlie said it was because he was good with the ladies. Well, that's just the movies for you. What I recall of the Brits was not being smooth with the ladies at all.

CHAPTER 35

THURSDAY, NOVEMBER 6, 2008

Charlie reached for his phone to ask his dad a question he knew he could answer. When Don picked up, he heard, "*Dad*. What was that movie with Victory in it? You know the one about the war, 'Nam, the movie you always liked so much?"

Don knew the answer but was curious why Charlie wanted to know. He put him on speaker before he went further. "You're on speaker so your brother can hear this. Now tell me, Mr. Incommunicado in California, what are you doing that requires that information?"

Ben slapped his dad on the back. Charlie heard that and began to defend himself. "Now just a minute. Things have been crazy busy over here. It hasn't been quite two months and there's a lot to do. And besides, there's Nick and Nicola and other scientists."

Don was laughing. "Okay, okay, just want you to know we think about you a lot. And we'll be there soon. Maybe even before Thanksgiving. So now…"

Ben burst in. "Why do you want to know about an old movie? What are you up to, and I bet this involves Nick, am I right?"

"Well, yes and no, but mostly yes. They show movies here every week, and Nick has been catching up on history and social stuff through the movies."

Ben was curious about the approach. "Like what movies?"

"Last night, it was one of the old James Bond movies."

Don smiled. "Which one?"

Charlie was chagrinned. "I'd have to check. They all seem the same to me."

"All the same? Are you kidding? Each Bond girl was different, and the locations and villains were so different!" Don was offended.

Ben weighed in. "It's okay, just right now tell us why you think the movie you asked Dad about is right for Nick to see."

"Because Victory is in it for one thing. And because the Vietnam War was so different from Nick's war. Because it was one of Dad's favorites, I thought maybe it would help Nick understand."

"Understand what, son?" Don couldn't see where this was going quite yet.

"A lot of stuff. That war changed the country. And after that war, the draft went away. It's just so different now. And it seemed to me that the way the story was told in that movie explained a lot." Charlie was frustrated trying to explain his great idea.

"I'm not thinking you're wrong, Charlie." Don was thoughtful. "But let's think this through. Nick would get to see his niece in a great performance in a movie made in 1977 about 1970. The movie showed a lot of sad and angry people. The country was still torn up about the war in 1977."

"But, Dad, it also showed how much people cared about each other. That maybe the country as a whole was screwed up, but one person could still make a difference for another person."

Ben nodded his head to his dad. "He's right on there, Dad. The relationship between Victory's character and that soldier was pretty powerful."

Charlie could see his Dad's smile when he said, "Oh, it was powerful all right. I fell in love with her watching that movie. Good thing I was watching it with your mother. I told her that she played that role for me. Without your Mom, I would have been a mess after the war."

Charlie jumped on that revelation from his dad. "You fell in love with her?"

Don chuckled. "Thousands of guys did. That movie changed a lot of lives for the better. And I think it was a help to your mom too. I couldn't easily put into words what that movie was able to convey."

Charlie went back to the original question. "And the name of the movie is?"

Ben and Don spoke at the same time. "*Less Than Nobody.*"

"And what was the name of her coffee shop?" Charlie prodded them.

Again, in unison, he heard, "All Ground Up."

"Ack, why couldn't I remember that? It's so great!" Charlie was excited.

"When do you think you'll play this movie for Nick?" Don and Ben were thinking ahead.

"I'd like to ask Jane to play it this weekend. Most of the movies are in the middle of the week to give people a mid-week break, but there are a lot of us here right now and having something special for Saturday night would be cool."

Don was nodding. "And you think Jane could find a way to show that ancient film so soon?"

Charlie arched his eyebrow in a way that he knew his dad could see him across the phone connection. "Jane is amazing. She knows everyone and can make anything happen."

"Do you think she could have one of the stars of the movie on hand for the showing?" Don was showing his cards, but he didn't care.

"It's like that now, Dad?" Ben was grinning like a Cheshire cat.

"It's like that now, yes." Don was both smug and shy about his new relationship.

Charlie was almost finished with the connection when he offered. "Okay, you guys plan to come over, and I'll ask Jane to put it all together. Agreed?"

"You're on." Ben and Don were both chuckling when Charlie broke the connection to start working on his plan.

CHAPTER 36

SATURDAY, NOVEMBER 8, 2008

Victory was taking extra time and care for the evening's activities.

Nicola was on hand to help, of course. "You look great, Tia Vic. Beyond great, absolutely beautiful."

"For a woman my age?" Vic was rueful.

"For a woman of any age. Don't sell yourself short. Besides, this is not going to be an audience of critics." Nicola wanted her aunt and friend to enjoy the evening. She knew what was planned.

"But this movie was made a little over thirty years ago. That's forever in Hollywood and maybe longer for an actress." Vic wasn't lying.

Nicola continued her relaxation approach. "This is a bunch of scientists, some from other countries. They're interested in watching a movie that changed a lot of lives. And not only were you in the movie, you were part of what was going on in the country back then, I mean at that time." A little slip in her approach made Nicola a little worried that she had lost her momentum with her aunt.

"For young people, thirty years is a lifetime. But I do understand that this particular movie was special. We had no idea when we made it. Just a small indie film with an unknown director and B-movie actors."

"But you did more than B-movies, Tia." Nicola was on the defense.

"In Mexico and Europe, yes, but in this country with my looks, A-list parts weren't offered." Vic shrugged at the recollection.

"But after this one, didn't you get better parts?" Nicola wanted to know what had happened.

"There were a lot of beautiful women available for movie parts back then. Most of them blond, slim, that look. Not my look. I was called exotic. Shorthand for 'not leading lady.'" Vic was just stating facts.

"That's unfair and not right." Nicola was angry.

"Now you know why I started my own production company." Vic squared her shoulders.

"Was this the movie that started it. PWP?" Nicola wanted to pin this down.

"Smart little science girl." Vic hugged Nicola. "Yes, the royalties from this movie have helped Powerful Women Productions fund a lot of other small movies with a lot of talented actors. And I'm proud of this one too. It's a good story."

Nicola picked up her purse and handed Vic her wrap. "All right then. Let's go show a little Hollywood glamor to some science nerds."

They laughed their way out of the house and all the way to The Institute.

CHAPTER 37

SATURDAY, NOVEMBER 8, 2008
AT THE INSTITUTE

Mitch greeted Nicola and Vic at the door. "You both look amazing." Then he caught himself. "Not that you don't always look amazing, but tonight you both glow."

Vic gave him a quick hug. "It's okay, Mitch. We like being noticed for taking special care for a special night."

His shoulders relaxed. "Close one there. I need to work on my 'smooth' around lovely ladies."

He guided them through the lobby toward an intimate auditorium used for scientific presentations and movie nights. A couple of visitors were standing at the doors waiting for them.

Don walked toward Vic to take her hand as Vic moved into his arms for a long hug. Ben, standing a few feet away, softly cleared his throat. Don pulled away slightly. "Was that a hint?" He grinned at Ben.

"I think you don't want to be part of the show, that's all." Ben had an idea that there would be more hugging at the back of the theater between those two, but now was time to get the movie started.

"Well then, let's get this party started." Vic took Don's hand and headed into the auditorium. The chatter in the packed hall lowered to a murmur. Jane was waiting near the screen to greet them. She had prepared a couple of words to say as an introduction for the audience members.

The lights lowered until the front of the room was the only place with light. Don stepped forward a half step.

"I'm Don Grant. Most of you know my son Charlie. More important for tonight's context, I'm also a veteran of the Vietnam War. This movie was life-changing for me and for many vets. If you don't know anything about that war, it tore this country apart. It broke a lot of men and women and families. This movie showed a lot of us a way through the pain, the wrongs, and the way to hope and love that could still be found."

Vic stepped forward to stand next to him. "When we made this movie in 1977, the wounds from the war, both physical and emotional, were still very raw. It was supposed to be a little indie film, made by a couple of unknown directors and actors who didn't have big names. In other words, we had a very small budget."

The audience laughed at her aside. "Given that setup, we had no idea what the impact of our little movie would be. Here we are thirty-one years later, and its humanity still connects. Even now I get letters thanking me. I'm humbled by the knowledge that a story, told on film, could be so powerful, so positive, and so lasting. Please step into the lives of the characters from decades ago. The time was 1970. The setting is here in Southern California." And the lights went dark as the screen lit with the opening newsreel.

Don had Vic by the hand and pulled a small flashlight from his pocket to guide them to their seats, as Ben had guessed, in the back row. His eyes glistened as he leaned in to whisper in Vic's ear, "I can't believe I'm here with you watching this movie."

"And I can't imagine watching it with anyone else but you." And she kissed him lightly.

Near the front row Nick leaned in to whisper to Charlie, "So you wanted me to see my niece on film and learn something about history, right?"

"Good catch, dude. Two for one night, and my dad gets to see his new squeeze." Charlie whispered back.

"Squeeze?" Nick was still learning current slang.

"Girlfriend." Charlie filled in.

"Ohhhh, really?" Nick grinned.

"Yeah, really." Nicola leaned from the other side. "Now shut up and watch the movie."

Nick's Notes, Sunday, November 9, 2008

Wow, last night, Jane showed one of my niece Victory's old movies. Not only did she come for the showing, but Charlie's dad and brother were there. The story was powerful, sensitive, and made me wonder what happened after my war. Victory's movie made it sound like soldiers were treated like heroes when my war was over. Not so much for Vietnam. It was sad to think about all those guys and gals, being hurt and coming home to scorn and protests. But the love story was beautiful and gave us hope. I'm not sure exactly why Charlie wanted me to see this one of Vic's movies, but I'm glad he did. She was and is a beautiful woman. Her character showed such warmth and understanding, and I think the person behind the character is just like that.

Charlie's father, Don, spoke briefly before the movie started. He told everyone that he was a veteran of the Vietnam War and what the movie meant for him and his friends. I kind of knew that he was a vet, but watching the movie gives me even more respect for him. I can't believe my luck at encountering him when I traveled. Of course, Theresa would tell me it wasn't luck at all.

Nick's Notes, Wednesday, November 12, 2008

Yesterday was rougher than I thought it would be. Now it's called Veterans' Day, the day the first big war ended, but now, all veterans are honored. That was supposed to be the War to end all Wars. We know that didn't happen. There are so many. So many men *and* women. My God, have we learned nothing? What's wrong with humans that we get to the point that we kill each other? Maybe this is the research we should be doing.

Tonight, Jane selected lighter fare for our movie enjoyment. Smart, given the somber tone of the day, at least for me. Watching Harry and Sally dance around each other was a tease, interesting, frustrating, but the story really helped me see how things between men and women are so different now. But I will not soon forget the scene in the restaurant and the laughter over "I'll have what she's having." Me too.

I talked with a couple of the women in the audience after the movie. Because they are scientists, I wanted to know what they thought. They laughed. They said that things are different in California. New York, where Harry and Sally lived in the movie, is its own special subset of American life. I wanted to know more. They told me I need to watch something on TV called *Seinfeld*. I'll ask Charlie about it.

THURSDAY, NOVEMBER 13, 2008, THE COMMONS AT THE INSTITUTE

Nick arrived in the Common area to grab a cup of coffee just in time to see Charlie and Nicola huddled over her laptop. Nicola was shaking her head and laughing.

Nick plopped himself on the coach across from them. "What's up. What's making you laugh?"

"Charlie thinks I need a life and that a personal ad in the *Daily Bruin* is my ticket to romance." Nicola was staring at the laptop screen.

"Dude, is this another thing to add to that list that never ends?" Nick was smiling at his friends.

Charlie grinned. "Nope, I can explain it right here and right now. A personal ad is just like it sounds. You describe yourself and your interests with an e-mail or phone number to contact you, or in the case of the *Daily Bruin*, maybe you e-mail the paper with the number of the ad that piqued your interest and then you get connected."

"Connected? Like you have a date?" Nick was still confused.

"Not exactly." Charlie was in full social guide mode now. "When you do get the phone number or e-mail of the person, then you call or e-mail them. Maybe the person you want to meet replies. Then you exchange more calls or e-mails. And after a while, maybe then you meet. Like for coffee. Not even a beer. Coffee is safer."

Nicola chimed in. "Yeah, coffee. I'm not meeting a stranger at a bar. That can be dangerous."

Nick was shaking his head. "A bar can be dangerous?"

"For a single woman? Oh yeah, it can be very unhealthy. Not to mention it can give someone the wrong impression. And you only get a first impression once."

"Okay, I'm very lost here." Nick still shook his head. "Bars are unsafe and give the wrong impression. Well, how do people meet nowadays and why would you bother with a personal ad in light of all of the dangers?"

Charlie stepped in. "She's being cautious, which is her way. Lots of times it's fun and safe. Maybe we should do an ad for you?"

Nicola stiffened her shoulders. "Wait just a minute. You said you'd help me. I need to be first."

Right about now, Fabian arrived and overheard this last bit of conversation. "Who's going first for what?"

Nicola was chagrinned to be caught in this breach of her personal life. "Oh, Charlie said he would help me write a personal ad for the *Daily Bruin*. I can't even get past the word 'single.' I'm not white, I'm not Hispanic, I'm not Asian. I'm all of them. What's the word for that?"

Charlie spoke. "Exotic?"

Fabian grinned. "Nah, that sounds like she's a stripper. Not exotic. Maybe just beautiful, smart, single woman looking for what?"

Nicola stared at him. "You think I'm smart and beautiful?"

"Well, are ye daft? Of course, you're smart and beautiful." Fabian was sincere.

Nick looked at the two of them and said, "Well, I may be new here, but when a guy thinks a girl is smart and beautiful and the girl is looking for a date…maybe an ad isn't necessary."

Nicola looked at Fabian. "But you've never made a move."

Fabian glanced at Charlie. "I thought you two…"

"Ack, no. Not even. He's like my brother." Nicola was almost physically pulling away from Charlie.

Nick got in between the two friends. "Okay, you two. It's good that you're friends. You don't need to be more than that. And you do spend a lot of time together. I can see where Fabian might have gotten the impression that it was more than friendship."

Nicola relented. "When you put it that way, I guess we could have given off a vibe that was misinterpreted."

Fabian was homing in on the opportunity he had just been handed. "So if the two of you aren't an item, does that mean you might be available for something?"

"Can you be more specific?" Nicola wasn't going to be too easy to catch.

"Would you like to go to a movie with me?" Fabian tried to sound casual.

"I've been wanting to see *Slumdog Millionaire*," Nicola suggested.

"And I'm interested in the new James Bond movie," Fabian countered.

Charlie offered, "Which one is the more romantic of the two?"

Fabian threw his head back. "Gah, do ye hafta even ask? Bond is sexy, not romantic. Although Daniel Craig is more nuanced."

Nicola almost screeched, "Nuanced? Nuanced? No James Bond movie is nuanced. *Slumdog Millionaire* it is."

Fabian raised an eyebrow. "So you want to see a romance movie with me, do ye?"

Nicola chuckled. "Okay, James Bond it is. Clever guy. Got wha-cha wanted."

Nick brought them back around. "Will you write an ad for me then? I think I'd like to meet a girl."

Charlie warmed to his task. "Okay. Let's do it."

"And just what are you going to do?" This time, it was Jane who had stepped into the room, looking for just this very group.

Charlie spoke up. "Writing a personal ad for Nick so that he can get a date."

"Not so fast here, young man. Nick isn't just some lonely guy looking to meet a lonely girl. We have to be a little bit more careful with the situation." Jane got to play Mom to lots of lonely scientists and had been down this path.

Nick looked at her. "Do you have something more important than my social life in mind?"

"That I do, fellas, and young woman. Don't you all have some pressing research to attend to?" Jane was already heading for the door as the group scrambled to follow her.

Nick's Notes, Wednesday, November 19, 2008

Plans have ramped up for the Thanksgiving celebration. I guess it's a big thing here. Jane says the holiday is big all over the country. We celebrated back then, but it wasn't that big of a deal. That said, I'm looking forward to seeing family. So strange to think of the family I now have. So different from what I would have pictured just a little more than two months ago. Jane says that after the war, lots of people moved around, or at least didn't go home. If they had been stationed somewhere, they might have gotten married and stayed there. Often, people like her folks got together because of the war and lived someplace new. So families are different because they no longer live close to each other. But they travel to see each other. Charlie says it's a pain because the roads are clogged with holiday drivers.

The movie tonight had many messages. *Moonstruck* was funny and touching. The older man trying to be younger with a too young woman. The older woman sad over her cheating husband yet at peace with herself. And the firecracker of a leading lady. I loved it when she slapped her lover's face and said, "Snap out of it." We could all use that from time to time.

I wonder if I need to "snap out of it." Sometimes I just sit and think about who I was and who I am now. I have no answers. I just keep getting up every day and try to solve the problem of what actually happened that morning.

CHAPTER 39

NOVEMBER 20, 2008,
VENTO JUNCTION

After the movie night at The Institute, Vic and Don had moved from e-mail to regular phone calls. Don called every morning. "Hi, V. How's your day looking?" was his typical greeting.

She would give him a rundown of what she had ahead. "Teaching a class of young women in a juvenile facility today. You know that drama is very therapeutic, right?"

"I know when it's you delivering the drama, it works on me." He flirted with her.

She laughed at him, enjoying the easy way they had with each other. It was like they had known each other for a long time.

"Any news from Ben and Michelle on their investigations?"

Don grew serious. "Not a lot to report, but we just heard the other day about a native kid who was picked up by some other kids around the time Nick showed up."

"And this is significant why?" Vic was curious. Don wouldn't bring it up unless it mattered.

"Because he was disoriented. Spoke about Los Alamos and not knowing how he got here." Don spoke deliberately.

"Oh my god. Does that mean that the experiment that brought Nick here could have affected a wider area?" Vic was growing alarmed.

Don reassured her, "We don't know. I tried to get in to speak to him, but my friends at the hospital are slow to respond to my request."

"Well, how can you get to him? What kind of excuse can you give?"

"Ben and Michelle and I are working all the angles. I'll let you know as soon as we have something to share."

"My, my, you are just full of surprises, Don Grant. I thought I had an interesting life before I met you. Now it seems utterly banal and mundane. I don't think I'll ever be the same."

"Good surprises, I hope. I know my life will never be the same since I met you." He was definitely flirting now.

They both said goodbye, ending the conversation on that sweet note.

Vento Junction Juvenile Facility

The hospital was at the edge of the small downtown in Vento Junction. It was here that they hoped to find the young man, who said his name was Tommy. His strange behavior meant he was being closely observed. Ben and Michelle were in the hospital parking lot looking at the front doors.

"Maybe they'll let me in if I say I'm doing a story on runaway youth." Michelle tried out an approach.

Ben shrugged. "It didn't work on the sheriff. You think it might work on the hospital staff?"

She stared at the automatic doors and the nearby security guard. "They may be interested in a positive story about their work. Law enforcement is always leery of the press."

"I called a friend yesterday who's in healthcare PR. She gave me a name of someone she knows who works here. I'll see if that connection might be the key we need to get in."

"If that works, there's something you're going to need to know before you meet him." Ben had discussed this with his dad this morning before he and Michelle had left for the hospital.

"You've been suspicious about Nick from the start, right?"

Michelle drew back in her seat to look directly at Ben. "Yes, you know I've been suspicious."

"And you've felt that there was something I hadn't been telling you, right?"

"I guess I haven't been good at hiding my frustration from you. Yes, I do feel like there's more going on. Are you finally going to tell me?"

"Honestly, it's been killing me not to share this with you. My dad, Charlie, all of them have been concerned. I thought all along we could trust you. Please tell me we can trust you." Ben was leaning forward as he said this.

"Of course you can trust me. I've come this far, haven't I? My God, Ben, we're close. I trust you with my secrets and my truth. If I trust you enough for that what in the world, could you tell me that's more sensitive than that?"

"It's just that there are major consequences to what I'm going to tell you if it gets out."

"But I need to know it before I meet this young man?"

"Yes, because this information might be what he needs to hear to help him know he's not crazy."

"Well, you're making me crazy. *Tell* me, just get it off your chest."

"Okay. Nick Brown is Nicholas Nishimura, and he time-traveled sixty-four years on September 8, 2008, and arrived here in Vento Junction. My dad found him and brought him home."

"I knew it! I just knew it. And you thought I'd go public if I knew the truth? Honey, they'd think I was a loon and I'd lose whatever credibility I have as a journalist."

"Well, when you put it that way, yes. We did worry, and you're right, any news organization not fringy would think you were pulling a stunt."

Michelle's mind was spinning. "If I get your drift on this guy in the hospital, you think he might have come along with Nick for the ride, so to speak?"

"So to speak, yes. My brother and the rest of the scientists at The Institute are trying to figure out how Nick got here, across time, and not just across Los Alamos. So if someone else from 1944 is here, well, it puts a whole new layer of unknown on the situation."

Michelle's eyes were getting moist. "That poor kid. Nick at least knew he was part of an experiment. If this guy was in 1944 one minute and here the next, he must think he's lost his mind. I have to get in to see him."

"Now you know why I had to tell you. And really, I had wanted to tell you for a while now. Please believe me."

Ben's earnest face and his hand gripping her convinced her. Her anger softened. "Okay, I'll consider forgiving you, but don't keep anything else from me. Not a thing from now on, agreed?"

"Agreed. And maybe now that you know everything…" Ben brought her hand to his lips and kissed her knuckles. She smiled and opened the car door to step out into the warm November day. The look she gave him sent a shiver through him. Now that the secret wasn't secret anymore, he was ready to let Michelle into everything he'd been holding back.

CHAPTER 40

AROUND THE KITCHEN TABLE AT DON GRANT'S HOME, LATER NOVEMBER 20, 2008

Don looked at Ben and Michelle. They seemed serious but also happy. He'd have to find out what that was all about, but right now, it sounded like they needed all hands on deck.

Ben spoke rapidly. "We've got to get him outta there. They think he's crazy, and that's going to make him crazy for real."

Michelle put her hand on Ben's. "Slow down there, Mr. Calm and Steady. I have a friend nearby, remember? And I think she may owe me. So let me make a call and see what I can do."

Don added. "If you don't, I know a few people over there, and my word is good with them. But more important, tell me why you think this is part of our secret."

Ben squared his shoulders. "So there's a teenager being held—and just saying that gives me the creeps—in that 'facility.' He says his name is Tommy Cisneros and he's from the pueblo near Los Alamos, New Mexico. He was hanging around a building where a bunch of guys in suits did stuff they wouldn't talk about. He and his buddies were having a smoke when a storm was starting. He thought he heard or felt lightning. He thinks he blacked out. Not really sure. And then he was here."

Don was studied in his approach to his concerned son. "Did you ask him about his family and facts we could correlate to what we know from Nick?"

Michelle said, "We did ask him about his family, but we don't know his parents' names, so then we asked why he was at the site. He said his sister was a maid and that the guys she knew were working in the building he was near."

Don leaned in. "And his sister's name is...?"

Ben and Michelle spoke softly together. "Theresa."

"My God. She's been holding this in all these years. Her brother went missing. Do you think it was the same time Nick traveled? Of course you do. That's why you're so worried about him." Don was shaking his head.

Ben had calmed. "If she's the shaman that we believe her to be, then she might not have been as agitated as someone else. We'll need to ask her. In the meantime..."

Michelle jumped in. "We need to get Tommy out of there and into a different place."

"What about Sky Ridge Ranch?" Ben was thinking out loud.

Don spoke up. "You mean the place Jane mentioned. The one Dick Stanton's wife started after the war."

"One and the same. It's a boarding school and protected. And Betsy knows the scoop." Ben warmed to the idea.

Michelle was making notes. "OK. I'll call my friend and see how and how soon we can transfer Tommy into our safekeeping. Don, it might be best if you're ready to assume guardianship of a young man. They know you."

Don nodded. "While you make your call, I'll make mine and see what it's going to take to spring our traveling friend."

They went separate ways, leaving Ben in the kitchen to think. Then he picked up his phone and dialed The Institute. "Dr. Jane Stanton please. It's Ben Grant in Arizona." A minute later, he heard Jane's voice.

"To what do I owe the pleasure, Ben Grant? Your brother is fine. Is he not checking in with you?"

"No, it's not that, but thanks for letting me know. Charlie isn't good at letting us know what he's up to. But we have a situation here. Dad got word through his friends from the high school that a young man, probably Native American, was found wandering around downtown Vento Junction telling crazy stories. Saying he was from near Los Alamos. That he doesn't know how he got here. His clothes are from another era. You get the picture?"

"I'm glad I'm sitting down. Are you thinking we have another time traveler?" Jane sounded excited and concerned.

"That's exactly what we think. And we think he's Theresa Cisneros's brother. He says his name is Tommy Cisneros and that his sister was a maid for the scientists at Los Alamos." Ben sounded calmer than he felt.

Jane went into director mode. "What's his status? How's his health? And what do we need to get him out of wherever he's being kept?"

"Dad and Michelle are working on two of their contacts as we speak. We were wondering if we could bring him to Sky Ridge when we get him out." Ben suddenly felt uncertain.

Jane's voice settled him immediately. "That's exactly what I was thinking. Whoever needs to talk with me about it, I'm here. I'll prepare acceptance paperwork for him right now."

"Thank you. That will be a relief. My God, do you think he's been in this time since Nick traveled? When Michelle and I spoke with him, we didn't ask him how long he's been around here. I can't imagine what he's going through. We didn't want to tell him the whole story. That can wait until we have him someplace safe. Oh, and I told Michelle everything. Now she's in on the secret. I figured it was time, and I couldn't figure out how to help Tommy without her knowing about Nick."

Jane smiled at his voice. "I'm sure you feel a lot easier now. How did she take the news?"

Ben was chagrinned. "She told me that if she reported the story to anyone, they'd think she was crazy and her reputation would be ruined. And that I could calm down, the secret was safe."

Jane chuckled. "Was that all she said?"

Ben blushed and was glad Jane couldn't see him. "No. She was a little pissed at me. She thought I trusted her. I think she knows why I couldn't tell her everything. I don't think I've totally screwed things up, but I'm going to have to work to earn back her trust."

Jane spoke with the wisdom that comes from having many young lovers turn to her "You're not wrong, and neither is she. The good news for you is that she's a smart girl. Give her some time. Call me as soon as you have an update, and I'll give the ranch school a heads-up that they'll be getting a new student soon."

Nick's Notes, Wednesday, November 26, 2008

All ability to focus went out the window by noon. The beer was flowing in the Common Room, and talk of football bounced off the walls. I hung out with the guys from Sweden and the UK. We all share a lack of connection to the festivities on the playing field. I don't even remember football from Stanford. Maybe we had a team, but it wasn't like it is now. I could, however, explain some of the food fetishes. I told them about the pilgrims and the first Thanksgiving. They all thought it was interesting and maybe just a bit favorable toward the invading white men. Can't argue with that at all.

Because so many family members are arriving, our movie was a matinee, so people would be free to have dinner with family. I had to explain that word to a few younger colleagues. We were all touched by the film about young men at a boy's boarding school. There are days that The Institute feels like such a school but with girls, of course. The wonderful teacher whose message to the students, "Carpe Diem. Seize the day, boys. Make your lives extraordinary." I do think we do that well here, and we are well served to keep in it mind. I know all too well how precious the days are.

I realize it hasn't been that long since I saw Don, Ben, Grace and the rest. It sure seems like a long time. Those first days of fear and excitement. Trusting that the people I met would not let me down. And they haven't. If I'm ever to figure out what happened on that day in September 1944, I think this is the place and these are the people to help me.

And Charlie told me about the teenager found in Vento Junction. I haven't seen a photo yet, but the way they describe him and his "delusion," he could have been caught up in the experiment. But I need to talk to him. I need to know. Well, the verb know is probably not the one to use. I need to find out how he might have been involved, if he was.

CHAPTER 41

THE INSTITUTE, THURSDAY, NOVEMBER 27, 2008

Thanksgiving was happening. TVs blared the Macy's parade. Coffee and bagels were handed around. A handful of scientists made their way to the common room to wake up and absorb this bit of Americana.

Preparations for the big meal were in full swing in the cafeteria and the dining room was being set for a large group. Jane was checking her list to make sure she had a handle on the visitor/VIP list. She knew of at least two newcomers who would be a surprise for Nick, Charlie, and Nicola.

Given the dietary preferences of the crowd, the menu went well beyond standard turkey, dressing, sweet potatoes, and cranberry sauce. This year, the heavy buffet table would hold Alaskan wild salmon, Atlantic mackerel, corn tortillas, chorizo and potato casserole, and some amazing pastries. California wine, of course, and she thought she had found some bourbon to echo the rough stuff that used to be served at the 1940s parties at Los Alamos. Her father-in-law would smile, maybe cringe, and maybe Nick would as well.

Mitch stopped her as she was leaving the cafeteria kitchen. "Mom, slow down. It's all good. We're more than ready."

"I know. I just can't help being a bit tense. The secret is still a secret to a lot of the people coming. What if Rick's dad or Betsy slips up? And they're bringing Theresa. When she sees Nick, will she give it away?"

"If it's just them, it's okay. Unfortunately, their age is an easy excuse. If it's any of the other crew, then we'll have some tap dancing to do. At least no one from the outside is coming this year."

Jane smiled ruefully. "No, we don't have any breakthroughs to announce this year, and that's actually a relief."

Mitch hugged her, engulfing her in his football-sized frame, and said, "It's going to be fine. And if we get a surprise, we'll handle it. Just in case, I'll scramble the cell signals for the time of the meal."

"Oh, that's good. I had forgotten you could do that. It could buy us time if something comes out."

"And I won't make an announcement. It will just happen like a natural phenomenon."

Jane nodded to him, and they split up to go to the next tasks on their busy day.

The timing of the meal was mid-afternoon, after the parade ended, half-time for many football games and warm enough to call the sun-kissed Californians in toward the table. Guests often began arriving just after 1:00 pm.

Don, Vic, Daniel, and Nicola came together. Charlie had driven her to her aunt's yesterday to do a little catching up before the big dinner. Shortly after they cleared the entry way, Ben and Michelle arrived, followed by Grace and Father Joe and a very excited Samantha Jane. Rick and his dad arrived next, with Feynman. The Irish Wolfhound had long ago been adopted as The Institute's mascot for all holidays. Betsy would be arriving with Theresa to bring up the late arrivals. Mitch was greeting them all and guiding them toward the festive dining hall. Feynman and Sam got fresh rawhide chewies from Mitch and were deliriously happy to head to the court-yard and play with the younger scientists, while the dining room filled with guests.

The dining hall echoed with conversations as Charlie, Fabian, and Nick arrived. They huddled with a few of the other visiting scientists, explaining the peculiarities of the holiday. They moved toward Mitch and Suzanne to grab a table. The big screen at the end of the room was set up for a Skype greeting from Mac and Martha. Jane discreetly met the two newest visiting scientists at the door. Twins Elizabeta and Mercedes Gonzales-Thompson had just arrived. Student waiters moved smoothly around the room, carrying trays of champagne-filled glass flutes. The courtyard crew ambled in as it approached 2:00 p.m.

Rick raised his glass. "Please help us celebrate today and all the days that led up to it." Sounds of glasses touching and murmuring began to fill the silence. Soon the serious moment passed. Trays of creative nibbles were handed from table to table, and greetings were exchanged.

Jane moved to rescue the twins and find them places to sit. "We follow an informal yet effective rule for seating. With our weekly Sunday suppers, we mix up our gaggle of folks deliberately making room for new connections and discoveries. So, you twins, please separate. Mitch will take Elizabeta to a seat, and Mercedes, please come with me."

Jane was heading to the table with Nick and Charlie. Mitch seemed to move a bit more slowly, guiding Elizabeta to a seat next to him at his table. Jane's eyebrow raised. This was unusual for Mitch.

Daniel Acevedo had found a new friend in Suzanne the wheelchair demon. Vic gravitated toward Betsy and Dick, exceptions to the Sunday supper rule in light of their decades of marriage.

Don joined Michelle and Fabian at Daniel's table. Suzanne shifted her gaze to Michelle and decided to get to know the "new girl." Don's eyes followed Vic as she sat with Dick, Betsy, Grace and the woman Betsy had walked in with. Ben was moving toward a table with several staffers and visiting scientists.

Mitch was introducing Elizabeta to Nicola, Charlie, and Rick as Charlie and Nick were moving toward their nearby table. Father Joe had been seated by Jane with Nicola, whom he knew, but Mitch, Beta, and Rick were new to him, although Grace had tried to fill him in on the drive from Indio. It helped to put faces and names together. The open seat at Jane's table was soon filled by a slender young woman in chef's whites. "Hi, I'm Elaine, your chef for the day."

Jane smiled at that. "She's actually overqualified in the kitchen. Her day job is head of our chemistry lab."

Elaine shrugged with chagrin. "Cooking is all chemistry. I love it. I can blend art with science. It makes me happy."

Charlie turned to introduce himself. "I definitely have to get out of the physics lab more often. I'm Charlie Grant."

Meanwhile, Nick was trying not to stare at Mercedes. She turned to him, extending her hand. "I'm Mercy, and my sister and I just arrived."

Nick took her hand, and a wave of familiarity washed over him. "Do I know you? I'm Nick Brown."

"I don't think so, but we've definitely met. My studies are in quantum consciousness and connections. What I felt when you took my hand says to me that we have a connection."

"What do you mean?"

"Maybe not in this life, but we're connected."

Nick shook his head. "And you're a scientist?"

"Oh yes, it's science, just not respected by everyone…yet. My time will come."

Jane was smiling when she decided to stir this pot. "Mercy and her sister grew up in New Mexico, not far from Los Alamos."

Charlie had not taken his eyes off Elaine. "Tell me about today's meal. What should I look forward to?"

Elaine nearly popped up out of her seat with excitement. "I had so much fun. I raided the garden here and then went to a few local farmers' markets. Everything but the salmon and mackerel is local. I didn't have to kill the turkey, but he *was* alive two days ago. I have friends at Skyridge Ranch who raise the turkeys and prepare them."

Jane added, "Skyridge Ranch is the school Rick's Mom Betsy and her friends started after the War. Mercy is familiar with it."

Mercy heard her name and adjusted to the new conversation. "Skyridge was where Beta and I went to High School. G-Ma wanted science for us, so went to boarding school and studied out here."

Nick was interested in her nomenclature. "G-Ma? That's unusual. I've heard of G-Men, but yours is different, yes?"

Mercy smiled warmly. "My grandmother. She was a teacher. She studied after the war. Then my mother followed her into teaching. But they both knew we needed more than Los Alamos could offer."

"Nick knows a lot about Los Alamos and that early history," Jane explained.

"Did you know that a lot of the Pueblo people played a part in what happened there?"

"Actually, I do, but it's been hard to find out what happened at the end of the war."

"Well, what happened after wasn't nearly as dramatic. G-Ma met an engineer who came out to work at one of the labs, fell in love, went to school. Came back to Los Alamos. There's still research happening today."

Nick had perked up. "What did your grandmother do during the war years?"

"She was only sixteen, so she couldn't do much. She was a maid to the scientists living at the lodge. She tells stories about it. Pretty crazy ones."

Nick was on the hunt. "How crazy?"

"Other experiments—not just the bomb. A guy who disappeared. And my Great-Uncle Tommy disappeared. They say he ran away, but G-Ma doesn't think so. That kind of crazy."

Slowly he asked. "What is your grandmother's name?"

"Theresa Cisneros-Johnson."

"She's not crazy." Nick spoke almost to himself.

Jane touched his arm lightly.

Nick continued, "My work here builds on work that was started at Los Alamos back then."

The room grew quiet, and Nick reluctantly looked away.

Mitch moved from table to table to collect Rick and Jane leading them to the front of the festive hall.

As they raised their glasses and looked up, the screen came alive, and Martha's smile warmed the room. Her Irish lilt still flavoring her speech.

"Welcome to you all, new friends and old. It fills my heart to see you all and to share the blessing my Mac wrote so long ago. Please lift your glasses." She paused while the room turned to her and raised their glasses. "Today we are thankful for freedoms, faiths, families, and friends and the fortitude to protect and defend them."

Mac loomed behind her, his hands on her shoulders and his smiling face peering around hers. He mouthed "Happy Thanksgiving" as Martha reached up her hand to clasp his and the screen went dark.

Jane's eyes glistened. Rick gripped her hand and squeezed. Betsy's shoulders shook with silent tears at the unfairness of the disease that was stealing Mac.

The murmurs slowly became conversations peppered with laughter following the momentary serious reminder of why they were all in the hall at all. Food was served, cutlery clinked, and the murmur settled as people began to eat. Nick turned again to find out more about his new friend Mercy. They talked about family and the crazy paths that brought them to The Institute. His through the survivalist parents of his fictional backstory and hers through long-ago connections, connections that were all too fresh for him. He would need to be careful not to reveal too much around this new friend.

Her eyes caught an arrival across the room. She jumped up and shouted, "G-Ma!" Beta did the same, and they both almost ran to the table with the vintage crowd. G-Ma, Theresa, rose to hug them and admonish their exuberant show of affection. Betsy and Dick held each other's hands and smiled fondly at the generations of Skyridge Ranch alums at hand.

"G-Ma, he's here. The one you told us about. At least we think he's the one." This was Mercy.

Beta shook her head. "It can't be him. That was more than sixty years ago and look at him. Okay, he's Asian and a scientist. A coincidence."

Theresa and Mercy smiled at her. "Really. That's what you want to believe?"

Beta continued, "Look, no one has said anything about time travel at The Institute and that would be what we're talking about, right?"

Dick and Vic both reached out their hands to touch the girls on their forearms and say, "You might want to lower your voices. People are beginning to stare, even for here."

The girls blushed and decided to continue the conversation with G-Ma after dinner.

Ben and Michelle watched the interchange with the twins and their grandmother closely. Having met and rescued Tommy from that facility in Vento Junction they wanted to talk with Theresa and find out if she knew anything specific about her brother's disappearance. Now that he was safe, they could come up with a plan to let him know what they think happened. Anything she could offer that might help them sort out the story of the mysterious teenager with the crazy story—one that they knew wasn't crazy at all.

When Mercy got back to her seat, Nick was staring intently at the older woman she had just left at the other table. "Who's that?"

"As if you couldn't tell from my exuberant greeting. That, my dear Nick, is the very woman we were just discussing. The one and only matriarch of my family, Theresa Cisneros-Johnson."

"Do I get to meet her?" Nick was both curious and concerned. If this was *his* Theresa, then what if she said something and his secret got out?

"G-Ma wants to eat her meal in peace. Apparently, her granddaughters do not create a peaceful place for her to eat." Mercy was not too happy about waiting, but this wasn't the first time her G-Ma had put order to chaos in the family.

Jane had retaken her seat next to Nick and quietly whispered, "It's OK, she knows not to say too much."

At this news, Nick relaxed and began to pay attention again to his first real Thanksgiving dinner since before the camp. And what a meal it was. Elaine gave them all a play-by-play of each dish, which enhanced the taste for everyone. Sometimes knowing is better than not knowing. Imagine that for scientists to realize.

Vic was enjoying listening to Grace and Theresa share stories of what it was like to be sixteen during the Great War. Dick leaned over to her and let her in on a key to Theresa's presence there. "Have you heard us mention Skyridge Ranch?"

Vic shook her head.

Dick continued. "After the war, Betsy and I came back here to start our lives, me at UCLA and Betsy—well, after teaching those Tennessee kids, she decided to start a school for girls out here. She knew girls weren't getting enough math and science, and she decided to change that."

Vic was curious about this. "What do you mean teaching the kids, and where is this Skyridge Ranch?"

Betsy smiled and told Vic about Oak Ridge and Susanna, the children, and her women friends who helped form the first teaching staff at the school to teach science and math to girls.

Dick grinned. "Land was pretty cheap back then, and with both of us having served, we qualified for a loan to buy this small ranch in the east edge of LA. It was before freeways, just a two-lane road but nice hills and a couple of buildings. Enough to start the school and be able to board a few students."

Vic wanted more. "And…"

Dick continued his tale, "We arranged to have this wonderful couple from Oak Ridge, our friends Susanna and her husband and kids, come out to manage the property and live on site. They had been the best part of our time in Oak Ridge. Because they were black, they never thought they would have a future outside Oak Ridge. We couldn't imagine building the school without them. Then I mentioned to Betsy that there might be some Reservation kids from the Pueblo at Los Alamos that we could help too. She was on board for all of them to come."

Vic was nodding. "OK, but why Theresa?"

"Oh, she was our maid when we were working on the Hill during the war. That's how we knew anything about the pueblo at all. She was so smart. When I told Betsy about her, we knew she needed to have a chance."

It dawned on Vic all at once. "Holy shit, Dick, you didn't let him know she was coming and now she's here? Did she know he would be here? Oh my god, oh my god."

Dick just smiled at her. "It's OK. She knew. He didn't. We thought it might be suspicious in this setting to put a youngster with an oldster. They'll have time after pumpkin pie and coffee to get reacquainted."

At that, Vic glanced over toward Nick and noticed that he was deep in conversation with Mercy and Elaine. Then she looked around a bit more. Mitch's head was lowered to hear what Beta was saying. Suzanne in the wheelchair was holding court with her brother, the Irishman, and Don and Michelle. Father Joe and Ben were sharing stories about Thanksgiving with a couple of the foreign scientists who were new to it all. So she relaxed and enjoyed her meal. Whatever would happen would happen later.

The noise level raised and lowered as food was brought out from the kitchen and plates that had been full began to empty. All too soon, the kitchen crew was clearing tables preparing to bring out the selection of pies. Mercy grabbed Nick's hand and said, "It's time for you to meet G-Ma."

"She's here?" Nick had been very much in the moment and enjoying getting to know this interesting person, and her announcement startled and reminded him.

"Oh yeah. She and Dick and Betsy Stanton are tight. Have been since Betsy started the Ranch school."

It wasn't a long walk to the table where the senior scientist and his wife were seated, but they stopped to greet friends on the way. When they got to the table, Mercy tapped Theresa on her shoulder. She turned and smiled at her granddaughter and rose to greet her friend from long ago. Nick stepped into her open arms for an embrace.

Theresa whispered to him, "I couldn't tell you then, but I knew you would be back." He squeezed her. Then she whispered, "Have you found the other one, my brother who went missing when you did?" A searing pain ripped across Nick's forehead. He tried to hold onto to Theresa as he lost consciousness and began to slip to the floor. The room erupted into chaos. The last thing he heard was her scream, "Help him!"

EPILOGUE

As people around the room looked at each other and tried to make sense of what had just happened, Father Joe leaped to help Theresa, saying as he moved, "I'm an EMT."

Grace moved to Nick's side, saying, "And I'm a nurse."

Nick was quickly stretched out on the floor as they began to assess his condition. Jane looked over at Mitch who was speaking into his lapel radio, "I need a gurney in the dining room, stat."

Grace listened to Jane who was saying, "We have a fully equipped infirmary here. We don't need to leave the building right now."

Mercy had come over to be near Nick. Her shamanic gifts, inherited from G-Ma, had gone on high alert when she saw her grandmother whisper to Nick. She was sensing a coming together and something else. Her guess was that the *something else* was behind Nick's problem.

Across the room, Nicola, Charlie, Ben, Michelle, and Fabian huddled.

"Do you think this has something to do with 1944?" Fabian voiced the question they were all wondering.

"Remember that road trip we talked about a few weeks ago? I think we have to go to Los Alamos and see for ourselves what the September 1944 anomaly could have been." Charlie was visibly shaken.

"I couldn't agree with you more." Nicola's voice quivered. "I don't think we can go any farther until we have more evidence from the site.

Ben spoke. "You should take Beta with you. She has the local contacts. You're going to need access to the elders who may have been there then. I think Mercy and Theresa should stay close to Nick."

"I'll e-mail you what I have from the New Mexico highway people. Might be useful." Michelle was firing up her ever-present smartphone.

"How fast can we get there?" Charlie sounded firmer.

Jane appeared at his shoulder. "Don't spread it around, but we have access to a private jet. We'll have you there in the morning. Now work on a plan so we don't waste any time."

Mitch had followed her over to the huddle and heard what she said. "I'll put a flight plan together."

Fabian raised an eyebrow. Jane filled in. "He's not just head of security. He's a commercially rated pilot. You're in good hands."

The groups began to separate and head out of the dining room. The gurney had arrived. Nick was lifted onto it with Grace on one side and Theresa on the other. Jane and Mercy stood behind them.

As they headed down the corridor toward the infirmary, Nick squeezed their hands. Grace looked at Theresa, just in time to see her begin to crumple and shout "Catch her." One aide stayed with Theresa and Jane, while Grace and Mercy continued toward the double doors.

After the aides rolled Nick into a treatment room, Mercy turned to Nick's sister, "Grace, right before G-Ma collapsed, I sensed something. Just like I did before Nick collapsed. I'm not sure, but it feels like they're connected."

Grace calmly took Mercy's hands. "I know they have a powerful connection. Perhaps it will be easier to sort this out with two of them like this. I'm glad you're here. I believe more than science is at play."

Teresa? Nick thought her name.

I'm here. Her thought answered his.

"Where is...here?"

ABOUT THE AUTHOR

Lynn Perez-Hewitt is an unlikely adventurer. A Catholic schoolgirl from Rockford, Illinois, a Bradley University graduate, and a PR professional with many traditional achievements, she nonetheless followed her heart and curiosity through five states and seven industries.

She came to writing novels late, though words and language have been themes throughout her life. Whether giving speeches, performing on stage, or persuading an audience to adopt new ideas, her craft is language, her canvas is people.

Constants in her life are love of reading, music, pets, and men. More books than music and more music than men, until finding the right man who plays music and loves dogs, cats, ferrets, and more. They live, play, write, and throw frisbees in Colorado.

You may find Lynn on LinkedIn at linkedin.com/in/perezhewitt

CPSIA information can be obtained
at www.ICGtesting.com
Printed in the USA
BVHW072354161120
593219BV00002B/8